# DEVILS DON'T FLY

## A LOVE ME, I'M FAMOUS NOVEL

## MICHELLE HERCULES

INFINITE SKY PUBLISHING

Devils Don't Fly © 2020 by Michelle Hercules



This book is a work of fiction. Names, characters, places, and incidents either are products of the author's imagination or are used fictitiously. Any resemblance to actual persons, living or dead, events, or locales is entirely coincidental.

Paperback ISBN: 978-1-950991-28-0

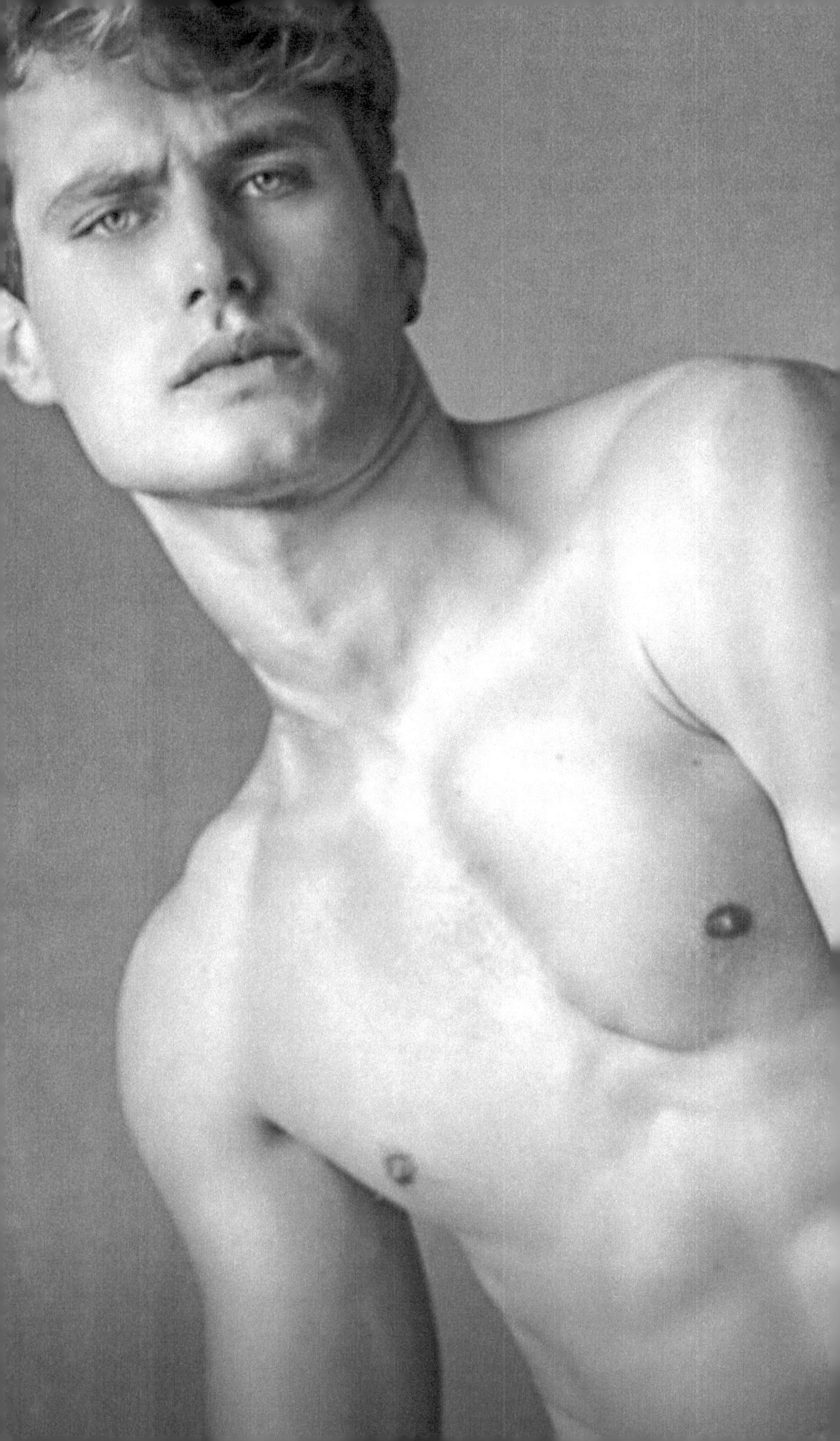

# CHAPTER 1
## SAYLOR

blink a few times as I stare at the complete stranger my mother just announced as my husband. My head feels like it's filled with cotton candy and nothing makes any sense. There's a huge gap in my memories, and I think I'll go crazy if I try to put the pieces back together now. Still, I stare at the man hovering between the bed and the door, uncertain of what he should do. He's attractive, just the type of guy I would usually go for, but I feel absolutely nothing as I look at him. I wait for my heart to tell me what my brain can't, but it doesn't respond. It's indifferent.

God, if I married him, I must have loved him. I feel like the worst person in the world. I can't remember anything about Oliver, the tall blond with the angst-filled eyes. What if I never recover my missing memories? What if I never remember our life together?

"I'm sorry. I can't, I… it's just too much."

His face falls and my heart constricts in guilt. He turns to the doctor and asks him what the next steps are. I half listen to what they're saying, having a hard time concentrating on anything at the moment.

"When can I take her home?" my husband—it's so odd to

even think that word—asks.

"Uh, considering she can't remember you, shouldn't she come home with me?" my mother intervenes, looking at me in search of support.

Shit, I hope this doesn't turn into a battle of wills. I don't think I can pick a side right now.

"Well, my advice is for Saylor to return to her former routine. It will be beneficial if she goes home with her husband. Her brain is still recovering from surgery, so it might only take a small object or a word to trigger the return of her memories."

Mom's lips become a thin flat line. She's not pleased about this situation at all. It seems our relationship has somehow mended during the time lapse I can't remember. I look in Liv and Sebastian's direction. Bas has his arm around her shoulder and she's hugging him by the waist. When did they get back together? My head begins to pound thanks to the infinite questions bouncing in there.

"I still think she should spend a few days with me first." My mother turns to Oliver. "She doesn't remember you. Would you force her to live with a stranger?"

I know Mom didn't mean to twist the dagger deeper, but that's what her words are doing.

Oliver rubs his face before his gaze searches mine. "If you'd prefer to go with your mum, I'd understand."

The accent. I just caught on to it. He has a beautiful British accent, and my heart warms a little for reasons I don't yet understand. Is it remembering? I stare at him intently, trying to absorb every single detail of his tall frame, of his perfect face. I want to know how we met. How long did we date before we got married? Did we have a big party or just a small reception? The hole in my memory seems so big and dark, I'm afraid to look closer. A part of me wants to go home with Mom, because she's right. Oliver is a stranger to me. I can't make this decision right now.

"I'd like some time to think about it," I finally say, watching the glimmer of hope in Oliver's eyes fade a bit. "I'm sorry."

"Nothing to be sorry about, sugar." He gives me a tight smile.

I frown. Why does he call me 'sugar' instead of 'Blue' like most of my close friends? Is there a meaning behind the endearment? *Stop it, Saylor. You'll give yourself an aneurism.*

The thought gives me pause. Why am I in a hospital in the first place? The side of my head itches and I raise my hand to it, feeling a bandage there.

"What happened to me?"

"You had a blood clot in your brain," Dr. Laurent answers. "We performed surgery to remove it, you were in a coma for three weeks.

"Three weeks?"

"Yes, but don't be alarmed. That's quite normal."

I try to bring my hands together to wriggle my fingers, but only my right hand cooperates. The left arm stays there, unmoving. I can't even feel it. I focus on moving a finger, *any* finger, and I barely twitch one. *What the hell.* I pinch my forearm and there's no pain.

"Sugar—I mean Saylor, what are you doing?" Oliver has moved closer to the bed, frowning at my useless limb.

"I can't feel my left arm."

"Doc?" He turns to Dr. Laurent.

The gray-haired doctor comes closer and does a series of examinations by touch. He asks me to try to move my legs as well. The right works fine. I have trouble with the left. It's numb, but when the doctor probes, I feel something at least.

"Why can't I move my left arm and leg?" I ask.

"Like I said before, the brain is a very complex organ and yours is still mending. You have some sensitivity on your leg, which is a good sign. You have no speech impairment, which tells me not all of your left side has been affected. That's very, very good news. I'm sure with physical therapy, you will be able to use your limbs again."

"I play the guitar, or I used to. Will I be able to do that again?"

"It's possible, but I can't guarantee it."

First the memory loss, now this. There's a sudden weight on my chest, caving it in. With my good hand, I massage the spot. My eyes begin to prickle. I don't want to cry—not in front of everyone, anyway.

I feel a light touch on my right shoulder and I look up.

"We've got this." Oliver smiles at me, but it's pained. He must be having such a shitty day too. I want to return that smile, but I can't bring myself to do it.

I'm so drained, and yet I don't want to sleep. I just spent three weeks dead to the world. What I want, what I *need*, is to get out of this hospital and discover what I've done with my life during the time I went and got myself a husband.

## OLIVER

I don't know yet how I should feel. Saylor has come back to me, and yet she hasn't. My mind is spinning like a top. When Dr. Laurent walks out of Saylor's room, I follow him.

"Doc, may I have word?"

"Certainly. Let's go to my office."

I follow the man, barely paying any attention to my surroundings. I keep thinking about Saylor's indifferent gaze as she looked at me, the anguish on her face when she discovered she couldn't move her left arm.

The doctor stops in front of the elevator and we wait for it in silence. He must sense I don't have the mind for small talk. The metal doors finally open, spewing a handful of people from the elevator. A young girl glances at me as she walks by and her eyes widen when she recognizes me.

"Oh my gosh. It's Oliver Best."

Without a word or a smile, I slip inside the elevator. I can't play the gracious celebrity right now. Dr. Laurent follows me and I sigh in relief when the doors shut again before the girl can recover from her shock and ask for an autograph.

"Will she ever get her memories back?" I blurt out.

"Possibly."

I clench my jaw and refrain from asking anything else until we're inside Dr. Laurent's office. 'Possibly' is not a good enough answer to me.

Once off the elevator, we walk for another minute before we arrive at our destination. Dr. Laurent takes his seat behind an immaculate desk and I sit opposite him.

"What are the next steps, Doc?"

"We'll keep Saylor here for observation for a few more days. If there are no issues, she can go home with you and start physical therapy sessions right away. Due to the memory loss, I recommend that she see a psychiatrist as well."

"Do you think she should go home with her mother? Be honest."

"I think Saylor should decide that without pressure from anyone."

"I would never pressure her to do something she didn't want to." My reply has more bite than I intended.

"I wasn't referring to you."

I shift on my seat and rub my face. Miss Carter and I will need to have a conversation. I shove that thought to the side for now.

"What if Saylor never recovers her memories? What if she never remembers me?"

Dr. Laurent leans back in his chair and links his hands together. He watches me closely for a moment before replying, "Then you'll have to make your wife fall in love with you all over again."

# CHAPTER 2
## SAYLOR

've been staring at my useless hand for ten minutes, willing it to move, when I hear a knock on the door. I look up and find Liv's ex-boyfriend standing there.

"Derek!"

"Hi, Blue. May I come in?"

"Of course."

He walks in, smiling from ear to ear while carrying a beautiful bouquet of flowers in his hand.

"I brought something to brighten up this room. I know you hate hospitals."

"Thank you."

I make a motion for the bouquet, but only one arm cooperates. My smile wilts and Derek notices the shift in my expression.

"What's the matter?"

"Didn't Dr. Laurent fill you in?"

"No. He can't. All he said was you were awake. I would've come visit you sooner, but... well I figured I should wait until your closest friends had a chance first."

"You didn't want to bump into Liv, huh?"

He smiles but it doesn't reach his eyes. "Or her husband. So, what's going on with you, Blue?"

The air exits my lungs in a loud exhale. "Well, I can't remember what happened to me in the past year. I have a husband who is a complete stranger to me. I can't move my left arm or leg. Shall I continue?"

"Partial memory loss is quite normal. I'm sure you'll recover your memories. Give it time. And with physical therapy, you'll be back playing your guitar in no time."

"Do you really believe so?" I can't help the hopeful tone in my voice.

"I do."

"I have my first physical therapy session today. I don't know what to expect."

"You'll do great. What time? Maybe I can join you for moral support."

Mom and Oliver had offered the same thing, but I told both of them no. I don't want either present when I struggle with my partial paralysis. I think Mom is the most upset with my refusal. Oliver is just going with the flow, trying his best not to show emotion when I do or say something that's probably upsetting the hell out of him.

"I don't know…."

"Don't tell me you're embarrassed." Derek gives me a cheeky smile.

"A little."

He rolls his eyes, something so out of character for him that it makes my giggle.

"Who's your therapist?"

"Dr. Makamoto, I believe."

"No way!"

"What? Do you him?"

"Oh, I know *her*. We went to school together. She's a drill sergeant. Trust me. You'll want me there."

"Already talking trash about me, Dr. Simmons?" A female

voice by the door has me looking over Derek's shoulder. A petite brunette is standing there with a medical chart in her hand.

"Since when is speaking the truth considered trash talking?"

Dr. Makamoto ventures into the room with a glint of amusement in her eyes. "Ignore Dr. Simmons. He's always been a bit *soft*."

Derek crosses his arms in front of his chest and watches Dr. Makamoto through slits. "*Soft?*"

She waves her hand dismissively. "Enough about you. Hi, Saylor. I'm Dr. Makamoto, but you can call me Cheryl."

"Hi."

Cheryl peers down at the chart in her hand, scanning through the document quickly, before looking at me again. "Still no sensation in your left arm and leg yet, huh?"

"Nope."

The doctor shakes her head. "We can't have that. We gotta get you playing your guitar again ASAP. I need more Wreck of the Day songs."

My eyebrows arch as my jaw drops. "You know my band?"

"Sweet girl, the entire country knows your band. Didn't your friends fill you in yet?"

"A little. I think everyone is afraid to dump too much information on me at once."

"Well, once we're done with our session, maybe I can tell you all about Wreck of the Day from a fan's perspective." She smiles before she claps her hands with a resounding smack. "Now, let's get cranking."

I manage to get to the wheelchair with minimal help. Derek made a move to assist, but I leveled him with a 'don't you fucking dare' look and he backed down. As Cheryl whirls me through the sterile hospital corridors, I can't help the accelerated drumming of my heartbeat. I'm worried I won't be able to do anything today.

The therapy room is a wide space, cheery and bright with large windows that give a nice view of the city. I hadn't realized we were so high up. Several weird-looking pieces of equipment are spread throughout the room, some that look like they would belong in a gym, others in a torture chamber.

A few patients are here, already grinding and grunting. My stomach twists into impossible knots. I expected to find the room empty, and the added audience is making me queasy. Cheryl parks my chair close to a set of parallel bars I recognize from TV. I've been filling my days watching daytime soap operas and it seems half the time, the characters are in a hospital recovering from a tragic accident.

"You're joking, right?" I say, glaring at the bars.

Cheryl puts her hands on her hips with pursed lips and a deep frown. "You only have one leg that doesn't work. This should be a walk in the park for you."

I turn my 'drop dead' gaze in her direction. "I haven't walked in over a month!"

"Your laziness is not my concern."

My jaw drops of its own accord. "Laziness?" I turn to Derek. "Is she for real?"

He doesn't need to answer, the smirk on his lips and the glint of amusement in his eyes are enough. No wonder he wanted to join my session.

Cheryl grabs my right arm and pulls me up. "Come on. Quit stalling. You'll get an hour with me no matter how late we start. I don't have any appointments after you."

It's futile to fight, so I let her drag my sorry ass off the chair, my right leg screaming in the process. I fall against Cheryl, but mercifully she's able to stabilize me. My face is in flames. I feel like a sloppy drunk who can't remain upright unassisted.

"I hate this," I say.

"You're doing great, Blue."

I whip my face in his direction. "Shut up, Derek."

He takes a few steps back, twisting his face into a frightened expression. "I better stay out of your striking range."

Cheryl helps me get to the bars, but since I can only use one arm, she stays on my left, helping me remain upright. Clinging to the right bar, I groan as my leg gets used to my weight again. I've never felt more useless in my entire life.

"All right, Saylor. I want you to put some of your weight on your left leg."

"But I can't feel it."

"Indulge me. Don't worry. I got you."

I shift my body weight, and by some miracle, I feel a slight tingle on my foot, as if my leg has gone numb but slowly the circulation is returning.

"How is it?"

"I can feel something."

"Good. Now I want you to shift your weight back to your right leg."

"Okay."

"How is your hold? Do you think I can let go?"

Locking my right knee tight and clutching the bar, I tell Cheryl I'm good. She steps away, but remains hovering nearby. My leg trembles slightly, but I don't lose my balance.

"You're doing very well, Saylor. Now, I don't want you to walk, just try to swing your left leg to the side. Do you think you can do that?"

Taking a deep breath, I concentrate on moving my left leg. Sweat forms on my forehead, but the damn limb doesn't fucking move. Frustrated, I let out a groan, but what I really want to do is cry. This is hopeless.

"I can't."

"Yes, you can. Come on. Try again."

Leveling Cheryl with a glare, I scream, "I fucking can't, okay!"

"You're angry. I get that. But lashing out at me won't make you play the guitar again."

I close my eyes and fight the tears that are threatening to spill. I hate being this pathetic. I'm not a weakling, I'm a fighter, but everything feels like it's too much right now.

"Cheryl, take it easy."

*Great, now Derek is coming to my defense.*

Without opening my eyes, I try to move my damn leg, focus every fiber of my being into making the muscle obey what my brain is commanding. I picture myself on a stage, ripping Rita while thousands of fans clamor for more. Of course, it's all my imagination since I can't remember what it actually felt like. The bar has turned slick under my sweaty palm, so when my left leg finally decides to move, I lose my grip on it and fall forward on my knees.

I turn to Cheryl. "What the fuck! I thought you were spotting me."

I don't understand the shit-eating grin she's displaying now.

"You did it, Blue!" Derek says.

"What, fall on my face?"

"No. Move your leg *and* arm."

"What?" I look down, and sure enough, I'm supporting my upper body with both arms. "How is that possible?"

The moment the question leaves my lips, my left arm slips from under me, making me fall onto my side.

"Ouch. Spoke too soon."

Cheryl helps me up, still looking super proud. "That was amazing! I've never seen a patient progress so fast."

"Really?"

"Really. You'll be playing with Wreck of the Day in no time." She turns to Derek. "Are you still doubting my methods, Dr. Simmons?"

"Not at all. You did well, Blue."

"When do you think I'll be able to play the guitar?" I ask.

"That's really up to you, Saylor. But this exercise just proved your body can become fully mobile again. It's just a matter of how badly you want it."

Her words give me hope. "Does that also apply to my memories?"

Cheryl's smile wilts a fraction. "That I can't answer. I'm sorry, Saylor."

I try not to let her honesty drag me into that self-pity hole again. Not having my memories sucks, but if I have to choose between having them back and playing again, I'll pick playing the guitar.

I can always make new memories.

# CHAPTER 3
## SAYLOR

Dr. Laurent told me I could go home today. The news cheered me up, but it also gave me a new bolt of anxiety. I can't hide the decision I've made anymore. It wasn't easy for me, but with everything that's going on, I feel I can't add more stress to my already complicated life. Now I have to tell my husband that I'm not coming home with him, at least not for the time being. My stomach is tied in knots, knowing it'll upset him deeply. God, I would be devastated if the situation were reversed. My heart might not remember him, but I hate to see him suffer.

Mom already knows she's taking me home with her, so I asked her to wait until I had the chance to explain to Oliver before she showed up at the hospital. He knocks on the open door to my room with a look of pure happiness on his beautiful face.

"Hey, may I come in?" he asks, still a little shy.

I sit up straighter and smooth my hair, suddenly conscious of my appearance. Despite not remembering actually being married to him, I don't want to look like roadkill.

"Sure."

Oliver has a bouquet of beautiful flowers. He's brought me a fresh one every day he comes to visit. He stops by the side of my bed, leans over, and kisses me on the cheek. I stop breathing for a second and my heart does a backflip. This is the first time he's touched me since I woke from the coma, and I don't know what to make of my body's reaction to it.

"You look pretty," he says with a cheeky smile. My face feels like it's in flames so I avoid his gaze, looking at the flowers instead.

"They're gorgeous." I make a grab for them with my right arm. I've made more progress thanks to Cheryl, but the left arm doesn't always want to cooperate.

"Ready to go home? I've relocated your stuff to Charlotte's old bedroom. The brat has finally moved out."

"Oliver, I… we need to talk."

The levity in his expression leaves his face as swift as a summer storm. "Oh. That expression never bodes well."

"I've decided it's best if I spend some time with my mother."

Oliver doesn't say anything, just keeps staring with an intensity I suspect only he can muster. "What about what the doc said? The little things that can trigger your memories."

I stare down at my lap. "I thought about it, and you said yourself that we haven't lived together for that long. My childhood home probably has more details to help me than your house."

"*Our* house, and none of those details you speak of involve me."

There's no accusation in his tone, but I detect something much worse—hurt. Shit. I was so hoping he wouldn't take it personally.

"It's just for a little while until I get to know you better."

Oliver swallows hard before looking toward the window. "I'm not going to lie to you. I'm not happy about your decision." He turns to me again with the saddest eyes I've seen on him yet. "But I'll do whatever it takes to make you happy. If that means not seeing your face first thing in the morning every day,

I'll cope. I guess my partner Allan isn't a terrible second option."

His lips curl upward. Even when his heart is bleeding, he manages to crack a joke. No wonder I fell in love with him. *Come on, heart, kick-start already.*

Dr. Laurent comes in with my mother in tow. "So, Saylor, are you ready to go home?"

"More than ready." I throw an apologetic glance in Oliver's direction. "I mean, I'm ready to get out of this hospital."

The corner of his mouth quirks up. "No need to explain, sugar. I know what you mean."

He called me 'sugar' again. I still need to ask why he likes to call me that. It's obviously an endearment only he uses. It sucks that I have to dissect every little detail of our interactions, that the questions won't stop piling up.

"Oliver, would it be possible for you to bring Saylor's clothes later today? I want her to feel as comfortable as possible," Mom says with much more kindness than I've seen her show Oliver in the past. I guess now that I've agreed to go home with her, she has no reason to feel resentment toward him.

"Of course, Miss Carter. I'll head home now and pack everything up." Oliver turns to me. "I'll see in a few, Saylor."

He leaves the room with shoulders hunched forward, the usual air of confidence I was beginning to associate with him gone.

I did that. I broke my husband.

♡ ♡ ♡

## OLIVER

As I head out of the hospital, I want to punch something. With the foul mood I'm in, I'm afraid if a stranger approaches me, I might bark like a rabid dog. I put my sunglasses on, striding with purpose toward my car.

Of course, it would be my lucky day that the paparazzi decide to make an appearance this morning. I'm sure some fucker at the hospital tipped them that Saylor would go home today. They see me, and like a pack of wolves, they're on me in a second, flashing their stupid cameras and firing off questions. One of them gets in my path, more determined than the others to get a statement from me.

"Piss off." I attempt to walk around the guy.

My angry attitude acts like blood in the water, and the other sharks close in. Suddenly I find myself surrounded by a mob of ruthless leeches who only want to get their money shots and sell them to the highest bidder.

"Get the fuck out of my way!" I push the guy blocking my path to the side.

He yells a complaint before getting into my personal space again.

"Where's Saylor? Is she coming home with you? We heard she's suffering from memory loss. Is that true?"

That last question makes me pause. We haven't released an official statement about Saylor's condition yet, so the fact that this wanker knows brings fire to my veins. I curl my fingers around his shirt, bringing his face close to mine.

"Who told you that?"

"I'm not going to reveal my sources. So it's true, then?"

"Tell me who's feeding you information and I promise not to beat you to a bloody pulp."

The paparazzo squints at me. "You don't fucking scare me, asshole. Craig was right about you."

"What did you fucking say?"

"You heard me. Now let go."

I do, but not before I grab his expensive camera and throw it to the ground with all my strength. It shatters into tiny pieces, giving me at least a sense of satisfaction.

"What the fuck! That camera is worth four grand. I'm so suing your ass."

I'm keenly aware that the other sharks are more than happy to register every moment of my interaction with their comrade, but I'm beyond the point of caring. My blood is boiling and I have murder in my gaze. I spot the flash memory card among the mangled pieces and step on it, making sure there's no way in hell he can sell the pictures he took.

"Bring it. I don't fucking care." I flip the other paparazzi off. "Bye, bitches."

They don't follow me and, looking over my shoulder, I can see why. The hospital has called the cops, the presence of the police cruiser making the paparazzi scatter like the worthless pieces of shit they are.

As I slide into my car, I think about Saylor. *Fuck*. I hope she stays away from gossip sites and magazines. I can already see the shit storm I'll have to deal with on top of everything else. Allan is going to have a cow.

# CHAPTER 4
## SAYLOR

om tries to engage me in conversation, but I'm barely listening to her. I keep staring out the window and thinking about Oliver. Did I make the right decision? Shouldn't I have at least tried to stay with him for a few days?

I don't remember being in love with him, but I've noticed how my body reacts when he's near me. Sure, it's purely physical attraction right now, but don't most relationships start that way? *Ugh!* Why can't I just stick to one decision without feeling so torn? But what if I succumb to the chemistry between us and ruin everything by giving Oliver false hope? The bleak reality is that I may never fall in love with him again.

The car finally stops, distracting me from the inner turmoil boiling inside me. I recognize the street. We're home. Mom tells me to wait so she can bring the wheelchair around, but the car is beginning to suffocate me. In the past week, I was able to regain most of the mobility of my left leg, so I open the door, getting out of the car before she has the chance to get to me.

My left hand is still pretty much useless, though. Bitterness pools in my mouth. The limb that I need the most is the one taking the longest to recover. Life is so fucking ironic.

"Saylor, I asked you to wait."

I'm using the car for support because I don't trust my leg completely yet. "It's okay, Mom. I don't need the wheelchair. I want to walk."

Mom loops her arm around mine and I let her help me walk to the house. I see the 'For Sale' sign and ask when she made the decision to sell.

"Just before your surgery."

I don't make a comment. I never understood why Mom never sold the house after—

I look up and freeze.

"Saylor? What's the matter?"

There's a loud buzz in my ears and I find it impossible to draw air into my lungs. All I can think about is him, how his breath reeked when he tried to kiss me, how his rough hands tore my clothes as if they were made of paper. I curl my hands over my stomach right before my legs give out, Mom unable to prevent me from dropping to my knees. Closing my eyes, I let out a cry that splits my soul in half. For whatever reason, I was brought back in time to a state of complete terror.

My mother is calling my name, but I can't hear anything over the loud sobs racking my body. Strong arms wrap around my shoulder and I fight the embrace at first, until a familiar scent reaches my nose. I remember that smell.

I open my eyes to find Oliver there, staring at me in panic.

"Sugar, talk to me." He touches my cheek.

"Ollie, I-I—" I can't finish the sentence, choosing to melt against his body instead. He hugs me tighter, and I bury my face against his chest. "Please take me home."

"You *are* home."

I shake my head while tremors run though my body. Pulling back, I look at him. "No, *our* home."

Oliver holds my face with both hands before running his thumbs over my cheeks, and I realize he's wiping my tears. I hold my breath as my gaze is ensnared by his. Slowly the tremor ceases and a wave of tranquility washes over me. I feel safe in his arms.

"Anything you want, sugar."

He helps me stand up and I cling to him shamelessly, without facing my former childhood home. Mom stands not too far from us, staring at me with remorse in her eyes. Her cheeks are wet, and I realize she was crying to.

"Mom, I'm going with Oliver. I can't stay here."

She nods. "I understand. I'm so, so sorry, sweetheart."

"Don't be. It's not your fault."

She shakes her head and I know my panic attack brought back all the guilt she's been carrying all these years. I hope I haven't set her back and that she doesn't shut me out again.

"Please call me once you're settled. I'd like to come by soon."

"Yes, of course."

Oliver clutches me tighter. "She's in good hands, Miss Carter. I won't let anything happen to Saylor. I promise."

"I know. You're a good man, Oliver."

I turn to him, noticing how my mother's compliment affects Oliver. He beams like he's not used to receiving such praise. I must be imagining things. Surely I told him how wonderful I thought he was many times. I can't imagine I would marry someone I didn't admire.

He takes me back to his car, a sporty number that must be a dream to drive. With his arms still curled around my waist, he opens the door for me. But before I slide in, I look into his eyes.

"Mom is right, Oliver. You are a good man."

He smiles, even though it doesn't reach his eyes. "We'll see if you think the same tomorrow."

I frown. "I don't understand."

He shakes his head. "You will soon enough."

♡ ♡ ♡

## OLIVER

I shouldn't have said anything, but I couldn't let Saylor believe I was some kind of perfect hero, favored by damsels in distress and their mothers alike. I'm rotten, and she needs to know who she's married to.

But now I find myself worrying about her. I almost lost my shit when I arrived at her mother's house to find Saylor on the ground, crying as if she was in terrible pain. All my problems took a back seat and I got tunnel vision. All that mattered was Saylor. I don't know how to broach the subject, though.

She keeps stealing glances my way as I drive, but so far hasn't said anything. I need to say something; otherwise, I'll go insane.

"What's going on in that beautiful head of yours?"

Saylor doesn't answer right away, just looks down at her lap. I grind my teeth while my knuckles turn white from holding on too tight to the steering wheel.

"I almost punched a paparazzo today," I blurt out. *Fuck it, might as well tell her how royally I screwed up earlier.*

"What happened?"

"He got in my face. I didn't punch him, but I ended up breaking his camera. I'm sure I'll hear from his lawyer soon."

"Does that happen a lot?"

"Me having confrontations with paparazzi?"

"No. Them hounding you like that."

"When I was in Boys Future, it used to be awful. Almost as bad as being chased in the street by rabid fans."

She whips her face my way, and I reward her with a wolfish grin.

"You were chased by fans?"

"Yup, but it only happened a couple of times. Anyway, after I quit the band and moved here, the fascination with me died down a little. That was until Wreck of the Day exploded and we started dating."

Saylor looks out the window, lost to her thoughts once more. I let her be. This is the most conversation we've had since she woke from the coma.

"Being at Mom's house brought back everything. All the awful memories I tried so hard to forget. It was like it had just happened."

A spike of rage stabs my heart. Thinking about what happened to Saylor makes me want to commit murder. If that piece of scum wasn't already dead, I would kill him.

I reach over and lace my fingers with hers. Her hand remains limp inside mine, but then I feel a slight pressure. I stop at a red light and looked down at our joined hands. "Did you just squeeze my hand?"

"I-I think so."

"Do you think that maybe you would like to invite the girls over for a jamming session?"

Saylor bites her lower lip, making me wish I was the one doing that. My cock twitches in my pants, even if wanting to bang my wife right now is completely wrong.

She doesn't answer right away, so I'm quick to add, "You don't have to."

"Actually, I love that idea."

"You do?" I don't want to sound surprised, but I did think she was going to say no.

"Yes, I miss them. I miss singing." Saylor's eyes spark for the first time since her surgery.

"Okay. It's settled then. I'll ask Allan to call them and order plenty of food. Let's make a party out of this."

Saylor nods as a smile unfurls on her face. A minute or so goes by before she speaks again. "What's the name of your aftershave?"

There she goes again surprising me. I squint at her. "I don't know, to be honest. It's some fancy shit my mother sends me every year for my birthday. Why?"

"No reason. When is your birthday?"

"It's coming up soon."

"Oh yeah?"

"Yep."

Trying to suppress a grin, I watch Saylor from the corner of my eye.

"Are you going to spill it on your own?" She's watching me through slits.

"Valentine's Day."

"Oh good." She faces forward, and now she has me curious.

"Uh, are you going to elaborate?"

"Sure. It means I only need to get you one gift."

"Yikes, I never knew you be so cheap, sugar."

"I'm not cheap. I'm practical. Besides, I bet you get tons of gift every year from your adoring fans."

"It's okay. There's only one thing I want for my birthday, anyway."

"What's that?"

"You, naked on our bed, with a red bow on top."

There's no reply from Saylor, and I realize a second later why. *Me and my dirty mind, fuck!* I turn to find sheer panic in her eyes.

"Ah shit. Sorry, Saylor. Force of habit. For a moment I forgot."

God, I feel like the biggest arsehole on the entire planet right now. Saylor has barely recovered from her panic attack and here I am making inappropriate comments.

"Don't worry about it. You caught me by surprise, that's all. No harm done."

She faces the window again and doesn't utter another word until we get home.

# CHAPTER 5
## OLIVER

texted Allan a few minutes before we arrived to ask him to give Saylor and me a couple of hours alone. I didn't want her to be too overwhelmed. It's weird to watch her walk into our home with hesitant steps and look at everything as if it's the first time she's been here. She only let me help her while going up the stairs, preferring to use the cane to walk around without me hovering nearby. It's amazing how fast she's progressed in just a week.

She stops in the middle of the living room and scans everything—the office desks, the promotion materials stacked on top of the filing cabinet, the floor-to-ceiling inspiration wall filled mostly with pictures of Wreck of the Day. They're mostly cutouts from magazines or professional ones taken during concerts. The band's official shots are also there. Saylor moves closer and scrutinizes every single one of them, lingering on the picture of the two of us singing at Wreck of the Day's first televised performance. That's my favorite of the bunch.

Saylor looks over her shoulder. "That's an intense picture. Were we already together there?"

"Yes."

You would have to be blind to not see the chemistry between

us in that picture. My chest is tight, my heart constricted in a painful way. I wish I could read Saylor's mind to know if any of those images are stirring something—if not a memory, at least a sense of familiarity.

I didn't expect it to be so hard to keep my distance from her, to not say anything inappropriate, to not touch her. It takes a Herculean effort not to pull her into my arms just like I did earlier when she was too lost in her panic attack to reject the gesture.

She moves on from our picture and focuses on the band's official image. Saylor is looking fierce front and center, flanked by her bandmates. Riley Michaels did a fantastic job capturing the band's essence.

Saylor points at the brunette holding the drumsticks. "Who is she?"

"Her name is Elisa Gutierrez, but everyone calls her Sticks."

"Is she good?"

"The best. You'll like her."

"Why do you run your business from your home?"

There she goes again calling our home mine. I don't correct her this time. "I bought this house with the intention of turning it into Renegades Productions' headquarters. Now I'm realizing it wasn't the best idea, not when the band practices here as well. It gets crowded sometimes."

Her eyes widen a fraction as she spins around, almost losing her balance in the process. "The band practices here? Where?"

"There's a studio downstairs."

"Why didn't you take me there first?"

I scratch the back of my neck. That would have been a better idea. "Uh, I don't know."

Saylor crosses the living room a little faster than before, but stops short right at the top of the stairs. "Damn. This is going to be a pain in my ass."

Moving closer, I stop next to her and offer my arm. "I don't mind helping you."

"I bet you don't." She doesn't look in my direction, just keeps glaring at the steps going down.

"I'm not sure if you're joking right now or if you're mad at me."

She faces me with eyebrows pinched together. "Neither. I'm just stating a fact. If I'm mad at anyone, it's at myself. I'm not used to not being able to do whatever I want, whenever I want."

"It's just a temporary situation, sugar. You've already done so well in such a short period of time."

Saylor lets out a deep sigh and faces downward again. "I know. I'm just cranky right now."

"Perhaps you want to check out your room first, get settled."

"Yes, that's a good idea. I'd like to wash off the hospital's grime too."

We head to the second-largest bedroom in the house, where my sister Charlotte was bunking at not too long ago. Of course, I would've given up the master suite if I thought Saylor would be comfortable there.

I let Charlotte redecorate the room to her style, so it's a bright room with the perfect mix of modern and classic furniture. The king-size bed with its million pillows and white cushioned headboard doesn't appeal to my personal taste, but it looks comfy enough.

I remain by the door while Saylor walks in, wanting her to know this is her space. I want her to feel at home.

"Pretty."

"I'll run to the car and get your stuff."

Saylor doesn't acknowledge me. Instead, she keeps walking until she disappears inside the bathroom.

"I have one of those shower stools," I say loudly so she can hear me from inside the bathroom.

She emerges a few seconds later, sitting on the edge of the bed. "I feel so tired all of the sudden."

"Why don't you take a nap? You've been through a lot today."

Shaking her head, she turns to me. "I'd like to shower first."

"Okay. I'll be right back."

♡ ♡ ♡

## SAYLOR

I've been trying my best not to show Oliver how much I'm freaking out right now. Seeing my pictures on that wall in the living room made me feel like a complete stranger to my own life. There wasn't a spark of recognition, no sense of déjà vu while I stared at myself living the dream I never thought I would actually achieve.

While I wait for Oliver to bring my stuff, I swing my legs, trying to make the left go as high as the right. I can't focus on the stuff I can't do; I have to rejoice in the things I can.

I switch my attention to my arm next. If I concentrate hard, I'm able to wiggle my fingers. I pinch the inside of my forearm, taking pleasure when I feel a little pain.

A strand of hair falls over my face and I catch a whiff of the god-awful smell clinging to it. *Shit. How am I going to wash it on my own?* At the hospital, the nurses or Mom did it for me. I still have stitches on the side of my head, and a bandage covering it. Even if I could move both my arms, I would still need help.

Oliver comes back carrying two huge suitcases. "Where should I put these?"

"Uh, just set them by the love seat. Did you pack all my stuff?"

"Not everything, only the items I knew you'd want."

"And now you have to bring everything up again. I'm so sorry for the trouble."

"Trust me. I'm glad to do it. You're not a burden, sugar. I don't want you to ever feel that way."

"Why do you call me sugar?" I might as well get that question out of the way.

"You don't like when I can you that?" he looks surprised.

"It's not that. I was just wondering if there was a special meaning behind it since most of my close friends call me Blue."

"I can't really say there's a special meaning. It's one of those things that happens naturally. Plus, I like that I'm the only one who uses that endearment."

My shoulders sag as I stare at the floor. I don't know why his answer is a little underwhelming. Perhaps because I have no memory of those little, natural progressions in our relationship.

"You look upset," he says.

"I'm not upset." I stand up, holding on to the edge of the bed for a moment until I trust I won't fall. "Do you mind helping with those suitcases? I need to find clean clothes to wear."

"Sure, no problem."

Oliver opens them both, pulling out a few neatly folded clothing items, as well as a smaller zipped bag with pink skulls all over it.

"What's in that?" I move closer.

"Uh, your underwear." Oliver doesn't glance my way. I'm glad he doesn't, for my cheeks are probably bright red right now.

This is so silly. He's my husband, for fuck's sake. Why am I embarrassed that he had to handle my panties and bras? I snatch the bag and hold it close to my chest as Oliver lays a pair of yoga pants and a loose button-down shirt on the love seat.

"Is this okay?" He points at the clothes.

"Yes, it's perfect. Thank you."

Unfurling from his crouched position, he looks everywhere but at me. "The bathroom is stocked with everything you need. I got your favorite shampoo and conditioner as well." He makes a move to leave the room, still not looking in my direction.

"Ollie?"

He pauses and I notice his shoulders tense. *Shit. I shouldn't have called him that.* He looks over his shoulder, his facial expression revealing nothing.

"Yes, sugar?"

"Uh, I'll need help with my hair. I can't…." I sigh, dropping my gaze to the floor.

"No worries. We can take care of that after your shower, okay?"

"Yes. Thank you."

I honestly don't know how I'll manage to shower on my own without falling on my face, but getting naked in front of Oliver terrifies and excites me at the same time. I just don't know which emotion is stronger.

# CHAPTER 6
## SAYLOR

Oliver set up a makeshift hair wash station in the kitchen by placing a cushioned chair in front of the sink and laying a plushy towel over the edge. My favorite brands of shampoo and conditioner are next to it.

"Feeling better?" he asks.

"Much. Wow, look at that."

"I know it's not hair salon quality, but I did my best."

"It's wonderful."

Before I take a seat, Oliver wraps a towel around my shoulders, keeping the edges tied together with a large hair clip. I stare at the base of his throat, trying my best to ignore how my body reacts when he's near me. I don't want him to notice and get the wrong idea. He's not just a guy I find attractive—he's my husband. If I let my body dictate my actions, I'm afraid I'll end up hurting him more.

I sit without making eye contact, leaning my head back. Now I'm staring at the ceiling.

"Are you comfortable enough?"

No. I'm so not comfortable with this situation at all. But I know that's not what he's asking.

"I'm good."

He pulls the strands of hair that got stuck between my back and the edge of the sink, spreading them out over the stone surface. In the process, his fingers graze the back of my neck. The light touch makes me shiver, and I begin to imagine what it would feel like if he touched other parts of my body as well.

*Shit. Why am I so horny all of a sudden?*

Oliver runs his fingers through my hair, moving the section covering the bandage on the side of my head out of the way. I bite the inside of my cheek to avoid letting out a moan of pleasure.

"Should I try avoiding getting this area wet?"

"Yes." My voice is weak, nothing but a whisper, and loaded with need. I clear my throat before I continue. "Dr. Laurent said he'll remove the stiches next week. I don't think the bandage needs to be changed yet, unless it's stained."

"Nope. No stains. That's a good sign, right?"

"Yes, it's a good sign."

"I should know all this." His tone is heavy with self-reproach.

I won't have him blaming himself for that. Feeling brave, I touch his arm. "Hey, don't beat yourself about it. You weren't there when I was discharged, and I wasn't supposed to come home with you, remember?"

Oliver stares at my hand for a couple of beats before his gaze connects with mine. "Okay."

I'm the first to look away, sliding my hand off his arm in the process. He turns on the water, using the faucet's pull-out sprayer to soak my hair. "How's the temperature?"

Closing my eyes, I sink into the chair. "It's perfect."

I can't keep myself from enjoying the experience. I've always loved having my hair washed at the salon. The fact that it's Oliver's fingers doing the job just brings an extra layer of satisfaction.

Careful not to get the bandage wet, he lathers my hair with shampoo, applying pressure on the right spots. I become boneless, unable to stop the little sounds in the back of my throat.

"Enjoying yourself?"

"Hmm?"

He chuckles and I smile without opening my eyes. "What's so funny?"

"Nothing."

I peel one eye open. "Don't get so cocky."

*What am I doing? Stop flirting, Saylor.*

"Sorry, sugar. I was born this way."

A snort escapes my lips at the same time soothing warmth spreads over my chest. "That was the corniest thing you've said to me."

"Not the corniest, but it's up there."

Willing to push through my fears, I ask, "Then tell me the corniest line you ever used on me."

"Blimey. Of all the things you could ask me, you want to know that?"

"Yes."

"Okay, fine. I once tried to seduce you using a Phil Collins song title."

"Oh my God. Which one? No, let me guess. 'Another Day in Paradise'?"

"Bloody hell. How did you know?"

I laugh and the bubble of amusement catches me by surprise. "Don't know. A hunch?" I open both eyes and find him staring at me, an enigmatic glint in his gaze. "What?"

"Nothing."

There's a noticeable shift in the air, a tension that wasn't present before. The levity of the moment is gone, leaving me confused as hell. Oliver finishes my hair without saying another word, and his silence makes my chest heavy. My eyes burn while a wave of sadness rushes over me out of nowhere. I barely notice when he turns the water off and motions me forward to dry my hair with a large towel. Then he turns the chair around, standing behind me to untangle my hair.

He tries to be gentle, but I flinch nonetheless when the comb gets caught in a stubborn knot.

"Sorry," he says.

"It's okay."

In another couple of minutes, his work is done. I don't look in his direction when I bolt from the chair and half run to my room. Locking the door behind me, I lean against the hard surface and finally let the waterworks loose.

*What's wrong with me?*

♡ ♡ ♡

## OLIVER

I keep staring down the hallway for minutes after Saylor disappeared into her room. My mind is reeling, and I don't know what I did or said that made her pull a one-eighty on me. Things were going great until she guessed the name of the Phil Collins song. Perhaps she saw something in my expression that freaked her out. Her lucky guess did take me by surprise. For a moment, I dared hope she was remembering.

The sound of someone coming up the stairs pulls me out of my head. A second later, Allan appears in the living room.

"Hey, is everything okay? You look like you saw a ghost."

"No, mate. Everything's fine."

"How's Saylor?"

"She's...." *Fuck, I don't know how to answer that.*

"Hey, remember this is all new to her. I can't imagine what it must feel like to not remember a big chunk of your life."

"I don't think I'm helping either. I keep forgetting she doesn't know who I am. I say things that make her uncomfortable."

Allan steps closer and pats me on the shoulder. "Perhaps you're focusing too much on your relationship. I think it will be good if Saylor starts playing with the band again."

"Yes, you're probably right. Did you contact the girls?"

"Yup. They should be here in a couple of hours. Everyone's excited to work again. It's been a rough couple of months."

I veer toward my desk and Allan follows me. "We need to look at the commitments the band made prior to Saylor's surgery and see when we can start honoring them again."

Taking a seat behind his desk, Allan fires up his laptop with a glint of determination in his gaze. "I've received several e-mails from reporters who want to interview her. Do you think she would be up to it?"

"We can ask."

"The sooner she grants an interview, the better. I don't want to sound like an insensitive bastard, but the band's momentum is waning. There's still interest thanks to Saylor's situation, but you know how fickle the public is nowadays."

Grinding my teeth, I stare at my curled right hand. Didn't even notice turning it into a fist. I've been in show business long enough to agree with Allan, but at the same time, I don't want to put too much pressure on Saylor.

Allan's attention returns to his computer, and moments later, his eyebrows furrow. "Oliver, is there something you forgot to tell me?"

Ah fuck. The paparazzi.

"Uh, I lost my temper this morning."

"You don't say." Allan stares at me like I'm a kid who did something really naughty and he's the parent.

"Someone at the hospital leaked information about Saylor's condition to the paparazzi. One of the douchebags knew she has amnesia."

"What? That's fucked up. We need to contact the hospital's administration. They need to start an investigation. That's a breach of patient confidentiality."

"I know."

"Well, how badly did you lose your temper? Did you hit the guy?"

"No. Just broke his camera."

Allan clenches his jaw and returns his attention to the

computer. "Call your lawyer. Let's be proactive about this. Be prepared to pay a hefty sum to make this mess go away."

"It's on my to-do list."

"You know this means we need to issue a statement. I'll draft the press release."

"Fuck." I drop my shoulders forward, leaning my elbows on my thighs. I should've kept my temper in check.

"I can spin this around in our favor. I'm going to sound like a son of a bitch, but I want you and Saylor in front of a camera ASAP."

Whipping my face up, I level Allan with a glare. "Are you fucking mental?"

"Oliver, to you and Saylor, her amnesia is fucked up, but to the public, it's golden. Think about it. After a whirlwind romance, the love of your life almost dies, and now she doesn't remember you. This is the stuff that makes the greatest love stories. People will eat this shit up."

"You want to monetize our personal struggle? What the fuck, Allan?"

"Listen, your problems will still be there no matter what. I don't want to monetize anything. I want to control the narrative. If we don't do it, people like Craig Hawthorne will."

I pinch the bridge of my nose, closing my eyes for a brief second. Allan's right. There's really no keeping our shit from the public eye.

It's times like these that fame is a fucking bitch.

# CHAPTER 7
## SAYLOR

After my breakdown, I didn't want to join my band members for practice, giving an excuse that I had a headache. I made Oliver more worried about me in the process, but I couldn't face my friends while trying to hold off the tempest of conflicting emotions swirling in my chest. I texted Tabatha and sort of told her the truth. She's been through a similar situation, so she understands what I'm going through.

I called Liv next and asked if she could take me to my first therapy session with the psychiatrist today. I planned to call an Uber and go by myself because I didn't want to tell anyone about it. But considering my emotions are all over the place, I need my best friend there in case the session is too much and I turn into a blubbering mess.

I barely acknowledge Oliver when I finally emerge from my room. I haven't seen him since he washed my hair yesterday, and his concerned gaze feels like a dagger striking my heart. Guilt is eating me alive. Thank God Liv is already waiting for me.

She meets me halfway and engulfs me in a tight embrace. "How are you this morning, Blue? Oliver said you had a headache yesterday."

I give her a tight smile. "I'm much better. I just needed some rest."

"Where are you girls headed today?" Oliver asks.

Instead of looking in his direction, I drop my gaze to my shoes.

"We're going shopping," Liv answers for me. I asked her not to tell anyone where we're really going.

"That sounds fun. Call me if you need anything."

"Will do."

Still not making eye contact with Oliver, I lace my arm with Liv's and spin us toward the stairs. "Shall we?"

"Sure. Bye, Oliver."

Only when we reach the pavement outside does Liv stop me to ask, "What was that all about, Blue? You barely looked in Oliver's direction."

"I-I…." I pause, taking a deep breath. "Every time I look into his eyes, I'm swallowed by guilt."

"Oh, Saylor. It's not your fault that you can't remember him."

"I know, but still."

"You just got out of the hospital. Things will get better, you'll see."

She wraps her arm around my shoulders and hugs me sideways. "Are you nervous about your session today?"

"I'm fucking terrified."

"Maybe you'll get a therapist like Billy Crystal in *Analyze This*."

I step out of Liv's embrace so I can better glower at her. "Are you implying that I'm the mob man?"

"Let's hope not. That would make me your minion." She smirks at me, making me roll my eyes.

"Okay, *minion*. Let's go. I don't wanna be late."

Once inside Liv's brand-new car—which I suspect was a gift from Bas—I pepper her with questions, mostly about her rekindled romance with the love of her life. After she's done filling me in, I ask, "Are you happy, Liv?"

"Yes, of course. I don't sound happy to you?" She frowns at me.

"You do, but... I don't know. I guess I'm a little bit pessimistic today. You know when you dream about something for the longest time, and when you finally get it, you realize that it wasn't exactly how you envisioned."

"Are we still talking about me?"

I shake my head and look out the window. "Not necessarily. I don't know what I'm talking about. Forget I said anything."

There's a pause before Liv continues. "To be honest, things aren't as picture-perfect with Bas as I thought they would be. Don't get me wrong, I love him so much, but since we got married, there's this new tension between us that I can't quite understand or fix."

"Have you truly forgiven Bas for what he did to you?"

"Yes. Well, at least I think I did. Ugh! I'm such a basket case. Maybe your therapist has an opening for me today."

I reach over and grab Liv's hand. "You're not a basket case. Life and relationships are complicated. Just look at me."

"I can't imagine what it would be like living with Bas without knowing who he is. How are you coping?"

"Terribly." I let out a shaky laugh. "Yesterday, I wanted to jump his bones."

"What? Shut up! Why didn't you?"

"Because I don't remember him. I don't think it would be fair to get physical with Oliver without the feelings." I sigh. "I know I sound crazy."

"Ah, I see. But it's a good thing you're still attracted to him."

"True, but what if I can't resist the guy? More and more his nearness makes me hot and bothered. Gosh, I don't remember being such a nymphomaniac before."

"You guy always had great chemistry. I think Oliver brings out that nympho side of you. Perhaps you're looking at things the wrong way."

"What do you mean?"

"Your amnesia sucks, I know. But it's given you the chance to experience falling in love with Oliver all over again. There's no greater feeling in the world. The butterflies in the stomach, the giddiness. I would kill to experience that again."

"I never thought about it that way."

The radio is on, and when a familiar melody fills the car, I freeze on the spot. "I know that song."

Liv turns the sound louder. "You should. It's your ballad with Oliver."

My heart begins to hammer violently inside my chest while my stomach ties in knots. I change the station.

"What's the matter, Blue?"

"I'm not ready to listen to it yet."

Liv peels her gaze off the road for a split second to watch me. Heat rushes to my cheeks and I look out the window, wondering if one hour will be enough to talk about all the shit that's been running through my head.

# CHAPTER 8
## SAYLOR

Oliver isn't home when Liv drops me off. I'm grateful for that, the session with the therapist having left me raw. We talked about many things, including my reaction to my mother's house. It was the right call to ask Liv to accompany me. We didn't talk much on the way back, but having her by my side helped soothe some of the anxiety clinging to my heart. I thought therapy was supposed to help, not make me feel worse. I'm not sure I'll return.

I hear the band playing the moment I open the front door, and my heart does a somersault in response. I missed playing with them so much. Perhaps that's the only therapy I need.

Before I make a conscious decision, I'm already moving toward the studio. The door is not completely shut, and all it takes is a little nudge with the cane to open it all the way.

Tabatha has her back to me, so Remi sees me first. She stops playing and shouts my name. Everyone freezes, sudden silence replacing the awesome jam they had going seconds before. Tabatha spins around. Before I know it, Remi crosses the gap between us, launching herself at me to trap me in a bear hug. I almost lose my balance.

"You're here!" she says.

"Yes, I am."

A rueful smile blossoms on Tabatha's face, eliciting a similar one from me. A pretty brunette walks around the drums and stops next to Tabatha. That must be Sticks.

Remi finally lets go of me to face our band members. "Do you remember Sticks?" she asks.

"No. Sorry. I have no memories of the past year."

"Ugh, sorry." Remi looks at me with a pained expression.

I don't like one bit that my handicap is making my friends uncomfortable. Unfortunately, I can't control people's reaction, so I just have to deal with it.

"Nice to meet you, Saylor." Sticks waves at me.

"I've heard you're a great drummer, the best we've ever had."

The girl shrugs and looks at her shoes. "I don't know about that."

"Sticks is very modest. But she kicks ass. We have Rori to thank for helping find her," Tabatha says.

"How so?"

"He organized an open audition at Closing Time. Sticks was the last contender."

Remi puts her hands on her hips. "Hey, what about my contribution? If it weren't for my intervention, Sticks would've never auditioned."

I laugh, completely at ease watching the banter between my bandmates. I hadn't realized how much I've missed this. Missed *them*.

"I sense that's a juicy story. I can't wait to hear it."

Tabatha drops her gaze to my cane. "How are your arm and leg doing?"

"My leg is better. I think I've recovered more than half of the sensitivity there. It's still numb, but I can walk around unassisted with the help of the cane. My arm is a different matter, though. Still super useless."

"But you still have your voice. You can jam with us," Remi says with a glint of excitement in her eyes.

"Yeah, I need to learn our new songs ASAP."

"Have you listened to any of them yet?"

I remember my duet with Oliver and wince. "Not all of them. Just the upbeat ones."

Tabatha stares at me through slits and I know she understands the message between the lines. "Let's start with those, then, and skip the ballad for now."

Understanding finally dawns on Remi's face. "Of course."

Listening to the songs I wrote and recorded without having any memory of doing so is weird to say the least. I can't believe I created them. I also sound a thousand times better than when the band first started. The songs are catchy and edgy. When I learn one of them is part of a movie soundtrack, pride fills my chest. Wreck of the Day has finally made it.

After listening to the new songs a few times, I'm finally ready to practice. My voice comes out as a croak at first and a bit off-key, but once my vocal cords warm up, I sound like myself again. And boy, does it feel good to be singing once more. I get so caught up in the moment that I forget one of my legs is lame. Holding on to the mic stand, I try to pivot and lose my balance in the process when my left leg doesn't cooperate. I fall to the floor like a bag of potatoes, but instead of feeling mortified, I start to laugh.

The girls stop playing to watch me warily.

"Oh quit looking at me like that. That was funny as shit." I push myself to a sitting position using my good arm before I wipe the tears of laughter that have rolled down my cheeks.

"That move was so ungraceful, it was painful to watch," Remi says with a smirk.

"Bite me. Try doing that with a lame leg."

"I wish I'd caught that on camera," Tabatha adds, and I stick my tongue out to her.

Bracing my hand against the floor, I try to stand up on my own, only to fall flat on my butt again. Remi starts to laugh.

"Shut up," I say, but it has no bite, not when I'm fighting to keep the giggles bottled in.

"It looks like you're drunk."

"Is anyone going to help me, or are you just going to stare and laugh?"

Tabatha puts her bass away, but instead of helping me, she crosses her arms in front of her chest and smirks. "Nah, this is just too much fun to watch. Come on, Saylor."

I turn to our new drummer. "Sticks, come on. A little help here."

The poor girl looks at me and then at Tabatha and Remi, not knowing what to do. "Uh…."

"What the hell is going on here?" Oliver shouts from the door, killing the fun in an instant. His eyes flash with fury aimed at Tabatha. "Why is Saylor on the floor?"

"Oh for fuck's sake. Will you relax?"

Oliver ignores Tabatha and strides in my direction, offering his hand when he's in front of me. I bat it away. "I don't need any help."

I'm so angry at him, I can't see straight. Why did he have to come in and ruin my fun?

"What happened?" he asks.

"I fell. No big deal."

He doesn't seem to get the message as he tries to help me again.

"Oliver, for fuck's sake. I don't want your help!"

I regret my harsh words immediately when I see the stricken look on his face. He unfurls from his crouch while the gleam in his gaze turns ice cold. "My apologies for worrying about you."

He's out of the room before I can apologize, leaving me feeling like a rotten cow.

"Fuck!" I rest my head in my hand. "I'm such a bitch."

I feel Remi's hand on my shoulder. "He'll be fine."

"I'm not so sure, Remi. How many more blows can Oliver take from me before he decides he's had enough?"

*Or he realizes I'm not worthy?*

# CHAPTER 9
## SAYLOR

never got to apologize to Oliver. After my outburst in the studio, he kept his distance, only speaking to me about work. Allan issued a press release about my condition, but the interview on camera he wanted Oliver and me to give never happened. Anyone could see the tension between us. It hurts to know I'm the cause, but every time I tried to reach out to Oliver, I chickened out, afraid to say something that would hurt him even more.

I fired my therapist after the second session. He was a moron who made me feel like everything I ever did wasn't good enough. Dr. Laurent and my mother disapproved, but mercifully, Oliver took my side—a fact that only made me feel guiltier.

My jamming sessions with the band are a much better alternative, and I have Liv to listen to me when I need to pour my heart out. However, the darkness inside my chest is still there, swirling without pause. Guilt and frustration are like a stone hanging around my neck, dragging me down.

I should focus on the positive aspects of my recovery. After ten days of physical therapy, I can now walk without a cane. Cheryl tells me every day how amazing I'm doing, but the perverse part of me refuses to let her words sink in. My arm is still useless, and there's no sign I will ever recover my memories.

Without anyone knowing, I've been waking up before dawn every day to practice with Rita alone. And with each day without progress, my frustration grows.

Today, I decide to do something drastic. Scrolling through Wreck of the Day's songs on my phone, I press Play on my duet with Oliver. My heart clenches again when the familiar and yet foreign melody fills my ears. The urge to cry comes unbidden. I clench my jaw and fight the feeling, managing to listen to the first verse where I'm singing solo without bawling my eyes out. It's only when Oliver's voice joins mine that I have to pause the song. Pulling the earbuds off with a jerky movement, I throw the device far away, hiding my face between my hands.

*Just breathe, Saylor.*

I focus on inhaling and exhaling, and nothing else. It takes a while for my heartbeat to return to normal, for the urge to cry to subside. I don't know why that particular song plays havoc with my emotions like that. Perhaps I should try writing a new one.

I've always kept a notebook inside Rita's case, and upon inspection, I see that it still holds true. As I pick it up, a folded piece of paper falls from inside. I set the notebook aside and unfold the loose sheet. My heart gets lodged in my throat. This is a work in progress, a new song I must have been working on right before the surgery. My eyes fill with tears as I read the verses. It's like a window to my state of my mind then, to my feelings. And it's also a love declaration to Oliver.

Hastily, I fold the paper again, shoving it back inside the notebook. I'm not ready for it, not by a long shot.

*Let's just focus on practicing, Saylor.* I pick Rita up, propping her on my lap and connecting to the amps. I move my right arm slowly, placing my hand over the strings, but I can't feel them. It's like my fingers aren't attached to my hand. I will them to move, to do anything, but they remain frozen there. Dropping my chin, I bite my lower lip in concentration.

*This is useless.*

A strand of hair falls in my face, tickling my nose. I try to blow the rebel wisp out of the way. It doesn't work. Irritated, I set Rita aside and stand up with a jolt. On a table nearby, I spot the pair of scissors Remi used yesterday to open a box. I make a grab for them, veering toward the small bathroom just outside the studio. There's a small mirror there just above the sink, and I hate the image reflected in it.

Dr. Laurent has removed the stitches, but the shaved area is still very much visible under the longer strands covering the spot. I look fucking ridiculous. Without pausing to think, I part a section of my hair and chop it off. It's a much harder task using only one hand, and the result is atrocious. I look worse than I did before. Dropping the scissors in the sink, I sit on the toilet and begin to cry. It's ugly and loud, but who cares, right? There's no one around to witness me crumble.

"Saylor?"

I wince when I hear my name. Of course, Oliver had to find me today of all days.

"Go away." I curl into a ball, giving my back to him so he can't see my face.

"No." He grabs me by the shoulder and forces me to stand up to look at him. "I won't let you shut me out anymore."

"You don't understand. I'm a fucking mess. I don't want to drag you down with me."

"Get it into your thick head, sugar. I'm not going anywhere. I've made a promise to you, and God help me I'll keep that promise, even if I have to fight you to do so."

"Why?"

"Because I love you. You're the air I breathe. You bring light into my life."

I open my mouth to argue, but he talks over me. "Yes, even in your darkest moments, you're still my guiding star."

"I don't deserve you," I whisper, dropping my gaze.

"Don't ever repeat that. I'm the one unworthy of you."

I bring my eyes to his face again. He stares at me with such intensity, it robs me of air. This feels like a moment for something epic. I want to throw myself into his arms and kiss the hell out of him. But I just drop my gaze again and wipe my wet cheeks.

"What were you trying to do?"

"I got sick of my long hair."

Oliver makes a sound in the back of this throat, drawing my attention to him again. His gaze is glued to the scissors and the chunk of hair in the sink.

"All right. Sit back down."

"What? Why?"

"Just do as I say, sugar." He grabs the scissors and stares me down until my ass is back on the toilet seat.

Oliver runs his hands through my messy hair, dividing it in sections. "Sugar, promise me something."

"What?"

"Don't ever try to play hairdresser again. You suck balls."

"Shut up. Try cutting your hair using only one hand. What are you going to do?"

"Even this mess out. Then I'm calling Monni."

"Who is Monni?"

He chuckles. "Aw, sugar. I better not spoil it for you. Monni is someone you should meet without expectations."

"You're making me curious, and that's just plain mean."

His lips twist into a crooked smile and something shifts in my heart, as if a small piece lodged back into place.

*Oh my God. Am I remembering?*

# CHAPTER 10
## OLIVER

I can't keep the grin off my face as I watch Saylor stare wide-eyed at Monni, the band's stylist. He's a little less flamboyant today, having paired a tight white button-down shirt with even tighter jeans. But it's the fake orange tan and all the gold accessories that are probably making Saylor's brain go haywire.

We meet the man at an upscale hair salon in Beverly Hills, and after he finishes hugging and kissing Saylor a thousand times, he leaves us alone to talk with the hair stylist.

Saylor yanks my arm, pulling me closer to her. "You hired that man to be in charge of the band's image?"

I don't speak for a few seconds, too distracted by the proximity of Saylor's mouth to mine. "Have you seen how badass you guys look in every single photo?"

Saylor glances at me, notices there's barely any distance between our lips, and steps away. Monni returns with Eduardo, who stares in shock at Saylor's hair.

"*Dios mio!* Who did that to you?"

I open my mouth to answer, but Saylor elbows my arm and says, "Self-inflicted. They had to shave part of my hair for surgery, and well, it was already a hot mess."

Eduardo wraps Saylor's shoulders with a black cape and steers her toward a leather chair in front of a tall mirror. Peering at her through the mirror's reflection, he picks up random strands of her hair. "I'm glad there's still some length left for me to play with. What kind of style are you looking for?"

"Uh, I was thinking perhaps cutting it chin length with a few layers. I also want to shave the side of my head."

Eduardo looks down at Saylor's hair and frowns. "Is your hair naturally this blonde?"

"Yup."

"*Niña*, half my clientele would die for your hair. How about we have some fun with it?"

"Meaning?" she asks, and I take a step closer.

"I'm thinking rainbow."

"Yes!" The word rushes from my lips before I can stop it. Saylor raises an eyebrow at me and the corners of her lips twitch up. I rub the back of my neck as heat spreads over my cheeks. "Uh, you had mermaid hair when I first met you."

"What color?"

"Some sort of aquamarine blue, like your eyes."

"Oh, pretty," Eduardo interrupts. "We can do different hues of blue on the inside layers and the bottom. It will look gorgeous."

Without taking her eyes off me, Saylor nods. "Sounds good."

I'm left speechless. Did she just agree to that color because of what I said? It's been a hell of month, and I don't dare believe she's actually going to let me in, but my stupid heart still beats faster than normal.

While Eduardo does his thing, I talk with Monni briefly, and when the stylist leaves, I make some phone calls. Maybe I'm jumping the gun here, but I want to take Saylor out on a date tonight. I make a reservation in one of the best restaurants in town. The place is usually booked for months, but I just need to drop my name to get a table.

Two hours later, Saylor appears in front of me a changed woman. Her long hair is much shorter now, and the shaved side gives her an edge that suits her well.

"So? What do you think?" She touches her styled hair, a little uncertain.

"Stunning."

"It's strange. I've never worn my hair this short before."

I stand up and stop in front of her, taking a strand of her hair between my fingers. "Sugar, you would look gorgeous even bald."

She twists her face into a frown. "That sounds like a bad pickup line."

"It's not a line, it's the truth."

"In that case, thank you." There's a brief pause during which Saylor glances at everything but me. "Do you mind driving me to the hospital? I have therapy in an hour."

"Of course, sugar. Can I come with you this time?"

Her eyebrows furrow in a deep V as she looks my way. She doesn't need to say anything. I have my answer.

"I would prefer to go alone. It's nothing against you, I just don't want you to witness another embarrassing moment from me."

Her answer does something to alleviate my disappointment. She can keep me out of her therapy sessions as long as she agrees to have dinner with me tonight.

I don't simply drop Saylor off at the hospital and leave, choosing to wait for her in my car so I can drive her back home. A little over an hour later, she walks out of the building accompanied by a young Asian woman. They are talking animatedly before they hug. I can't sit in the car for another second. Burning with curiosity, I step out and make my way to the duo. Saylor's companion notices me first and her eyes widen.

"Oliver, what are you still doing here? I told you I could get an Uber."

"It was no big deal. I got a lot of work done in my car."

The woman next to Saylor clears her throat, making Saylor blush in response. "Ah, sorry. Oliver, this is my physical therapist, Dr. Makamoto."

"Nice to meet you, Doc."

We shake hands and she says, "You can call me Cheryl."

She keeps staring at me without saying a word, making me uncomfortable. I rub the back of my neck and glance at Saylor, who is watching the doctor with amusement in her eyes. *Did I miss something?*

"I'm sorry. This is so rude of me," Cheryl finally says. "I didn't mean to stare at you like that. I'm not some crazy fan, I swear. It's just a bit surreal to meet a Boys Future member in person."

"No worries. I get that all the time."

"You owe me five bucks," Saylor tells the doctor.

Cheryl rolls her eyes and retrieves a fiver from her back pocket. "Oh, all right."

"What kind of bet did you lose?"

"It's too embarrassing to tell."

Saylor chuckles before she continues, "Cheryl claimed she was above being starstruck, that she could meet you without acting strange."

The woman crosses her arms in front of her chest and glares at Saylor. "Laugh all you want, Saylor. Don't forget I have your ass for another month."

"Ugh! Don't remind me."

"How is she doing, Cheryl?" I ask.

Saylor hits my chest with the back of her hand. "Hey! I'm standing right here."

That's all it takes. Just a touch from her, even a meaningless gesture like that, sends my heart into overdrive. Cheryl watches everything with a hint of smile on her lips.

"Saylor is doing fantastic. She was able to flip me off with her left hand today."

I choke on my own saliva, which turns into a coughing fit.

"Hey, are you all right there?" Saylor asks.

"I'm okay. I would love to see that."

"See what?"

"Your left-hand birdie."

Saylor watches me through narrowed eyes while her lips make a flat, thin line. "Keep pushing me and you will."

We say goodbye to Cheryl, heading to my car. When I follow Saylor to the passenger side to open the door for her, she stops to glower at me. "What are you doing? I can open my own door."

Ignoring her, I pull the door open. "I know, but can't I be a gentleman?" I don't even try to hide the grin of mischief.

She squints at me. "You're trying to get me to flip you off, aren't you?"

"Me? Of course not."

"Right." She enters the vehicle still glowering at me.

I join her a moment later, still with a shit-eating grin on my lips. I've missed this easy banter between us.

"So, what do you have planned for today?"

"More practice with the girls." Saylor looks out the window and rubs her hand against her yoga pants.

"What is it, sugar?"

"I'm getting the itch to write new songs, but without being able to play Rita, it feels like I have paper but no pen."

"I could help you out. Our last collaboration was a hit."

I hear her loud intake of breath, which makes me turn to watch her face. She turns to me and our gazes lock. "I haven't been able to listen to our duet yet."

The euphoria exits my chest in a loud whoosh, leaving me hollow. "Why is that?"

She shakes her head and looks away. "It hurts too much."

My hands curl tighter around the steering wheel. I don't like that answer at all.

"I'm afraid to look too closely at what I'm missing," she

continues. "I want to remember you, Ollie. I want to remember *us*."

Tears suddenly prick my eyes, and I have to blink repeatedly to keep them at bay. Curling my hand over hers, I say, "You will, sugar. You will."

# CHAPTER 11
## SAYLOR

let Oliver help me up the stairs because I think he needs to feel useful right now. I didn't mean to tell him about the duet. It just came out. I know the truth hurt him deeply, and I'm tired of doing that to him.

*I'm such an idiot. I should just keep my mouth shut from now on.*

The girls are already downstairs in the studio playing, but I need a shower and a change of clothes. Before I head to my room, Oliver stops me.

"Do you feel like debuting your new hairstyle tonight?"

"What do you mean?"

"Would you like to have dinner with me?"

The way he asks me, as if his entire world revolves around my answer, makes my heart flutter. He's my husband and he's making me as giddy as a high school girl.

"Yes, I'd love that." *Ugh, could my voice sound any weaker?*

His eyebrows shot heavenwards. "You would?"

"Yes, Ollie. Why is that so hard to believe?"

"Okay then. We have reservations at seven."

"Wait, what? You made a reservation already?"

He gives me a wolfish grin, and if possible, the butterflies in my stomach become more savage.

"I didn't know you would say yes, but I was hoping. I guess I pulled a Bon Jovi and lived on a prayer."

I stare at him unblinking for a couple of seconds before a burst of laugher escapes my mouth. I laugh so hard, tears form in my eyes. "Oh my God. That was awful."

"Making memories here, sugar. I have to add to my repertoire."

"Have I ever say something corny to you?" I cock my head to the side, ignoring the voice in my head telling me to stop flirting.

"Nah, you're too cool for that. But there was that time you got sloppy drunk...."

My jaw drops. I was never a sloppy drunk. "I call bullshit. I can handle my liquor."

"Apparently not when you're partying with the Goulas."

"Ugh, Oliver. Now you have to tell me what I did."

He walks backward, grinning like a fool. "Maybe I'll tell you tonight if you play your cards right."

I flip him off and when he looks stunned, I realize I used my left hand again to do it. His smile stretches wider and his eyes dance with glee.

Without another word, I spin on my heels and head down the hallway. Alone in my room, I lean against the closed door and take deep breaths to calm down my out-of-control heart. I don't know what's happening to me. Was it just this morning when I was ready to do something stupid? The constant one-eighties are making my head spin. If I still had a therapist, I could ask him if these types of mood swings are normal or if the surgery did irreparable damage to my brain. Perhaps I should find a new therapist, someone who isn't a douchecanoe.

♡ ♡ ♡

liver knocks on my door at 6:00 p.m. sharp. I've been ready since five, but I was too chicken to leave my room until the very last moment. It took me forever to pick the right clothes for the occasion. I want to impress him, but I have no idea what he likes. When my hand brushed against a light, billowing skirt, I recognized it from the picture in the living room.

Now that I'm wearing the exact same outfit from the night of our very first televised performance, I don't know if it was the smartest idea. I'm terrified of Oliver's reaction, but it's too late to change now. With a deep breath, I open the door wide.

Holy shit, Oliver looks hotter than sin wearing a crisp button-down shirt paired with a navy jacket and slacks. The heady scent he favors makes me dizzy in a good way.

His gaze drops to my shoes before slowly traveling back up the length of my body. There's a myriad of emotions swirling in his blue gaze, but I can't hope to decipher any of them.

"Ready?" His voice is restrained, thick, and I wonder if he's feeling the same pull I am.

*Shit*. Maybe agreeing to go out on a date with him wasn't the smartest idea.

"Yes."

His Adam's apple bobs up and down before he nods. "After you."

I walk ahead of him, self-conscious all of a sudden. My back is tense as my body and mind are at war with each other.

We don't say much on the way to the restaurant. I only make a meaningful comment when Oliver pulls up in front of a busy restaurant. This was so not the place I was expecting him to take me.

"This is it?"

"Yes. It's one of the best restaurants in town."

"It looks… busy."

"You sound disappointed."

I'm not sure if disappointed is the right word. Perhaps I was expecting something else. I smile at him, hoping it doesn't come across as fake. "No, not at all. It's just been a while since I've been surrounded by so many people."

"You'll be fine, sugar. I'll be your knight in shining armor if anyone tries to bother you."

"I bet you would love that."

My door opens and a valet guy helps me out of the car. Oliver hands over his key to another man before walking around the car to place a warm hand on my lower back. He leans closer to my ear. "You look stunning, by the way."

Heat spreads through my cheeks at the same time a spark rekindles in the pit of my stomach.

"Thanks. So do you."

Oliver leans back and smiles from ear to ear. "You think I look stunning?"

"Ugh. Shut up. Shall we go in already?"

"Of course, sugar."

After we're greeted by the hostess, she leads us to our table, which I note is one of the best in the restaurant. I'm conscious of all the eyes on us, and it's a great effort not to squirm under the scrutinizing gazes. I feel much better once we're seated.

Our waiter comes by and introduces himself. Oliver asks if I want to drink something. It's a tempting offer—it would definitely help with my nerves—but I still have that sloppy drunk story hanging over my head, so I just order water.

I pretend to be distracted with the menu, not knowing what to say to my husband. I feel his scorching gaze on my face, though, so after a minute of trying my best to ignore him, I finally shut the menu and lock eyes with him. "What?"

"Nothing. Just admiring your new haircut. It looks so badass."

My cheeks burst into flames. It seems I can't take a compliment anymore, especially one coming from him.

"Eduardo did a good job."

Oliver nods with a smile before looking at the menu. "What are you in the mood for?"

"I honestly don't know. Probably something light. I'm not that hungry."

"The salmon is really good here."

I follow Oliver's suggestion and order the salmon. Once the waiter is gone, I lean forward and narrow my eyes at Oliver. "All right, husband of mine. Out with it. Tell me that sloppy drunk story. I still think you're lying."

Oliver leans back and grins at me. "I'm not sure you're ready for it."

"Try me."

"Okay. It happened at the farewell party the Goulas threw for you and Remi. You know you used to work there, right?"

"Yes, Remi filled me in."

"Apparently, you can't handle your Greek wine."

"What did I do?"

"Well, you could say we were on a break at the time. I came by the restaurant to talk business with you and you pretty much sexually assaulted me."

"I did what?"

"You were all over me, sugar, like a hobo on a hotdog."

"Shut up!"

Oliver bursts into laughter, and it's the most glorious sound ever. I get caught up in the giggles as well.

"I swear I'm not lying."

"And what happened?"

"What do you think? Nothing, of course. I may be a rascal, but I don't take advantage of intoxicated girls."

I freeze when he says 'girls', a spike of jealousy surging through my veins. "You were quite the player, weren't you?"

Oliver's gaze narrows and his expression loses some of its levity. "Yes, but all the other women ceased to exist to me when we got together. You're the only one I want, sugar."

"The one I need, oh yes indeed," I sing, and the smile returns to Oliver's face.

I'm so captivated by him that I don't notice we have company until a woman's voice interrupts our moment. Looking up, I find a bimbo in a tight dress staring at my husband as if she wants to eat him for dinner.

"Oh my gosh, it is you. I couldn't believe my eyes."

"Uh, hi?" he says, a bit too friendly for my taste. Why isn't he glowering at the blow-up doll who had the audacity to interrupt us?

"Would you mind signing an autograph for me?"

"Sure, luv. Do you have a pen?"

"Yes," the woman says with too much excitement, completely ignoring the death glare I'm aiming her way. She gives the pen to Oliver and leans forward, shoving her fake boobs practically in his face. "I don't have a piece of paper. Do you mind signing it here?" She points at her cleavage.

I can't control my tongue any longer. "You have got to be fucking kidding me!"

My outburst makes her jump back, as if she's noticing me for the first time. "Oh, I'm sorry. I didn't see you there."

I curl my good hand around the fork, ready to stab the bitch's eyes out. "Get lost before I have you arrested for solicitation."

She puts a hand over her unnaturally enlarged chest as her face twists into an expression of outrage. "How dare you!"

I spot the waiter not too far from our table, and somehow I'm able to flag him using my left arm. It seems the muscle only cooperates under stressful situations. The waiter comes to our table, and yet the bimbo still doesn't take the hint.

"Is there a problem, ma'am?"

"Yes, this woman is bothering us. I thought this was a distinguished restaurant."

The waiter promptly takes action, and with as much discretion as he's able, he guides the overenthusiastic fan far away from us. But it's too late now. She's managed to ruin the evening.

I can barely hear anything over the sound of my pulse roaring in my ears. When my gaze connects with Oliver's, I find him grinning.

"You think that was funny?"

"That woman shoving her tits in my face? No. But your reaction to it? Priceless."

I stand up, not feeling like staying in this stupid restaurant for another second. I sense all the stares aimed at our table, which only makes me feel worse.

"Where are you going?" Oliver asks, catching on that I'm not in the mood for jokes.

"I'm leaving."

I pray that I won't trip as I walk out of the restaurant with all the dignity I can muster. I don't look back to see if Oliver's following me. I honestly don't care.

Once outside, I ask one of the valet guys to call a taxi for me. Oliver appears by my side and says it won't be necessary. He gives the guy his ticket and together we wait in silence for his car.

"Sugar—"

"Don't."

He swallows whatever he wanted to say. He also doesn't try to speak to me again during the drive back home. I stare out the window the whole time, drowning in the anger that won't go away.

Okay, maybe I'm overreacting. Oliver didn't do anything wrong besides feeling amused at my expense.

When he parks in the garage, I'm the first to get out, stomping all the way to the stairs. I don't wait for him, confident that I can make the trek up unassisted. I feel his presence looming close behind me, though, and thank fuck I don't fall flat on my face.

"Saylor, come on. Are you going to give me the silent treatment now? I wasn't going to sign that woman's breasts."

"But you still looked."

"They were right in my face!" I hear laughter in his voice, so I spin around to glare at him.

"Don't lie to me and say you weren't enjoying the attention."

"I couldn't give a fuck about her. What I did enjoy was your jealous reaction."

My spine goes taut. "I'm not jealous."

"Are you sure? It's okay to be."

"Ugh! Stop being so cocky."

He takes a step closer, grin growing wider. "Why? You love when I'm cocky."

*Danger. Danger. Abort. It's time for you to go, Saylor.*

I take a couple of steps back, the anger quickly turning into something that feels a lot like desire.

"I can't remember loving anything. Good night, Oliver."

I spin on my heels so fast, my skirt gets tangled with my legs and I almost eat the floor, managing to catch my balance at the last minute.

"Whoa, are you okay there?"

I don't answer, striding down the corridor without a glance back.

# CHAPTER 12
## OLIVER

Saylor didn't speak to me the entire weekend. She locked herself in the studio with the girls, and I decided to make myself scarce to avoid more conflict. Despite her overreaction to the incident on Friday, I can't say I'm not happy about it. She got jealous, which gives me hope.

I will get my wife back.

She didn't say goodbye to me before she left to her therapy session, and I decide enough is enough. She's had plenty of time to get over whatever's eating her arse. It's not only jealousy that's making her act in this erratic manner—one time she seems happy and relaxed, the next she wants to bite my head off.

I take care of my to-do lists in the morning and head out, planning to surprise Saylor at the hospital. Once there, I buy the biggest bouquet of flower the hospital's shop has, which works bloody fantastic as a shield. I'm not in the mood to be recognized right now.

After getting directions to the physical therapy room, I find the door open. From the hallway, I can hear animated voices, and I recognize Saylor's laughter right away. *Excellent. She's in a good mood. Let's see if my presence here will make it turn sour.* I step into the room and the first person I see is that wanker Derek, sitting all smug in a chair, watching Saylor do her exercises.

*What the actual fuck.*

I lower the bouquet and glare at the doucheface. With a jolt, he jumps from his seat and has the gall to approach me with an outstretched hand.

"Hey, Oliver. How's it going?"

I drop my gaze to his hand, then stare at him again with murder in my eyes. The smile on his face wilts at the same time he drops his offending appendage.

"Good to see you, Oliver," Cheryl says, but I'm too lost in my anger to acknowledge her.

Derek turns to Saylor. "I'd better go. Good luck with practice, Blue."

I make a guttural sound in the back of my throat, which makes it clear I'm two seconds away from smashing his Ken doll's face in. Without another word, he walks around me and leaves. Now I aim my annoyance at Saylor, who's staring at daggers at me. Why am I not surprised?

"What are you doing here?"

"I could ask the same question about that wanker. I thought you didn't want an audience."

"Derek just dropped by to say hello. It's not like he can come visit me at the house."

"You got that straight. I don't want that preppy doctor anywhere near our place."

Saylor stalks in my direction, stopping in front of me to poke my chest. "Get it into your thick head, Oliver. Derek is a friend. Why do you hate him so much?"

"Why? Have you forgotten what he did right before Bas and Liv's wedding?" The moment the words leave my mouth, I realize my mistake.

"Yes, I did forget!" Saylor steps back.

"Guys, please calm down." Cheryl stands between us.

Saylor's reaction makes the anger inside my chest deflate like a balloon. What the hell am I doing?

"I'm sorry. Of course you can't know. That guy rubs me the wrong way for more than one reason."

"You need to get over it because Derek isn't going anywhere." The glint of defiance in her eyes tells me she's dead serious about it.

"Here, I brought this for you." I drop the flowers on the seat Derek was occupying a minute before. "I'll wait for you in the lobby."

"I'm not going home with you."

Clenching my jaw, I keep from saying something idiotic like 'Yes, you will.' Enough with the caveman attitude.

"All right, luv. I'll see you at home."

## SAYLOR

I'm still riding the anger wave when Oliver walks out of the room. But once he's gone, I want to collapse to the floor and cry like a baby. It didn't escape my notice that he called me 'luv' instead of 'sugar.' Somehow, I know it's a terrible sign.

"Those are beautiful flowers."

Through tear-filled eyes, I stare at the bouquet, guilt sneaking into my already bruised heart. *He must have come here to apologize for last night. I shouldn't have lashed out at him. I'm such a hypocrite. Didn't I get mad jealous not twenty-fours ago for something Oliver didn't do?*

"Ugh. I'm a fucking cow."

"Hey, don't beat yourself up for it. Oliver did overreact about Derek's presence. What's his beef against him anyway?"

"Derek used to date my best friend, Liv, who is now married to Oliver's best friend, Bas. There's more to it but it's a long story. I need to go after Oliver."

I pick up the flowers and practically run out of the physical therapy room. It's not until I'm already at the hospital's main lobby that I realize I forgot my purse. Cursing loudly, I spin on my heels to find Cheryl running in my direction.

"Forgot something?"

"You're a lifesaver."

"Is he gone?"

I turn toward the sliding doors. "Probably. I hope he went home."

"Why don't you call him?"

Shaking my head, I pull my cell phone out to call an Uber instead. "No. I need to speak to him in person."

A message pops on my screen. I just missed a call from Emma. A second later, I receive a text from her. **Do you want to meet up for lunch?**

I haven't seen Emma since she came to visit while I was still recovering. I'm tempted to blow her off, but on the other hand, maybe going out with her is exactly what I need.

I text her back, saying I'm still at the hospital. A second later, she offers to pick me up.

"Are you going to be all right? I have another appointment in five minutes."

"I'm good, Cheryl. A friend is picking me up. Thanks for bringing me my purse."

"No problem. And Saylor?"

"Yes?"

"Go easy on that boy, will you? He's clearly madly in love with you, but love doesn't thrive if it isn't nurtured."

Her wise words make my stomach clench. She's one hundred percent right. Memory loss or not, I've been acting like a total bitch to Oliver and he's been taking it without complaint.

While I wait, I scroll through the pictures on my phone, something I haven't allowed myself to do until now. There are way too many pictures of us that are painful to see. We were so in love. How do I get that back?

*Can I get it back?*

The picture that really puts my heart in overdrive is the close-up of our hands, showing off our wedding bands. A lonely tear escapes my eye, but before it rolls down my cheek completely, I wipe it off. Enough with the trip down memory lane. I have to accept I may never recover my memories. It's time to make new ones. If my reaction yesterday was any indication, I want Oliver in my life.

I send him a quick text message. **I'm sorry.**

A minute later, he replies. **No worries, sugar. I'll see you at home.**

*At least he didn't call me 'luv' again.*

# CHAPTER 13
## SAYLOR

"Why do you always like to come here when you're in town?" I slide into the booth and Emma does the same across from me.

"Uh, because they have amazing burgers?"

I watch her through slits. "Somehow I don't believe that."

Emma rolls her eyes. "Fine. I was hoping Rori would be here today. He's so dreamy."

"Aha! I knew it. But wait. When did you meet Rori?"

"We came here one night, after Liv's wedding dress fitting." Emma stops abruptly and her face changes. "Ah shit. Sorry, Blue. It's so easy to forget that you don't remember the past year."

"It's okay." I shrug. "It's better than people walking on eggshells around me. Please tell me you didn't sleep with Rori."

Emma hunches her shoulders forward and lets out a loud sigh. "Sadly, no. You didn't even let me say hello to him properly."

"Good. I like coming here. I don't want it to be weird."

I'm surprised when Emma doesn't fight me on it. Instead, she seems distracted as she looks around the semi-empty pub.

I reach out and touch her hand. "Hey, are you okay?"

The weird glint in her eyes vanishes, replaced by her usual

cheerful one. "Yes. Everything's great. I'm finally moving back to Cali."

"That's amazing. But what about your job?"

"Well, I still need to give notice, but it's not like they can't live without me."

"It will be great to have you back."

"Yeah, it'll be nice to have my friends near me again. Plus, Dad needs company. You know he got divorced again, right?"

"No, I didn't know that. How long did that one last?"

"Not even a year."

I look down, not wanting to think that perhaps I'll be divorcing in less than a year.

"What's up, Blue? Besides the whole gap in your memories. Is everything good at La Maison Best?"

"Maison Best?" I raise an eyebrow at her.

"It suits it. Better than calling it Renegades HQ."

Toying with the condiments on the table so I don't have to look in Emma's eyes, I say, "Things are strained at best. Sometimes it feels like we have this great bond, Oliver and me. Things are so easy. But then he does or say something that reminds me that I don't actually remember him and I crumble like a house of cards. I feel like I'm walking with a constant dark cloud over my head."

"Would it be so bad if you didn't remember the past year? Couldn't you make new memories? You can't possibly say you don't get hot and bothered around your husband. That man is yummy."

I know Emma is only joking, but a spike a jealousy still surges through my veins. I clamp it down.

"That's the problem. I constantly have to watch myself. Every time he's near me…." I pause to lick my lips and close my eyes. "Let's just say I have to take a cold shower afterward. I've never been so horny."

"What's keeping you from jumping his bones?"

"I don't want to give him the wrong idea. He's not only a guy

I find irresistible, Em. He's my husband. I need to at least feel something more than pure lust."

Understanding dawns on her face. "Ah, I see. And do you think you could fall in love with Oliver again?"

Her question makes me pause. Sometimes I think I'm already falling for him, but the anger at the universe keeps swirling in my chest and clouding everything.

"I-I don't know." I glance at my hands.

"Saylor, look at me."

With a loud exhale, I do as she asks.

"You have been given a second chance at life with a man who worships the ground you walk on. Are you going to throw it all away, or are you going to grab this chance and never let go?"

I squirm under Emma's intense stare. "When did you become so insightful?"

She twists her face into scowl. "I've always been insightful."

I give her a pointed look and she continues. "I hide it well."

Her lips split into a smile before she drops her gaze to the menu. "Well, since it seems I'm not getting my eye candy today, I better stuff my face with the most delicious greasy burger they have."

I end up ordering the same ten-thousand-calorie burger as Emma, but don't even eat half. I'm so nervous, I lost my appetite. Emma doesn't seem to notice, talking a hundred miles an hour about her life in New York and her many conquests. I listen to her partially, my mind going back to Oliver. What am I going to do about him?

The house is eerily quiet when I open the front door, so I call out Oliver's name as I come up the stairs. Reaching the landing, I find the main room empty. Allan's laptop is gone. Maybe he had an appointment.

Oliver comes into the living room a moment later with a

towel wrapped around his waist and nothing else, his chest still gleaming wet from the shower. He's drying his hair with another smaller towel in the most relaxed manner, as if prancing almost naked into his office isn't a big deal. What if the girls were here?

"What's up, sugar?"

I open my mouth to reply, but I'm hit with a sudden flash of memory—Oliver standing in front of me in the exact same manner. The image is gone before I can place it, leaving behind a blinding headache. A dizzy spell hits me, forcing me to take a side step to keep my balance.

Oliver is in front of me in an instant, his warm hands holding my upper arms. "Saylor, are you all right?"

His lemony scent hits my nose at full strength, almost making me whimper. I stare at the base of his throat, taken over by a sudden desire to lick the droplet of water still there.

*Calm down, Saylor.*

"Yes, I'm okay. I came up the stairs too fast."

"Would you like to sit down? I'll grab you a glass of water."

Taking a step back, I look at everything but him. "I'm fine. Clothes would be good."

I don't need to glance in his direction to know he's grinning. "What? Is my hot bod bothering you?"

"As a matter of fact, yes. Your glistening abs are very distracting. You look like you've been Photoshopped."

Oliver bursts out laughing, the sound creating havoc in my heart. I turn to him and wish I hadn't. I'm two seconds away from tackling the guy. God, I sound like a hormonal teenaged boy who can't control his sexual urges.

"What's so funny?"

"That's a line from *Crazy, Stupid, Love.*"

Wrapping one arm across my middle, I glare at him. "So? Do you have exclusivity rights to borrowing lines from songs and movies in this relationship?"

His smile grows bigger. "No, sugar. You can lay all your corny lines on me."

I walk toward Allan's desk and sit down, needing to put a barrier between Oliver and me. "Where's your right-hand man today?"

"He went to San Diego to check out a potential band."

"Oh, so you're looking for new talent." I can't help the disappointed tone in my voice. "I guess that makes sense."

"Hey, don't be like that. Renegades is a production company. We've always intended to add more talent to our roster."

"What's going to happen to Wreck of the Day if I can't play?" I stare at my semi-useless hand. I can feel some tingling sensation, but my hand's only cooperated on a few occasions.

"You still have your voice and your talent to compose music. If needed, we can find a guitarist."

I whip my face in his direction. "Hell no!"

"Calm down, sugar. It's just a contingency plan. I have complete faith that you'll recover the movement in your left hand. You can already flip me off with it."

Hunching my shoulders forward, I concentrate on wiggling my fingers. Surprisingly, they obey.

"Did you want to speak to me?" Oliver asks as he sits on the edge of the desk, the towel on his waist parting in the middle.

My gaze drops to his crotch as my cheeks become hot as lava.

"Saylor?" Oliver probes again.

Clearing my throat, I peel my gaze from his nether region. "I'm sorry I didn't tell you about Derek before."

Oliver loses his relaxed stance, his spine going rigid. "Was he there during every session?"

"No. He joined the first time. He went to med school with Cheryl, you know?" Looking up, my gazes connects with his. I want Oliver to read the truth in my words. "The reason Derek was there, why his presence didn't bother me, is because I don't care if I screw up in front of him. I don't want to impress him."

"Are you saying you want to impress me? Sugar—"

"Ollie, please, let me finish. Derek has no hold to my heart whatsoever. Your jealousy is misplaced."

Oliver keeps staring at me without saying a word for what feels like an eternity.

"All right, I'm going to put some clothes on before you combust on the spot." He hops off the desk with the grace of a cat. "If you want to change, do so now. I'm taking you somewhere."

"Where?"

His lips twist into a crooked smile. "Ah, it's a surprise, sugar."

# CHAPTER 14
## OLIVER

Saylor keeps staring at me, as if by doing so, she'll be able to read my mind. I try my best to maintain an impartial expression, but it's hard not to smirk a little. I'm smug, but I shouldn't feel that way. I don't know if I'm doing the right thing here.

I can tell Saylor is impatient when we drive by the welcome sign to Littleton. She can't sit still.

"Have I ever told you I don't like surprises?" she says.

"Everyone likes surprises."

"I don't."

"Relax, sugar. I'm not taking you to a sex shop, if that's what has your panties in a bunch. Actually, is there even one in this village?"

"Hey, don't dis Littleton. It's a great city to live in."

"Would you like to come back here? We could easily buy a house."

"No!"

"Wow! So much for your love of your hometown."

"Please tell me that's not what we're doing here."

Chuckling, I signal to turn onto the street Saylor once brought me to. "Nothing quite as dramatic. Here we are."

Saylor looks out the window before she turns me, her eyes round as saucers. "How did you know about this place?"

"You brought me here once when I was having a hard time. I can tell you all about it another day. So, are you ready to go on a treasure hunt?"

Without another word, Saylor gets out of the car. This time, we don't have to jump the wired fence to get in Blueberries' Antiques. Pity, I was kind of looking forward to climbing Marvin again.

I wave to the tree as I follow Saylor in. "Hello, Marvin."

Saylor stops and spins around so fast, I almost bump into her. "You know his name?"

"Oh yeah. Marvin and I go way back."

Squinting, Saylor pokes my chest with her index finger. "You're telling me that story when we get home."

I chuckle, grabbing her hand to kiss the knuckles without taking my eyes off her. The glint in her eyes turns from annoyed to molten in a split second. I never wanted to kiss Saylor more than I do now. I'm about to succumb to the pull that's stronger than me when the bark of a dog interrupts me.

Saylor turns, pulling her hand from my grasp in the process. "Oh my God. Xander, I can't believe you're still alive.

The German shepherd jumps on her, dirty paws smearing mud all over her clothes. She doesn't seem to mind. Instead, she laughs like a little kid as the dog proceeds to lick her face.

"Okay, okay, down boy."

He listens to her command, only to attempt to do the same to me. I step out of his way, less inclined to have my clothes smeared.

"What? You don't like dogs?"

"Dogs are brilliant. Their dirty paws and wet kisses, not so much."

Saylor wipes her cheek with the back of her hand. "Yeah, it's a little disgusting. But I couldn't reject the poor guy. I haven't seen him in…." Her eyebrows furrow. "Ugh, I hate this."

I move closer, placing a hand on Saylor's lower back. "It's okay, sugar. It hasn't been that long, only a few of months or so."

She nods once before stepping out of my reach to peruse the backyard. The rows of broken furniture and other gnarled pieces are just as bad in the daylight. But Saylor used to love this place, so I figured she would like coming here again.

I'm not surprised when she makes a beeline toward the same spot she did on the night she brought me here. However, there's only an empty space now where the old swing used to be.

"Oh no. It's not here." She sounds so disappointed.

"What's not there?" I pretend to be clueless.

"The old swing. It was my favorite piece in this place. I used to play in it while my mother looked around."

"I'm sure it's standing in someone's backyard, making another little girl happy."

"Or it could have just corroded completely and turned to dust."

"Way to think positive, sugar."

She looks over her shoulder to stick her tongue out to me. My cock twitches in my pants. *Fuck me.* All the wicked things I have planned for that sinful mouth. *Patience, Ollie boy.*

"Do you want to look around? Maybe find a piece for a DIY project?"

Saylor turns around, looking at everything and nothing. "I haven't done those in a very long time."

"I know."

"Are you going to help me?" There's such a vulnerable glint in her gaze that I want to pull her tight against my chest.

"Help with what? Picking out something?"

"That and also help work on it."

Rubbing the back of my neck, I glance at the closest piece of junk next to me. "Uh, I've never done anything like that. I'll probably fail miserably at it."

Saylor lips twist into a smirk. "Oh my God. Did Oliver Best just admit he's not good at something."

I take a couple of steps in her direction with all the swagger I possess. "I'm good where it counts."

I drop my eyes to her lips and once again, I notice Saylor's reaction to my proximity. It's the hitch in her breathing, the way her lips part just a fraction, as if she's unconsciously inviting me to taste her cherry-flavored Chap Stick.

The magnetic pull between us is too strong, and I'm tired of fighting it. I lean closer, determined to kiss my wife today. Her eyes focus on my mouth, and when her pink tongue darts out to lick her lower lip, I almost lose my shit. There's barely any gap between us now. My heart feels like it's going to explode.

At the last minute, Saylor seems to wake up from the lust fog and steps away.

Clearing her throat, she says, "Uh, I think I saw a table that could use some love."

She scurries away with the dog close on her heels before I can stop her.

*It's okay, sugar. Your walls are crumbling down tonight.*

## SAYLOR

My heart gallops at full speed the entire trip back home. I don't know what to do, I'm fidgety, and my palms won't stop sweating. There's some overwhelming energy swirling in my chest that I haven't felt since I was a teen. It's crazy, but I think I have a crush on my husband. How many people can say that? The question is, should I give in and see where it'll lead?

The tension in the air surrounding us is palpable; it's an electricity we can't deny. I avoid looking at Oliver at all costs as I walk ahead of him, which only proves to be a terrible idea. His gaze on my back scorches my skin. It makes me feel vulnerable, but it's also like a soft caress. Chills run all over my body.

I have every intention of hiding in my room, but Oliver won't let me escape so easily.

"It's a lovely day. Shall we hang out by the pool for a little bit?" he asks.

"Sure." The answer leaves my lips before I can process the ramifications. I *am* a silly girl crushing on the hottest guy in school. I have no free will anymore.

*Cut the bullshit, Saylor. You're dying for a taste of Oliver Best.*

He walks around me to open the sliding door. The chilly gust of wind barrels through the opening, and I shiver inside my jacket. "Perhaps going outside isn't such a great idea after all."

"Aw, come on, sugar. I'll start a fire. Maybe we can toast some marshmallows."

I'm immediately sold on the idea. I do love those gooey sweet treats. "How about some hot cocoa too?"

"Consider it done. Let me start the fire first."

I follow him outside, but it takes me a moment to realize Oliver had ulterior motives to bring me there. The old swing that used to be my favorite thing in that secondhand store is standing on the other side of the pool. It looks a little worse for wear, but I recognize the chipped red and white paint, the rusty chains. One of them is broken, and the seat is hanging at an angle.

I peer at Oliver, my vision already blurry. "You bought my swing?"

"Sure did, sugar. I thought it could be my DIY project. I know I have my work cut out for me. Do you like it?"

"Do I—" A huge lump forms in my throat and the words get stuck there.

My feet start moving of their own accord until I stop right in front of Oliver. I have to crane my neck to stare into his eyes. Breathing is almost impossible with the way my heart is beating at full speed. Oliver keeps staring at me with a sweet smile on his lips and a promise in his gaze.

Raising on the tip of my toes, I give him a soft, chaste kiss on the lips. Holy cannoli, it doesn't matter. Heat spreads through my body like wildfire, uncontrollable and devastating.

I try to take a step back, but Oliver wraps an arm around my waist, keeping me in place.

"Not so fast, sugar."

His warm palm cradles the side of my face right before he brings his lips to mine again. His tongue darts out, teasing the seam. I'm too weak to fight my own traitorous body, so I lean closer, melting against his chest and succumbing to Oliver's invasion with glee.

If there were awards for first kisses, this would take first prize. It's heady and is making my head spin. Raw energy crackles just above my skin, curling around my limbs in a sensual dance. I grab his arm so I can remain upright. I've never been so lost and found at the same time.

Oliver is the one who pulls back first. If it were up to me, I would never stop kissing him.

"Now that's better."

Heat rushes to my cheeks. I'm embarrassed that I so easily lost control. I think if Oliver hadn't stopped, I would've jumped his bones right here and now.

"I-I-I'm cold. I'd better get back inside."

"What about the marshmallows and hot cocoa?" Strangely, he doesn't seem disappointed.

"Maybe some other time."

I run back into the house as fast as I can because I'm one second away from ignoring all my self-imposed barriers and demanding Oliver continue what he started.

# CHAPTER 15
## OLIVER

Saylor locked herself in her room yesterday and didn't come out again. When I woke this morning, her door was still shut. Perhaps I should be worried about her reclusion, but I'm too fucking happy about yesterday's kiss to let concern dampen my mood. As it is, Allan finds me whistling when he comes into the office. It takes him all of five seconds to ask why I'm so cheery.

"No reason," I say.

"I don't believe that for a second."

"How was the trip? Fruitful, I hope." I quickly change the subject, wanting to keep my progression with Saylor on the down-low.

A glint of excitement shines in Allan's eyes. "Well, the band I went to see was a total bust. But then I wound up at this local bar where a brother and sister duo were playing. They were freaking awesome."

I pull up a chair and take a seat. "Go on."

"They're twins. She plays the piano and he's the voice. Both very talented."

"I take it you have an idea for them?"

"Oh yeah. I think they could make a great dance-rock band.

We just need to find a drummer and a guitarist."

"And what did they think about that idea?"

"Are you kidding me? After the stratospheric success of Wreck of the Day, they were freaking excited."

"All right. You should arrange for them to come over. Maybe they can jam with the girls."

"Sticks would love that."

There's a different tone in Allan's voice when he says our drummer's name, and it gets me curious. "How are things going between the two of you? No more awkwardness?"

"To be honest, I haven't had a chance to talk with her properly. I think she's avoiding me."

"I'm not going to beat around the bush here. Are you interested in her?"

The way the color drains from Allan's face is almost comical. "What? Why would ask that?"

"I don't know, mate. You change every time you mention Sticks. Listen, I don't care if you do, and I have no problem if you two decide to hook up. As longs as the feeling is mutual, I'm cool with it."

"Now I'm seriously offended. I would never force myself on any woman. I'm not a worthless bastard."

"Sorry, I didn't mean to offend you. But you didn't answer my question. Do you like the bird or not?"

Allan's cheeks turn a deep shade of red. He can't hold my gaze. "No, Ollie. I do not like her in that manner."

"Hey, mate. Poker? Not your game."

## SAYLOR

I wait until I'm certain Allan is around to finally venture out of my room, not trusting myself around Oliver alone. I couldn't sleep last night, just kept reliving that unforgettable kiss over and over again. I wonder if our actual first kiss was that intense, that consuming. If it was, then I'm glad I got to experience it all over again. It turns out there's a silver lining about my memory loss: I get to relive my firsts with Oliver all over again. Finally, I don't feel completely broken that I can't remember the last year.

Oliver and Allan are talking animatedly when I enter the living room. Oliver pauses briefly to look in my direction, and his lips break into a grin. "Good morning, sugar. Sleep well?"

"Marvelously." I veer toward the kitchen so he can't see the deep dark circles under my eyes. Not even makeup could hide it. I need caffeine stat.

"I'm glad to catch you. I want to discuss Wreck of the Day and our future plans," Allan says.

"Sounds good. Let me get coffee first and we can talk."

Five minutes later, I'm sitting across from Allan. Oliver has pulled his chair next to mine, but mercifully he left a little gap between us.

"You know the CW has included one of Wreck of the Day's songs in their new series, right?"

"Yes, Tabatha filled me in. That's amazing."

"It really is. They've started filming the series and the writers had mentioned earlier that they would love it if the band could make a cameo appearance on the show."

My stomach twists in knots because I know what Allan is going to say next.

"They need us ASAP, right?"

"Yes. We're talking early next week."

"So soon? I-I can't play Rita yet."

Oliver moves closer and places a hand on my arm. "Hey, sugar. Don't worry. You don't have to play live. They add the sound later."

I drop my gaze to my left hand and manage to curl into a fist. "Still, I have to pretend I'm playing the guitar."

"I've spoken to one of the producers. He's aware of the situation and he guaranteed it won't be a problem."

I can't keep postponing the band's comeback. I've been too selfish lately, only caring about my problems.

"Okay," I say.

"There's another thing I'd like to run by you. I've found a potential new talent in San Diego, and I would like to invite them to play with the band."

"Oh, that's cool."

My reply is a little less enthusiastic. Why am I being so petty? Renegades is a production company. Wreck of the Day wouldn't remain their only talent forever. I should be happy they've found other people to work with.

No longer in the mood to talk business with Allan, I stand up. Music is calling to me. "I'm heading to the studio."

I feel Oliver's frown aimed in my direction, but I don't acknowledge it. I also need to think what about my next move when it comes to him. Are we dating now? I snort in my head. The thought is ludicrous. How can someone date their husband?

As soon as I enter the studio, I receive a text message from Liv. **Hey, I'm not sure if you know already, but Oliver's birthday is coming up.**

I pause in my tracks. "Crap," I say out loud.

I don't bother typing back, but call her right away. She answers on the first ring. "I'm such a cow."

"Hello, good morning," Liv replies.

"Sorry, good morning."

"I take it you didn't know about his birthday."

"I did, but it totally slipped my mind."

"But it's on Valentine's Day. How could you forget? Oh, that sounded so mean. I'm sorry."

"No, be mean all you want. I deserve it. Time has gone so fast. I didn't realize the day was approaching."

Liv laughs. "It's okay, Blue. Do you want to do something? Maybe we could all go out to dinner?"

I think about Oliver's sweet surprise yesterday, and I want to repay him in kind. That's what I propose to Liv, a surprise birthday party for Ollie. She's completely on board, naturally. I also tell her about the swing.

"That's so sweet," she says.

"I know. There's more."

"Oh do tell."

"I kissed him."

Liv yells so loud I'm forced to pull the phone away from my ear.

"That's awesome, Saylor. Ollie must be over the moon."

"I don't know. I kind of bailed afterward. One more reason for me to do something amazing for him. He's taking so much shit from me."

"Don't worry, Blue. Oliver's party will be epic."

# CHAPTER 16
## SAYLOR

Oliver and I haven't kissed again only because I avoided being alone with him in the past week. There were lingering touches and caresses on both our ends, but things were busy enough that it didn't seem like we had regressed in our relationship. At least I hope he doesn't think that was the case. But every time I caught him staring at me, I saw written in his eyes the promise that he would have me soon enough. The thought excited and terrified me at the same time. Oliver is a hot enigma I won't be able to fight much longer.

We filmed our cameo appearance last week. It took the entire day, mostly because there was a lot of waiting between shots. Tiring but also fun, and we got to meet the cast.

Today, I gave Oliver an excuse and headed to Liv's place so we could plan his surprise birthday party. Liv had the brilliant idea to throw a themed party since his birthday falls on Valentine's Day, so it's going to be a "Love Shack"-styled party full of hearts, cupid, and glitter galore.

She's driving me back home now, and I'm covered in the stuff. Oliver is going to notice, no doubt. He sees everything, and I don't have an excuse to justify the amount of pink and red glitter all over my hair and clothes.

"Why does it have to be so clingy?" I rub my hands against my jeans.

"Beats me. I think I even have glitter in places the eye can't see," Liv replies.

"Well, if Bas shows up with glitter on his tongue, I'll know why." I laugh and Liv smacks my arm.

"Take your mind out of the gutter, will you?"

"I can't. I feel like I'm on the verge of exploding. You have no idea how hard it is to live under the same roof as Oliver without getting any action. I've never masturbated so much in my life."

"Why are you keeping him at arm's length, Blue? Are you still denying that you've fallen in love with him?"

"What makes you say that?"

"Oh come on. I'm not blind. I see the gleam of excitement in your eyes every time you say his name."

"The thing is, I'm afraid the feeling isn't real, that it's just the lust talking."

"That's the stupidest thing I've ever heard. Don't be afraid to put yourself out there. You deserve to be happy."

I look out the window, mulling over Liv's words. Maybe I should stop fighting the current pushing in Oliver's direction. I'm sure he would love it if I was his birthday present.

I shake my head. Having sex with him doesn't seem enough. The surprise birthday party doesn't seem enough. What can I give him that will show how much he means to me, even if I can't bring myself to say the words out loud yet?

Like a spark in the dark, the idea comes to me. The work-in-progress song I found a few weeks back. What if I finished it? Anxiety turns my stomach into knots; I don't know if I'm ready to work on it. Even as I balk at the idea, it takes hold in my head. That's it. If I can't bring myself to finish that song, I have no business entertaining the idea of having sex with Oliver. It's all or nothing.

Up ahead, a guy wearing a dog costume catches my attention. He's carrying a sign advertising a dog shelter event nearby.

*Hmm, cute dogs sound like a great distraction right now.*

"Hey, Liv. Do you want to check that out?"

"Puppies? Heck yes."

"Well, it's a dog shelter event. I'm not sure if they have puppies there."

"They're all puppies to me."

Liv turns onto the street the sign is pointing at. Farther down the road, several cars are parked on each side of the street. Colorful balloons and white tents make the event's location hard to miss.

"How crazy would it be if we both brought dogs home?" Liv asks.

"Bananas crazy."

Getting a dog never crossed my mind. I love them, but I've always felt they were too much work. But it breaks my heart seeing all those abandoned dogs and hearing their stories from the volunteers. It does make you want to take them all home.

Liv sees something that catches her attention and veers in that direction without a word to me. A woman on a mission.

I continue alone, stopping in front of the last cage on this trek. Inside, there's a German shepherd, sitting on his hind legs. He reminds me of Xander. I read the name written on the sign: 'Felix.'

"You were named after a cat?"

The dog makes a noise that sounds like a snort, as if he understood me. Then he lies on his belly, resting his muzzle on top of his paws. He turns slightly onto his side, allowing me to see the jagged white scar on the side of his head. Just like mine.

"Hi, there," a volunteer greets me.

"Hi. What's his story?"

"Oh, we're not quite sure. He broke into someone's yard and they brought him to the shelter. He was emaciated and covered in fleas. The folks who brought him in were kind enough to pay for the vet bills."

"And that scar?"

"He already had it."

"How long has he been in the shelter?"

"Six months. He's very smart. Unfortunately, he's not a social dog, and it's hurting him finding a new home. If we don't place him with a family soon, he'll have to be put down."

I stare at the guy, appalled. "You mean you're going to kill him?"

"It's awful, I know. Hopefully we can find him a home today."

I turn to the dog, and then I crouch in front of his cage. "Can I take him out?"

"Uh, I'm not sure."

I level the guy with a glare. "How do you expect him to be social when you keep him locked in a cage?"

"Hey, you look familiar."

My cheeks turn hot and I avert my gaze. I'm not used to the whole fame thing yet. Liv finds me then, carrying a furry ball in her hands.

"What's that?"

"Saylor, meet Fritz Coleman."

"You adopted a dog?"

"I sure did. What do you think? Isn't he the cutest?" The dog wags its tail and licks Liv's face.

"That's the ugliest dog I've ever seen."

"Shut up."

"I knew I recognized you from somewhere," the volunteer interrupts. "You're Saylor Blue from Wreck of the Day."

"Yes, she is," Liv is happy to rat me out. I give her my death stare, which she promptly ignores.

"Holy crap. I love your music. Can I take a selfie with you?" The guy already has his phone out.

*Fine, if there's no way out of this, I might as well get what I want in return.*

"You can if you let Felix out."

"Duh, of course."

Oh my God, what a one-eighty in attitude! People are so silly when it comes to celebrities. The volunteer opens the cage, but the dog doesn't move from its prone position. He truly isn't a social dog.

Well I'm not having that. Getting onto my knees, I venture half in the cage.

"What is it, boy? Are you shy?"

Reaching out, I scratch the back of his ear. Felix closes his eyes, enjoying the caress.

"Wow, he never lets anyone near him. He must like you," the volunteer says.

I'm not sure what it is about the dog that draws me to him, whether it's his refusal to be a happy-go-lucky dog when he clearly has been through some serious shit, or the scar.

I get out of the cage and turn to the volunteer, still on my hands and knees. "What do I need to do to take him home with me today?"

"You want to adopt Felix?" The guy's eyebrows shoot to the heavens.

"Yup."

"I'm not sure. This is my first time helping out. I'm doing it to fulfil my fraternity's charity work requirements. Let me get a supervisor."

It turns out taking Felix home is super easy. Red tape is usually involved—a fact no one bothered to tell Liv. First and foremost, the shelter wants proof that a person can actually take care of a dog. But since I'm willing to use my fame to promote the event, the supervisor approves Felix's and Fritz's adoptions on the spot.

On the way home, we stop at a pet superstore and Liv and I go crazy. Her car is filled to the brim with pet toys and food. When we finally arrive at Renegades, we see Sebastian's car parked in front of the house.

"Did you know Bas was coming over?" I ask.

"Nope, he didn't say anything."

"This is going to be epic." I smile

"We couldn't have planned it better." She matches my devilish grin.

# CHAPTER 17
## OLIVER

hear the front door open but don't think much of it. My face is buried in the fridge, looking for the damn bangers I thought I still had. It's not until I hear Bas curse loudly that I turn around. *What the fuck!* We've been invaded by a couple of fur balls.

"Surprise!" Liv yells from the top of the stairs.

"What the hell is that?" Sebastian points at a tiny dog going ballistic in my office.

"That's Fritz Coleman, our newest dog," Liv answers with a cheeky smile.

"What?" My mate's reaction is comical. I would've laughed my ass off if it weren't for the other, much larger dog in my house.

"What about that one?" I point at the German shepherd.

"Well, that's ours." Saylor moves closer to me, smiling from ear to ear.

"You got us a dog?"

My jaw drops. Of all the things she could've done, this is a total surprise, especially when we're still unclear where we stand as a married couple.

"His name is Felix. Do you see the resemblance?" She points

at the scar on the dog's head and then everything becomes crystal clear to me.

I never thought I would own a dog one day. But seeing the happiness on Saylor's face makes me fucking ecstatic that she got him. I walk out of the kitchen and stop in front of the dog. He stares at me, cocking his head as if he's unsure if he likes me or not.

"Is he friendly?" I ask.

"He is to Liv and me."

I raise my hand to pat his head, but the dog barks a warning. I pull back quickly. "I don't think he likes me very much."

Saylor scratches his head and the dog melts under her touch.

"It seems you've got some competition there, Ollie," Bas says.

"Blimey. I can't win."

Saylor surprises me when she pulls me into a side hug, the most affection she's shown me since the kiss. "No competition here."

"Aw, look at you guys," Liv says.

I turn to Saylor. "Really, sugar?"

She glances up, looking into my eyes. Her gaze glints with mischief. "None. Felix wins."

Her lips curl into a grin and I narrow my eyes at her. "Oh yeah? Can he do this?"

I wrap my arms around her waist, pulling her closer to steal a kiss. As usual, I find myself lost in the taste of her. She doesn't fight me and I wish we were completely alone. When the dog begins to bark like mad, I step away, not wanting to lose a limb.

"It seems you have a cock-blocker there, mate." Bas laughs, earning a smack upside the head from Liv. "Ouch, what did I say?"

Saylor's face is a serious shade of red as she crouches in front of the dog to calm him down. "It's okay, boy. Oliver wasn't attacking me."

The dog barks twice and I shit you not, it looks like he's smiling at Saylor.

*Fuck, I truly think I have competition.*

"I never realized you wanted a dog. I could've come with you to pick one," I say.

"I wasn't shopping for a dog." Saylor stands up. "I saw a sign on the side of the road about the dog shelter event and something just prompted me to go check it out. I think I was meant to find Felix."

I narrow my eyes at the dog. "You better be nice to me. Otherwise I'll cock-block *you*."

"Oh my God. Can you stop talking about cock-blocking?" Liv says, and her strange dog agrees by barking several times.

"Well, at least you're a good-looking fella," I say to Felix. "You could look like that chap over there. What is that, anyway? A cross between a mop and a Gremlin?"

Saylor snorts and Liv glares in our direction. "Fritz is not ugly!"

"Of course not, baby. He's exotic," Bas says with a straight face.

I stare at him like he's lost his mind. When Liv walks outside, taking her ugly-ass dog with her, he adds, "What? I don't want to be banished to the doghouse. I like having sex with wife."

"Oh yeah? So, you're not going to tell her you've decided to join Renegades?"

The levity leaves my friend's face as he stares out the sliding doors. "Of course I'll tell her."

Saylor tilts her head to the side. "Am I missing something? Why would Liv be upset that you decided to work with Oliver?"

"She doesn't want me to return to showbiz. She thinks it corrupted me."

"Did it?"

"No. If anything, it helped me. I was in a bad spot for a long time, Blue. Granted, I did some stupid shit while I was in the band. Ollie's a witness."

"Witness? More like an accomplice." I turn to Saylor. "I was bad, sugar. I want you to know who you married."

Saylor seems embarrassed as she glances away. "Well, I know."

"You do?"

"I googled your name after you told me about the paparazzi."

"Hello? I thought we were talking about me." Bas waves a hand between Saylor and me, but he's not smiling. "Anyway, Liv is really against the idea, even if I would be working behind the scenes."

"Bas, I'm sure if you explained why you want to do it, she would understand. Maybe you have other unresolved issues."

"What? Did she say anything?"

"No, I just noticed something was off."

Bas looks out the door again where we can see Liv playing with Fritz.

"I—you're right. Things are strange between us. I barely see Liv. She works so damn much."

"You'll work things out. Your love is of the legends."

Bas smiles at Saylor, then looks over her shoulder at me. "Yours too, Blue."

He goes after Liv, leaving Saylor and me alone to deal with that statement. Slowly, she turns to me. "Is he right? Was our love of the legends?"

"Not was. *Is*. I'll prove it to you, sugar."

She stares at me without blinking for several beats, her face revealing nothing, until she gives me the best answer I could hope for.

"Okay."

# CHAPTER 18
## SAYLOR

Mandy called complaining that she hasn't seen me since I left the hospital, so I asked her if she'd like to come to physical therapy with me. Now that I don't suck so much anymore, I don't mind an audience.

Cheryl runs me through some leg exercises, and when I'm able to keep my balance standing on my left leg, she's satisfied with my progress. We move on to focus on my hand, which is taking the longest to improve. First she tests each finger to assess my motor coordination, then gives me a stress ball.

"Seriously?"

"What? They're great to rebuild your muscle strength."

"Yeah, I know. You gave me one weeks ago and I've been using it daily."

"Don't get snappy me with now, Mrs. Best."

It's the first time anyone has called me by my new last name. It's so strange to be called Mrs. Best.

Cheryl's phone ring, which is odd because she never brings it with her during our sessions. She looks at the screen, then, without glancing in my direction, says, "I'm sorry. I have to answer this."

She walks out of the room, leaving me alone with Mandy.

"She seems nice."

"She's awesome." I keep squeezing the stupid ball. I do hate these exercises.

"Is everything okay, Blue? Have you remembered anything?"

"Things are good, and no, no memory recover. Although, I had a flash of a possible memory, but it happened too fast for me to be sure."

"Really? Have you told anyone?"

"No, you're the first one to know. It involves Oliver and me, and well, I don't want to get his hopes up."

"How is he handling things? It can't be easy for him."

"Oliver's been great despite it all. I can see why I fell in love with him before."

"Is it still past tense?"

I let out a loud exhale as I press the ball harder. "I don't know yet. He makes me feel things I can't explain. It's possible I'm falling in love with him, but I want to be certain before I say anything, you know?"

Mandy nods and looks down at her lap.

"What's up with you? How is school?"

"School is great. Grandma's in a nursing home now. Connor's as busy as ever with work."

"And how are things with you, missy? No boyfriend?"

"No boyfriend, but I did meet someone."

"Oh, please share."

Mandy bites her lower lip and begins to pick at her nails. "There was one night I stayed with Emma at her hotel. I couldn't sleep, so I went to the rooftop area to do some writing. He came in and we talked."

"And?" God, getting anything out of Mandy is like pulling teeth. She was always reserved like that.

"I let him read what I had been working on."

"No way! You've never let anyone read your stuff. I mean, you didn't a year ago."

"I'm still kind of shy about my writing, which is stupid since my dream is to be a screenwriter."

"So what compelled you to share that part of you with a mere stranger?"

"I don't know. Maybe because it was dark and I couldn't really see his face. Or maybe because something about him made me feel safe. Am I crazy?"

"No, chica. You're not crazy. But you don't even know what he looks like? Or know his name at least?"

"Nope. After he read my stuff and said he liked it, I bolted out of there like a chicken running from the big bad wolf."

She looks kind of sad, so I try to cheer her up. "Hey, if you're meant to see this guy again, you will."

*God, I'm so full of baloney.*

"Do you really think so?"

"One hundred percent. I'm living proof that miracles do happen."

The smile that illuminates her entire face makes my white lie totally worth it.

♡ ♡ ♡

Mandy drops me off after the therapy session because she needs to finish a school assignment. I don't mind; in fact, I'm glad. I was worried about leaving Oliver alone with Felix for too long. The dog did get used to him —no more angry barking, at least—but you never know with dogs that have been abused before.

I call out their names as I walk up the stairs. The only answer I get is a string of curses not aimed at me. Then a couple of barks follow. The noise came from the master suite. What the heck are those two up to?

The bedroom is empty, so I continue to the bathroom. It's mayhem central. Water and foam are everywhere. Felix is inside the tub, shaking soapy water all over Oliver, who is soaked to the bone. It's the most ridiculous scene I've ever witnessed.

Oliver doesn't notice my arrival, so I clear my throat while leaning against the doorframe. "This is what happens when I leave the dog with you?"

He turns to me, frustration showing in the clench of his jaw and the furrow on his forehead. "Who did this dog belong to before? Satan?"

"Why are you giving Felix a bath in your tub? What's wrong with the hose outside?"

"The water is too cold. I'm not an animal abuser."

I roll my eyes, pushing myself off the doorframe. "Oh please. Why did he need a bath in the first place?"

"I was working on the swing, and this guy here decided it would be fun to play with the paint."

Putting my hands on my hips, I look sternly at the dog. "Felix, why did you do that?"

The dog jumps out of the tub to greet me properly, splashing water all over me as well before dashing off.

*Fuck!* I look down at my soiled clothes. I'm soaked through and smell like a wet dog. "Ugh! Stupid dog. Now I'm all wet."

"Join the club." Oliver points at his own drenched shirt and jeans.

I narrow my eyes at him before pushing him all the way into the tub. He falls on his ass with a loud splash.

"There, now you can complain."

"You want to play games, sugar? It's on."

His arm snakes out in a blur, grabbing a handful of my T-shirt before I can escape.

He drags me into the tub and I go under like a sack of potatoes. *Motherfucker!* The lukewarm water soaks the rest of my clothes and hair, and gets into my mouth. Disgusting.

In retaliation, I grab a handful of dirty foam and smear it all over his face. Things become messy and slippery, and Oliver has the advantage of being stronger. He can use both his arms, easily over-powering me. I become trapped by his tight embrace and things go from harmless fun to smoldering hot in zero-point-one second. We're both breathing hard when we lock gazes, the air surrounding us crackling with energy. I'm keenly aware of every place his skin touches mine. I won't be able to fight the pull this time.

Oliver's gaze drops to my mouth right before he crushes his lips against mine. Holy fuck! This is the type of kiss that inspires songs, that becomes legend. It's hot and demanding. His hands are everywhere, his restraint gone. So is mine. My hand goes under his shirt, my long nails scratching his abs. When Oliver's fingers graze the underside of my breasts, sinful fire concentrates between my legs, causing a delicious ache there that only his touch can soothe.

"Sugar, I've missed your taste so much," he says between kisses.

I can't even form words to reply. I don't remember what it was like before, but I know I'll keep coming back for more. Screw taking it slow, screw my stupid need to know for sure if I can fall in love with Oliver again. We're going down today.

Breaking the kiss, I try to tell him I want to move things to his bed, *our* bed. But my wish gets lodged in my throat as a scream interrupts our moment. Then Felix's angry snarl puts the nail in the coffin.

"What the hell!" Oliver yells right before he jumps out of the tub.

I follow him, much slower than I would've liked, almost falling onto my knees when I slip on the wet surface.

"Get this monster away from me!" I recognize Charlotte's voice despite only meeting her a couple of times since I came back from the dead.

Barreling into the living room, I skid to a stop, taking note of the chaotic scene in front of me. Charlotte's on top of Allan's desk, trying to fend off Felix with her tiny Chanel bag. If it weren't for her undeniable fear, I would find humor in the situation.

"Felix, down, boy," I say.

The dog barks a couple more times before backing away. He runs in my direction to circle me playfully as if he hadn't been on the verge of biting off one of Charlotte's limbs.

Charlotte glares at her brother, then at me. "You got a watchdog and didn't tell me? Are you fucking mental? He could've mauled me to death."

"I'm sorry."

I do feel terribly guilty. Charlotte is still shaking as she steps down from the desk.

"That teaches you not to come barging in, sis. You don't live here anymore." Oliver crosses his arms in front of his chest, not showing an ounce of remorse.

His dynamic with Charlotte isn't something I'm used to. Being an only child, I only have Liv's and Remi's family as a guide, and their relationships with their siblings are miles away from what Oliver has with Charlotte.

"I wouldn't have dropped by if you had picked up your phone."

"What was so urgent that you couldn't have waited for me to return your call?"

Her face changes in an instant, giving me a bad feeling.

"It's about Dad. He had a heart attack, Ollie. It's bad."

Pressing my hand against my chest, I turn to Oliver. The color vanishes from his face and it seems he's stopped breathing too.

"When?" he chokes out.

"I'm not sure. Mum didn't say. But she expects us to fly home as soon as possible."

Oliver runs a hand through his hair and curses, then looks at me, regret written all over his face. "I have to go, sugar."

It's like he doesn't expect me to join him. My heart twists inside my chest, a sharp pain that robs me of air. I'm his wife and he believes I'll abandon him in his time of need. It makes me so fucking sad. I've done that. I've kept him at arm's length. But no more.

I breach the gap between us and touch his face, making sure I have his undivided attention when I say, "I know. I'm coming with you."

# CHAPTER 19
## SAYLOR

look out the window with bleary eyes. Light rain peppers the glass, distorting the view of a countryside covered partially by gray fog. This feels like a surreal dream.

Everything happened so fast, I barely had time to process what I was doing. I can't believe I agreed—no, volunteered to travel to another country with a husband I still don't know. Never mind that I left my bandmates to hang dry. Allan had already planned a bunch of appearances for us, things he had canceled before due to my surgery, and now he'll have to reschedule again. The length of our stay in England is still unknown.

Despite the problems my sudden departure caused, I don't regret my decision. This feels right. Oliver needs me, even though he's acting like he has everything under control.

Yesterday, he operated like an automaton, barking orders left and right. The fire I usually saw in his gaze was gone. His face was frozen solid, rigid with a ruthless determination I confess frightened me a little.

Before I left, I managed to call Liv and my mother to give them the news. Liv offered to call our friends and cancel Oliver's party. I was grateful for it because in the uproar, I forgot all about our plans. Before I had even ended the conversation with her, Bas had called Oliver. Surprisingly, he took the call, but locked himself in his room. I know they go way back, but the fact that Oliver felt the need to talk with his best friend in private hurt a lot. Have I lost his trust?

After we arrived in foggy London by means of a private jet, a couple of town cars were already waiting for us. Yes, we needed two cars, because even with only a few hours to pack, Charlotte managed to fill three suitcases. We also had Felix to contend with. I couldn't leave him behind.

Now we're headed to the family's stately home in Hertford-shire, a town near London where his father is now recovering from surgery. It turns out the heart attack happened last week and his mother only bothered to contact her children now. Oliver, who was already closed off before, became even more withdrawn at that news. I tried to comfort him, but it was like trying to breach a solid ice wall.

The car leaves the main road to pull into a gravel pathway surrounded on each side by tall trees that are currently gnarled and sad. It must be beautiful here in the spring and summer. At the end of the road, I can see a grand red brick building, and once the car gets closer, my jaw drops as I take in the size of house. No, not house—mansion. I didn't realize Oliver's family had so much money, but then again, I never bothered to really ask anything about them, so focused I was on my recovery.

There's a man standing in front of the house wearing a dark suit, and I can only assume that's the butler. Surreal.

Charlotte's car pulls up first, and *Jeeves* opens the door for her. She exchanges a few words with him before venturing into the house without a glance back. The butler opens my door next, extending his gloved hand to assist me.

"You must be Mr. Best's new wife. Welcome to Longview Manor."

The way he says 'new wife' sounds like Oliver has had multiple wives before me and I'm the newest model.

"Thank you," I say.

"Where's my mother?" Oliver butts in without so much as a hello.

"She's in the tea room."

*Tea room?* Jesus fucking Christ. Did I marry into royalty or something? I should've asked Liv for more intel on Oliver's family. I have to call her—or better yet, Bas—as soon as I get settled.

Oliver takes a step toward the house, then stops and turns in my direction as if I'm an afterthought. "Gilbert will take you to your room. I must speak with my mother."

Without waiting for my reply, he disappears inside the house just like his sister did, without a glance back, leaving me alone and forlorn. Who is this man? He's nothing like the Oliver I was getting to know.

*Stop with the pity party, Saylor. His father almost died.*

The chauffer walks around the car and opens the trunk. Felix jumps out, running a circle around the guy before coming to stand next to me.

"What's that?" the butler asks, the disgust in his tone evident.

"A dog. His name is Felix."

"Mr. Best knows his mother does not tolerate animals in the house. He should've known better than to bring that *thing* here."

*Okay, I so do not like this guy.* "Felix is not a *thing*. He's a dog. And you can't possibly tell me there isn't a place on this vast property where Felix can stay. I thought British people liked dogs. What about your fox hunts?"

Gilbert puffs his chest out and watches me through slits. "The Best family does not hunt."

"Well, unless you want to make me look bad for bringing Felix inside the main house, I suggest you find a solution to our dilemma."

"How about looking for a dog hotel?"

"How about not?" I cross my arms in front of my chest and glare at the pompous man.

"Oh, fine. I was instructed to give you a room in the main house, but assuming you want to stay close to your pet, I can arrange for you to stay in the guesthouse."

*A guesthouse far away from Oliver's strange family? Sign me up.*

"Sounds marvelous. Lead the way, Jeeves."

His closed-off expression turns even more sour. "My name is not Jeeves, it's Gilbert."

"Potato, potahto."

A strangled noise comes from the butter, but at least he refrains from making any more comments. If an employee acts with that sense of entitlement, I can't imagine what Oliver's parents must be like.

Gilbert takes me to the guesthouse, which turns out to be a mini version of the main building. It has three bedrooms, a kitchen, a living room, and even a small game room with a pool table. With only a quick glance, I can tell everything is top quality, from the polished dark wood furniture to the state-of-the-art appliances. The master bedroom is almost as big as Oliver's room in California. The bed looks comfy and inviting. It beckons me. I feel very tired all of a sudden.

Felix makes himself at home, jumping on top of the pristine couch to Gilbert's clear dismay.

"Linus will bring your suitcases in a moment. Since I didn't think anyone would be staying here, the kitchen is not stocked yet, but if you let me know your preferences, I can arrange for food to be delivered within an hour."

"Should I write down a list?"

"You can send it to my e-mail. Here's my card."

He hands me a fancy business card with his full name, cell phone, and e-mail address on it. *Holy smokes, how things have changed.*

Despite my annoyance with the guy, I thank him and promise to send him a list of things soon. It doesn't happen. The long hours of travel have made me weary, and the last thing I want is to make a grocery list.

I check on Felix and find him snoring already. Then I head to the master suite, undressing until all I'm wearing are my panties. I have a change of clothes in my bag, but I'm too tired to bother grabbing it so I get under the covers as I am, almost naked. The cool sheets against my skin make me hiss, and I curl into human ball until I get warm. The moment my eyelids shut, I'm dead to the world.

♡ ♡ ♡

I wake hours later, feeling lost. *Where the heck am I?* I spot the silhouette of someone near the bed and my heart jumps to my throat. I scream, scooching up on the mattress and hitting my head against the headboard in the process.

"Relax, sugar. It's me."

Heart still stuck in my throat, I rub my blurry eyes. "Oliver? What time is it?"

"It's almost suppertime. Why are you here? I thought my mother had arranged a room for you in the main house."

"Gilbert didn't think your mother would appreciate Felix's presence."

"Ah, I see. He's right. In that case, I'll have my stuff brought here too."

Oliver's tone is softer, and it lifts a weight off my chest. He sounds like his normal self again.

"How's your dad?"

"Stable, at least that's what Mom says. I haven't seen him yet."

I sit up and cold air brushes against my naked chest, turning my nipples as hard as tiny pebbles. *Shit.* I had forgotten I wasn't wearing a shirt. Oliver's gaze drops to my breasts before a hissing sound whooshes from his mouth. I pull the sheets up quickly, covering myself as heat rushes to my cheeks.

"Sorry. I didn't mean to give you a peepshow."

"Sugar, never apologize for flashing me your glorious rack."

My face turns even hotter, and I'm glad it's dark in the room.

I clear my throat to disguise any signs of embarrassment. "What's the plan? When do I get to meet your mom?"

"Oh, in an hour or so, at dinner. There's someone else here who is dying to meet you."

"Who?"

"Grandma Adeline."

My stomach twists into knots. I hate meeting the family. I don't speak for a couple of beats.

Oliver turns the lamp on and looks closely at my face. "You look like you're about to puke. Are you feeling okay?"

"I'm fine. Just a little hungry. I guess I should be getting ready, then?"

"You know," he starts, lowering his gaze to my lips, "the tub is pretty big. We could finish what we started."

The hot memory comes to the surface and my body reacts accordingly. But the idea of meeting his grandma just after having sex with Oliver makes me extremely uncomfortable.

"Tempting, but I don't think that's a good idea."

Oliver's face falls right before he stands up. "Right. Well, I'll come get you in a half hour?"

"Sounds good."

He turns on his heel with shoulders a little hunched forward.

"Ollie?"

"Yes, sugar." He pauses but keeps staring ahead.

*Come on, Saylor. Say that this rebuff means nothing. Confess what's in your heart.* But the words get lodged in my throat. I'm such a coward.

"What should I wear?" I ask instead.

*Ugh. Kill me now.*

"Anything you like."

Well, that doesn't help me much.

Oliver is gone before I can say anything else.

# CHAPTER 20
## SAYLOR

"Liv, I totally screwed up. Not only did I turn Oliver down, but I didn't even wish him happy birthday. I'm such a cow."

"Don't be too hard on yourself, Blue. I don't think he's thinking about his birthday right now."

"It doesn't matter. Plus, I'm totally freaking out about meeting his mom and grandma. You know how I hate meeting the family. I have the feeling they'll have a quick look at me and find me lacking."

"You're stressing over nothing. So what if they don't like you. It's their loss. Oliver is crazy about you. That's what matters."

I pinch the bridge of my nose. Liv is not getting my anxiety. I don't want to add more problems to Oliver's life; I've already made him go through hell and then some.

"I don't know what to wear."

"Saylor, listen to me. Stop and take a deep breath. Trust your instincts. You've always killed in the fashion department. You'll slay your look tonight."

I sit on the edge of the bed, surrounded by scattered clothes. "It's not only that. I know nothing about his family, what to expect. If I'm to judge by their butler alone, I'm probably about to enter the set of *Dynasty*."

"Bas told me he met Oliver's parents once and they were snob assholes."

"Gee, exactly what I wanted to hear."

"Since when do snooty people scare you?"

"It's not. It's just… I don't want to give Oliver more stress by having his family hate me."

"Hold on a second. Bas is saying something."

I stare at my clothes while I wait. I'm leaning toward dark jeans and a heavy sweater. It's casual, but at least my clothes won't offend anyone. Unless they're the type of people who wear cocktail dresses to dinner. *Crap!* I'm back to worrying.

"So, Bas told me that Oliver's grandma is actually quite nice and she's the only person Oliver likes in the family. So if you're aiming to make an impression, focus on the old lady."

"Okay. Make Granny love me. Should be easy enough."

*How come I don't feel an ounce of confidence?*

"Knock, knock," Oliver says from the door, making me jump. I drop the phone in the process.

"Shit. You scared me."

"I see you're not ready, unless you're planning on wearing boy-shorts and a tank top. Not that I'd mind."

"You weren't very helpful before." I pick up the phone from the floor. "Hey, Liv, Oliver's here. I gotta go."

She says goodbye and I toss the phone onto the bed. Oliver is already looking though my clothes and while he does, I take a moment to check what's he's wearing. Jeans and a dark gray sweater with a button-down shirt underneath. Casual and preppy. I've never seen him dress like that. He looks so proper and British. Even his hair is styled in a more conventional way, no out-of-bed look.

He turns to me and catches me staring. His lips twist into a grin. "Charlotte is wearing a dress, if that helps. Maybe you can wear this one."

From his index finger dangles a dark red, vintage-style dress that I had planned to wear at his birthday party. It has a full skirt and sweetheart neckline. The fabric has some shimmer to it; it's definitely a cocktail dress. I stare at the garment for far too long without speaking, so Oliver continues.

"Uh, it's my birthday today, in case you forgot."

I snap my face to his once more, finding him smiling. But his eyes, oh God, his eyes shatter my heart in tiny fractures. He's so sad. I want to hug him and say all the right things, but if I did so right now, I'm afraid he might think it's an action driven by pity, not love.

*Jesus Christ. Did I just admit to myself that I love him?*

"I know. I'm sorry that, with everything, I forgot to wish you happy birthday." I walk to my suitcase and retrieve a letter-sized envelope. "Here, this is for you."

He raises an eyebrow before taking it. Without taking his eyes off me, he rips it open. His eyebrows furrow when he pulls sheets of music from inside. "What is this?"

"I found them inside my guitar case. I must have been working on a new song before my surgery. I finished it a couple of days ago."

Oliver reads the sheet with focused attention while my heart lodges in my throat. I didn't tell anyone I found that work in progress, not even Liv. It was my little secret.

"Is this about us?" He looks at me.

I glance down at my feet, unable to withstand his intense stare. "Yes. It's probably different than what my pre–memory-loss version intended, but well…. I know it's lame—"

Oliver cuts me off by grabbing my face and crushing his lips against mine. The assault takes me by surprise, short-circuiting every nerve in my body. I have to step back to keep my balance, but Oliver wraps his arm around my waist, keeping me in place. Electricity surges through my veins, leaving my skin tingling in the most sinful way. Our tongues mingle in a dizzying dance as a wave of desire travels up my back.

He ends the kiss all too soon, taking a step back. I stare at him through hooded eyes, confused as to why he would start something and not follow through. I'm so ready for more.

"It kills me to do this, but we really can't be late for dinner. My mother's tongue lashing will ruin everything."

My rebellious mind is shouting 'fuck her.' It's impossible to think about a stuffy dinner when Oliver still has his arm wrapped around me.

"Plus," he continues, "when we do have sex again, I want to have all the time in the world so I can properly worship your body."

Fuck if he didn't just make my body melt with his words.

"I need a shower," I say when I finally find my voice.

Oliver chuckles, dropping his arms from my waist. "Me too, sugar. I'll wait for you in the living room. I need to have words with Gilbert. The cupboards are still empty, and Felix needs food too."

"To be fair, he was waiting for my grocery list, but I fell asleep and never sent him one."

"That's no excuse. He's been working for my family for a long time, and I'm afraid it's made him more arrogant than he already was. He is still the help, so don't be afraid to put him in his place."

"The help? That sounds awful."

"It's warranted. That's what I call him when he's acting particularly rude."

Oliver doesn't make a motion to leave the room, just remains staring at me as if he's trying to read my mind.

"Uh, okay. If you don't want us to be late, then go." I make a shooing motion with my hand.

"All right, all right. I'm leaving."

♡ ♡ ♡

've never dressed so fast in my life. With the clock ticking, I just hopped into the shower to rinse the travel's yuck, and to also douse the lust-induced fire running through my veins. I didn't bother washing my hair, knowing it would take too long to dry and style. Instead, I used dry shampoo. The blue is already almost gone, and the shaved side has grown a bit so now my scar isn't as visible as before. I wonder what Oliver's mom and grandma will think of my look. Too rock 'n' roll for their conservative tastes?

Oliver is playing with Felix when I walk into the living room. He turns to me and freezes, his gaze dropping to my feet before slowly traveling up the length of my body. Then he whistles.

"Is that all for me?"

"Well, besides your birthday, it's Valentine's Day as well. Or have you forgotten?"

"Sugar, I think I want to skip dinner."

I wiggle my finger. "No way. I don't want to start my relationship with your mom on the wrong foot."

He takes a step closer, his eyes narrowing. "I want to make something very clear before we venture into that lion's den. I don't bloody care what my mother thinks, so don't bend out of shape to impress her. She's not a very nice lady."

"And your grandma?"

Oliver's frown vanishes and he smiles. "She's brilliant. Don't worry about her. You've got her in the bag. She's a fan, you know? She told me earlier that she's listened to Wreck of the Day's album on repeat since it debuted."

"You're joking."

"No, I swear to God. Now, where's your jacket?"

After Oliver helps me into my coat, we walk to the main house. The air is chilly and even with the extra layers of protection, the cold air seeps through the barriers, making me shiver. Oliver throws his arm over my shoulder and I lean against him. My heart is beating at warp speed. I can't believe he can't hear it.

I'm nervous about dinner, but I'm more nervous about what's going to happen afterward. Tonight is the night, and the anticipation is killing me.

We find the front door unlocked, but soon Gilbert appears to take our coats. "Mrs. Best is waiting for you in the living room."

"Thanks, Help," Oliver says, and I elbow him on the side.

When he looks in my direction, I give him a look that says, 'Be nice.'

I barely have time to absorb my surroundings, too focused on putting one foot in front of the other without stumbling. My legs are suddenly shaking. It feels like all the progress I've made with Cheryl has gone down the drain. But from the corner of my eyes, I notice a few pieces of classic décor that scream wealth. Oil paintings wrapped in golden frames remind me of a museum. Double doors open to the living room, a space that is almost the size of the entire guesthouse. Expensive-looking furniture is placed strategically throughout the space. Over every surface, I find ornaments and small decorative pieces that I'm pretty sure cost an arm and a leg. Man, dusting off this place must be a bitch.

We find Oliver's mother sitting on a long couch near the fireplace. She's wearing an impeccable light gray suit, her hair swept up in a perfectly coiffed up-do. I have no idea what Oliver's dad looks like, but when his mom turns to us, I can see where Oliver gets his coloring. Her blonde hair is almost as light as mine, and her blue eyes are the exact electric shade as Oliver's. However, while Oliver's blue eyes have fire in them, hers are ice-cold. I swallow the sudden lump that's lodged in my throat.

Opposite her, Charlotte is sitting next to an older lady also dressed to the nines, but with a less severe expression on her face.

"Good evening," Oliver says.

"You're late." His mother narrows her eyes at us.

Without missing a beat, Oliver continues. "Mother, Nana, I would like to introduce you to my wife, Saylor Blue."

His mother makes a disapproving sound in the back of her throat, making me feel like an insignificant insect. Oliver places a hand on my lower back, his touch helping with the nerves.

"Ignore my daughter-in-law. Come closer, child. Let me see if you're as pretty as the pictures I've seen online."

The warmth in her gaze is what pulls me out of my paralyzing discomfort. With careful steps, I approach the couch where she sits.

"Char, scooch over. I want Saylor to sit next to me."

"Gee, it seems I've been replaced." Charlotte stands up, going for the liquor trolley near the couch.

I sit next to Oliver's grandma with a stiff back, not knowing where to put my hands. She keeps watching me with a small smile on her lips.

"I like what you did with your hair. Very edgy," she finally speaks.

I touch one of the strands, a silly automatic reaction whenever someone comments on my new do. "Thanks."

"Now, let me see that scar."

*What?* No one has ever been so blunt about the red line across the side of my head. But I know people stare at it plenty when they think I'm not aware.

"Grandma doesn't beat around the bush. I forgot to warn you about that," Oliver says.

Feeling uncomfortable as hell, I turn my head and let the woman inspect the scar at will. I wasn't going to say no to her.

"Oh, that's a good one. Your doctor did an excellent job. It's healing quite nicely. I also have a scar on the back of my head from the time I fell on wet tile and hit the edge to the tub. Mine isn't so pretty as yours, mind you. It happened in the seventies and the doctors were vile then. That asshat did such a shoddy job."

"No one wants to see you scar, Grandma," Charlotte says.

"How long did you know my son before you decided to elope?" Oliver's mom cuts in like a ruthless banshee. For a moment, I had forgotten she was there.

"Uh, a little over a year."

She watches me through narrowed eyes while she plays with the pearl necklace hanging around her neck.

"Not quite long enough to marry someone, is it? I'm sure the fact that he's the heir of a considerable fortune didn't factor in at all."

"Mother, that's out of line."

"I couldn't care less about Oliver's money," I say through clenched teeth. If I cared about that, I wouldn't have given up my rights to my biological's father fortune.

"So, are you saying you signed a prenup?"

*Shit.* I don't know. I turn to Oliver with a plea for help. He's glaring at his mother.

Before he can say anything, his grandmother chimes in. "Lydia, if you're going to be insufferable, I'll have to ask you to have dinner with the staff."

"This is my house. You can't tell me what to do."

"No, this is my son's house. A piece of property you have no rights to. You know very well that when he dies, Oliver and Charlotte will inherit it, not you."

"Solid burn, Nana," Oliver says.

There's a flash of fury in Lydia's eyes, but to give her credit, she recovers fast, returning to her constipated bitch look.

"Semantics. You know what I mean." She waves her hand dismissively.

Not wanting to be the cause of a family argument, I change the subject. "So, Oliver tells me you listen to Wreck of the Day's music."

The tension leaves his grandma's face immediately, and her eyes shine with excitement.

"Oh yes. You're quite the talented musician. I love all your songs, but my favorite is your duet with Ollie. It's so beautiful."

The song I still haven't been able to listen fully. I drop my gaze to my lap. "Thanks."

"Saylor wrote a new song. It's just as good," Oliver pipes up.

"Oh, you did? Wonderful. We have a piano here. Perhaps you would like to sing it for us after dinner?"

Panic seizes me. I look wide-eyed in Oliver's direction, trying to convey to him how not ready I am for a public performance. In fact, I can't believe I had the cajones to give him the new music sheet in the first place.

"Maybe another time, Nana. She hasn't even played for me yet. I'm calling dibs on the first performance."

Gilbert enters the room and announces that dinner is served. We all stand up, but Oliver and I hang back and wait for everyone to leave the room. He moves closer, placing a warm hand on my hips. "How are you holding up? Do you need a drink?"

"No, I'm okay."

"Sorry about my mother. My father's illness only made her worse than she already was."

"I can handle her. It's your grandma I'm worried about."

"Why? She's clearly taken with you."

"I know. That's the problem. I'm afraid she's going to ask again for me to sing one of my songs. I'm not ready for that."

"Hey, sugar. Don't worry. I've got your back." He leans closer to whisper in my ear. "The only singing you'll be doing tonight is a thousand yeses when I make you come so hard, even the mile-away neighbors will hear you."

He takes a step back to watch my face burst into flames. His sinful lips turn into a wolfish grin. Blast Oliver and his dirty mouth. Now I'm all hot and bothered. I'll need a bucket of icy water to cool down.

But two can play this game. I casually brush my hand against his crotch as I walk around him and say, "I can't wait."

# CHAPTER 21
## OLIVER

Despite my mother being the usual stuck-up bitch, dinner is a pleasant affair. Thank all the gods for Nana, who diverts Mum's not-so-veiled insults at Saylor. Using her sarcastic sense of humor, she annihilates Lydia. You can't win against Adeline Best.

Saylor is laughing at something Nana said, but I've missed the joke, too busy staring at my gorgeous wife. I can finally see the woman I fell in love with. Before, it felt like she was hiding from me, maybe even hiding from herself. Now she glows.

My hand sneaks under the table to squeeze her thigh over the fabric of her dress. I won't dare doing anything more scandalous, not wanting to put Saylor in an uncomfortable position.

There's no birthday cake for me, as my family knows better. I haven't had a cake to celebrate the occasion since Harry's passing. My chest is tight as I think about my brother, and being in this house doesn't help. The ache is always there, a dull reminder of my darkest sin. No matter what I do, I will always carry that burden. It will never allow me to soar to a place where guilt doesn't exist. Devils don't fly.

Mum places her napkin down and looks pointedly at me. "Your father would like to have a word with you."

I haven't seen the man since I arrived. Mum told he was too tired for visitors, so why the change of heart?

Grandma makes a tsking sound, leaning back in her chair. She's openly glaring at Mum.

"You said he was too weak to see anybody," Charlotte says.

"Well, considering it's your brother's birthday, Frank is willing to make the sacrifice."

*Just twist the dagger a little deeper, why don't you?*

Standing up, I say, "It's okay. Might as well see what the old man has to say."

I don't bother glancing in my mother's direction as I walk out of the dining room. She probably looks like she's sucking on a sour grape.

My parents' country house is the same as I remember, even though I haven't been here since I was old enough to go off on my own, and they couldn't drag me back. There are too many god-awful memories. If I close my eyes, I can still hear Harry's hurried steps as he tries to catch up with me.

*Don't think about him now.*

With each step I take up the stairs and then down the hallway toward my father's room, I vest myself in an imaginary protective armor. Steeling myself is the only way I can cope being in the presence of my father. He was never a kind man before Harry's death, but afterward, he turned vile.

I don't bother knocking before I push the door open. The room is surprisingly bright with all the lights on. The plasma screen mounted on the wall is showing some type of game show, but the sound is too low for anyone to hear anything. The original bed has been replaced by a hospital setup, currently in a semi-reclined position. Dad is asleep, but if it wasn't for the monitoring machine next to his bed showing his steady heartbeat, I would think him to be dead. His skin is ashen, almost translucent.

His eyes flicker open once I approach, watching me in silence until I stand next to his bed. They're glazed and red, the dark circles under them a stark contrast against his sickly pale skin.

"You wanted to see me?" I force out.

"I heard you got married." His voice is weak, not the booming one that used to put fear in my heart when I was a kid.

"Yes."

"I would congratulate you if I thought it was something that deserved any praise."

"Did you ask me to come here so you could tell me how disappointed you are in my actions? I guess almost dying hasn't changed you at all."

Ignoring my comment, he continues, "Did you have her sign a prenup, at least?"

I clench my jaw hard before I respond. "No."

"You irresponsible cad. I don't care what you do with the filthy money you 'earned' by shaking your ass to a bunch of deranged girls, but I'll be damned if I'll let a low-class gold digger have a dime of my fortune."

Hot rage makes my blood boil. How dare he insult Saylor. My nostrils flare as I take a deep breath, holding it in while my hands curl into fists by my sides. It takes a Herculean effort to not yank the oxygen tube from my father's nose. It's probably what's keeping him alive.

That's Frank Best, able to make me want to commit murder even from his deathbed.

"I don't give a damn about your fucking money."

"Good, because you aren't getting any. It's a pity your brother left us too soon. God took away the only child who was worth anything."

*Oh yeah. Here we go again.* It's not the first time he's flung that horseshit my way. I bet if the roles were reversed, if I had died and Harry was alive, Frank Best would say the exact same vile things to him.

"Hate me all you want, but what did Charlotte ever do to you?"

My father snorts. "That little leech? She's your mother's project. She's not a true Best."

I stare at my father with mouth agape, trying to figure out if he had a stroke as well.

"What do you mean she's not a true Best? Because she's a girl? You disgust me."

"The feeling is mutual."

"Rot in hell." I turn, ready to get the hell out of the room.

"Harry was always the better son. I wish you were the one who had died."

Clenching my jaw tight, I step into the hallway, closing the door with enough force to rattle the pictures on the wall. *God damnit! Why did I let him get to me like that?* I thought his hateful words could no longer affect me, but boy, was I wrong. I feel like punching something.

I can't let Saylor see me like this.

I veer toward the secondary set of stairs, the one that leads into the kitchen. There I find the family's private chef cleaning up the place. He stops what he's doing to glance at me.

"May I assist with anything, Mr. Best?"

"Yes, where do you keep your stash of alcohol?"

"What kind? We have wine, whiskey—"

"Give me the whiskey."

The guy ventures into the storage room and comes back with an unopened bottle of Chivas Regal. I don't thank him when I curl my hands around the dark bottle, too focused putting as much distance between me and my father. I step into the back courtyard, the cold winter air immediately going through my sweater and chilling me to the bone. There's no way to retrieve my coat without walking by the dining room, so suffer I must. The whiskey will keep me warm.

The darkness around me thickens until it's almost absolute. The sky is cloudy—shocker—so I get nothing in terms of celestial illumination.

That's fine, I know this place like the back of my hand. I veer toward the edge of the forest that surrounds the property, hoping the old tree house is still there. Our childhood chauffeur built it for Harry and me. It used to be our favorite hangout spot until I got too old and stupid to want to play with my baby brother. That's my biggest regret, not treating Harry better.

I break the seal of the bottle, bringing the rim to my lips. The whiskey burns my throat as it goes down, but it's a welcome pain. Warmth spreads throughout my limbs and some of the tension melts away.

"Much better."

After a couple of minutes walking through the thick vegetation, I can finally make out the silhouette of the tree house out in the distance. In the gloom, I can't tell what shape the structure's in. Do I fucking care? Not one bit.

Once under the house, I test the wood planks nailed to the tree trunk—the makeshift ladder. The planks are a bit wobbly, but I think they can handle my weight. Cradling the bottle in one arm, I climb up until my head breaks through the opening in the floor of the house. No critters are bunking here, so I push myself all the way up. We used to keep toys, blankets, and snacks here, but they're long gone. It's only me and Chivas tonight.

*Happy birthday to me.*

# CHAPTER 22
## SAYLOR

s soon as Oliver leaves the table to see his dad, we relocate to the living room to sit by the fireplace and drink. Lydia doesn't linger long, and when she retires to her room, the change in the atmosphere is palpable.

I don't mind Oliver's absence. It gives me the chance to get to know his grandmother better. She's a hoot, so clever and funny. Her wicked sense of humor has me in tears more than once. Time flies without me noticing, and it's only when she declares she's tired that I realize how late it is. Oliver's been gone for two hours.

"Do you think Ollie is still with your dad?" I ask Charlotte.

"Shit, he's been gone for a long time, huh? I don't think so. Oliver and Dad don't get along. I doubt their conversation went smoothly. He probably went back to the guesthouse."

"Maybe," I say without really believing my statement. A sense of foreboding drips down my spine. Oliver wouldn't bail like this without cause.

With a sense of urgency, I head to the entry hall. Gilbert appears like magic to hand me my coat. He also has Oliver's.

"Have you seen Oliver?"

"No, ma'am. But our chef informed me that Mr. Best stopped

by the kitchen earlier and commandeered a bottle of whiskey before he went for a stroll."

"He went out in the cold without his jacket? Is he insane? It's freezing out there," I say.

"Mr. Best is not known for being a sensible lad."

I grab my coat from him, stepping out into the freezing night before I finish putting it on. Then I break into a run, hoping to find Oliver in the guesthouse. Something happened. I know it in my bones.

I call his name as I open the door, but the only greeting I receive is from Felix. He comes bouncing my way, wagging his tail and barking with joy. I rub his head, then go check every single room with the dog close on my heels. As I feared, Oliver isn't here. I call his cell phone and it goes straight to voice mail.

*Shit. Where did he go?*

There's nothing around for miles, and I don't think he drove into town. I would've heard the noise if a car left the property.

An idea strikes me. I go back into the room Oliver claimed and grab the first piece of clothing I can find, a white T-shirt. I bring it to my nose, inhaling his signature scent. This should work. Next, I go to my room to change from my high-heeled shoes into sensible boots. I grab a hat as well. If I'm going to brace the cold weather, I ought to be prepared.

"Come here, boy." I signal to Felix, placing Oliver's shirt in front of his nose. "Take a good whiff of this. Let's go find Daddy."

I have no idea if Felix will be able to do that. I'm sure dogs require training in order to track specific scents, but it's the only idea I have.

We venture back out and I use the flashlight app in my phone to illuminate the way. Felix takes off, and I have to run to keep up with him. I hope he's leading me to Oliver and not on wild-goose chase. When he disappears through a cluster of trees, I curse out loud. Going into a forest in the middle of the night is not how I envisioned the evening ending.

*The things I do for you, Oliver.*

I call Felix's name when I can no longer see him, and he barks a response farther ahead before coming back to me. He runs in circles a couple of times, then takes off once more. I think he wants me to follow him. I increase my pace, careful not to trip over an exposed tree root or hole in the ground. It wouldn't do to fall and twist an ankle. Losing mobility again would suck balls.

I find Felix barking at a tree, more specifically at the tree house that sits on top.

"Oliver, are you there?"

"Go away, sugar. I don't want you to see me like this" comes his slurred response.

*Oh, for fuck's sake. He's drunk.*

I turn off the flashlight and put my phone back into my pocket. Climbing up the makeshift steps proves to be a challenge. I can move my left arm, but I still have difficulty making my fingers cooperate, so I ball my hand into a fist instead of trying to grab the wooden plank. I scratch my knuckles in the process, but at least I'm making progress. I'm glad I'm no longer wearing heels, though.

Once I reach the top, I find Oliver sitting in a corner with a bottle of whiskey in his hand.

"I asked you to go away, Saylor."

Leaning on my elbow, I pull myself all the way up. Then I throw Oliver's coat at him. "No, you ordered me to go away. Too bad I don't take orders from drunk asshats."

He doesn't move, just keeps staring at me with his mouth partially open while I tower over him, glaring.

"Well, at least you finally get to see who you married."

He brings the bottle to his lips again, making me see red. Before he finishes his first sip, I take it from him.

"Hey!"

"You've had plenty."

I sit next to him, making sure the bottle is out of his reach. Without glancing at his face, I ask, "What happened?"

"The usual. I was reminded how worthless I am."

"You're not worthless."

He snorts. "You know nothing. You *remember* nothing."

I wince. My eyes prickle, but I won't cry over such a childish insult.

"That was harsh."

"It's the fucking truth, isn't it? You know I had a younger brother, right? Did you know that he's dead because of me?"

"I don't believe that."

"Open your eyes, sugar. I'm a monster. If you were smart, you would pack your things and run away while you can."

"What did your father say to you?" I glance at his profile, noticing the hard-set of his jaw.

"It doesn't matter."

I pinch his chin with my forefinger and thumb, forcing him to look at me. "It *does* matter."

"He told me *again* that he wished I was the one who died. Happy now?" He pushes my hand away and makes a motion to stand up. I jump on his lap, straddling him and keeping him in place.

"No, I'm not happy. I'm fucking sad. No one deserves a parent who wishes them dead. I don't know your father and quite frankly, I don't want to ever meet the man. He's vile and blind." I touch Oliver's cold cheek. "I don't remember the past year, but in the short period of time we've lived together, I saw you. You're a wonderful person, Ollie. Patient, caring, loyal. Yes, you have a colorful past, but so what? It doesn't matter to me."

"Saylor—"

I place a finger over his lips, silencing him. "The world would've been a sadder place if you weren't in it, Ollie. I wouldn't have fallen in love with a man twice if he wasn't worthy."

"What did you say?"

I bring our foreheads together, holding his face between my hands. "I love you, Oliver. So damn much."

Our restraint breaks loose, the stretched cord finally snapping, and Oliver's mouth is on mine. I get a taste of his whiskey-flavored tongue, but it doesn't matter. I surrender to that kiss, tasting the saltiness from tears as well. Whose, I don't know.

Everything happens in a blur. We're all tongues, teeth, and limbs. Oliver's hand is already under my skirt, traveling to where I so desperately need it to be. When his fingers swipe against my core, I moan loudly. I've been craving his touch for so long, it almost sends me over the edge. As much as I love foreplay, I don't care for it in this moment; I need to feel Oliver inside of me so I can believe this is finally happening.

I slide off his lap and lie on the hardwood floor, rolling the thick tights off my legs. Oliver watches me, paralyzed, as if he too can't believe this is happening. I want to make it very clear to him so I pull my dress up, bunching the fabric waist-high, and open my legs as an offering.

"I want you inside of me, husband. Fast and hard."

"A woman after my own heart. Wish granted, wife."

Oliver makes quick work of his pants, his rock-hard erection springing free in the next moment. I don't have time to admire his length before he's between my legs, the tip of his cock teasing my entrance. He brings one of my legs over his shoulder, kissing the inside of my knee before leaning over me, his nose brushing against mine.

"You have no idea how much I've missed having you under me like this, sugar. How much I've missed your taste."

"I'm so sorry, Ollie. I wish I could've pulled my head out of my ass sooner."

"Don't apologize to me, Saylor. Not about that." He moves his hip and his cock slides in an inch.

Pleasure shoots up my spine and I hiss.

"What's the matter, sugar? Too much?" He does it again, going in very slowly.

"Oliver, if you don't quit with the teasing, I'll have to take matters into my own hands."

"Oh, is that a threat?"

"You bet your ass it—"

I don't get to finish that sentence as Oliver slides all the way in, cutting off my train of thought. I groan instead.

"You were saying?"

"Quit talking and fuck me already."

"I love when you talk dirty."

He kisses me hard, the tempo of his tongue matching the tempo of his hips pumping into mine. I regret the layers of clothes; there isn't enough contact between our bodies, and we're generating enough heat to keep us both warm. The old wood floor creaks with the motion, giving me visions of the house collapsing with us inside.

"Ollie, how stable is this construction?" I say between kisses.

"Fear not, sugar. It'll hold." He kisses down my neck, leaving a trail of goose bumps in his wake.

"Oh God. This feels so good." I arch my back, offering my entire body for his taking.

He grunts in response, an animalistic sound that sends me over the edge. I hold on to his arms for dear life. The pressure builds to impossible heights down below right before a wave of the most blissful orgasm hits me with a vengeance. The small tree house begins to spin out of control, forcing me to shut my eyes for a moment. I think I'm screaming, but I'm too lost in the moment to know for sure.

"That's it, sugar. Come for me."

Oliver moves faster, and I feel his cock getting even harder inside of me. I'm hit by another wave of pleasure, less intense this time but just as good. I don't think I've ever had back-to-back orgasms in my life—not that I remember, anyway.

"Jesus fucking Christ," Oliver says right before his entire frame shakes and his cock pulses inside of me.

He keeps fucking me, faster and faster through his release

until, with a final jerky thrust, he collapses on top of me, bringing his mouth close to my ear. His warm breath fans over my skin, fast and out of control. It matches my own erratic heartbeat. Slowly, I slide my leg off his shoulder. It tingles as the blood starts circulating again. I didn't realize it had gone numb.

Oliver pulls out, rolling onto his side. He keeps his arm across my stomach, hugging me tight.

"Thank you," he says.

I turn my face to his because that's the only part of my body I'm capable of moving right now.

"For what?"

"For coming back to me."

"I made a promise that I would."

"Do you remember that?" There's hope in his tone.

"No. The work-in-progress song I finished told me that. I'm sorry."

He pulls me closer and I rest my head on his chest. His familiar scent hits my nose, bringing everything into focus. The jumbled pieces of my life fall back into place. *Home.* Oliver is home to me.

"It's okay, sugar."

"It still makes me sad that I can't remember the past year of my life. I can't remember how we fell in love. But I've decided to stop obsessing about it. I have to let go so I can move forward. We shouldn't be looking toward the past. We're not heading there."

He kisses the top of my head. "We'll make new memories, sugar, and they'll be more epic than before."

Felix barks several times down below. "I think our dog is done being ignored."

"Did he lead you here?"

"Yes, I gave him one of your T-shirts and Felix just took off."

"Of all the wonderful things you've done in the past week, adopting that dog tops them all."

"Really?" I raise my head so I can look into his eyes. "It tops even the last ten minutes?"

Oliver's lips twist into a crooked grin. "The jury is still out on that one. I'll need a reprise to be sure."

I roll on top of him, leaning my forearm against his chest. "You seriously didn't put me in the same category with Felix, did you?"

"Aw, sugar. Are you jealous?"

"Mega."

He touches my cheek with the tips of his fingers. "Don't be. No one else can compete with you, sugar. Not even the smartest motherfucking dog in the world."

"Boy, that statement makes me feel so much better."

"Should I John Legend it for you?"

"How about you Oliver Best it for me?"

His fingers tangle in my hair before he pulls me closer for a scorching, take-no-prisoners kiss.

I guess we're having a reprise after all.

# CHAPTER 23
## SAYLOR

I don't remember how long we stayed in that tree house, but by the time we got back to the guesthouse, all the muscles in my body were frozen solid. Oliver drew a warm bath, and despite the tiredness that had finally caught up with me, I couldn't refuse.

We didn't make love in that tub, but our restless fingers did have their fun. When we hit the sack, thawed and pruny, it was lights out for me immediately.

I wake up to soft kisses on the back of my neck. Oliver's arm is curled around my waist, trapping me against his naked body. His erection presses against my butt, and a brand new ache develops between my legs.

I make a soft noise in the back of my throat that sounds a lot like a cat purring. *Yikes, could I be more embarrassing?* It only seems to encourage Oliver further. He proceeds to leave a path of hot kisses down my spine, thoroughly waking up every single nerve in my body. When he reaches the middle of my back, my kneejerk reaction is to try to squirm away.

"Stop, I'm ticklish down there."

"Really? That's something I didn't know."

He continues to torture me despite my pleas. It's impossible to escape his assault when I'm weak from giggling. "Oliver, come on. Not fair."

"Where else are you ticklish?" He rolls me on my back right before he attacks the sides of my ribs with his torturous fingers.

"No!" I grab one of his wrists, laughing nonstop. "You're evil."

He straddles me, capturing both my hands and pinning them above my head. "I'm evil? You were the one who wore a dress last night that left me in a state of permanent arousal the entire time."

"Shut up. I did not. Besides, that dress is not that sexy."

"Oh, sugar. You make every single piece of clothing sexy." His gaze drops to my breasts and a new glimmer of hunger appears in his eyes. "Although, I prefer when you wear nothing at all."

He leans down and sweeps his tongue over my nipple, turning the nub hard as pebble. I arch my back, urging him to do more than tease. He chuckles against my breast before he brings the nipple to his mouth, sucking and licking the sensitive spot as if it were a popsicle.

I try to break free from his hold, but he won't let me go. "Easy there, sugar."

"I want to play too," I say, almost breathless.

"You will, but let me taste you for a little longer."

He switches his attention to my other breast, doubling the throbbing between my legs. I don't know how we got anything done before. I never want to leave this bedroom.

Letting go of my nipple with a pop, he leans back and searches the room.

"What are you looking for?"

Without answering, he jumps off the bed. It only takes me a second to find out what Oliver's up to.

"No way."

His smile turns devilish when he twists my scarf into a makeshift rope. "Oh yes."

Before I can sit up, Oliver is straddling me. I don't put up a fight when he ties my wrists to the wrought iron headboard. A rush of excitement runs through my veins as desire unfurls in the pit of my stomach. Anticipation is making my breathing shallow, short-circuiting my nerves.

"Now, where was I?"

He returns to my breasts, lavishing them with more attention than before. While his mouth and tongue are busy with one, his hand plays with the other. I don't know what's worse, being at his mercy or not being able to touch him.

"Ollie…."

"Yes, sugar."

"I have an itch."

"Oh yeah? Where?"

"Down below."

"Hmm." He runs his tongue across my breast. "Here?"

"No, farther down."

He continues on, peppering my feverish skin with sinful kisses that ought to be illegal.

"How about now?"

"Not even close."

Chuckling, he moves farther down until his hands are splayed over my hip bones. I'm glad I decided to get a Brazilian wax before our impromptu trip.

"Fuck, sugar. The sight of you makes me want to weep. So beautiful." He licks my outer lips and I buck my hips, the zing of pleasure almost too much to bear. He keeps me in place with his hands. "And also so delicious."

His tongue finds my clit this time and it's an explosion of sensations. I let out a cry as I lose the power to control my body. I'm at his mercy.

"I love the sounds you make." He sucks my clit in his mouth at the same time his fingers find my entrance.

It's just too fucking much, and I'm ashamed when I can't hold off any longer. I scream his name and close my eyes, trying to milk every drop of this devastating orgasm. Oliver's skillful ministrations don't waver. No, they get better. He only stops licking me when my body melts against the mattress and I let out contented sigh.

"Nothing turns me on like the sight of you coming."

I bring my knees up, opening myself to him. "Come and get what's yours."

With a groan, he's on top of me faster than lightning, his cock sliding in with ease. He kisses me hard, my taste still all over his tongue. I fight against the hold on my wrists. He abandons my mouth to stare into my eyes, flashing me a lopsided grin.

"Something bothering you, sugar?"

"I want to touch you."

His eyes zero in on the scarf around my wrists. "Have you noticed how tight your left hand is holding on to the scarf?"

"What?" I twist my neck, trying to see. Sure enough, the knuckles are already white from the strain. "Oh my God. I didn't notice."

"I think we should play this game more often."

He pulls out almost completely only to hammer back inside of me with a precise thrust, cutting off the reply on the tip of my tongue. I let out a moan instead.

"What's wrong, sugar? Feel like yelling my name again?"

"Yes," I hiss.

"Good." He silences me with a kiss, and not much later, I do scream his name, many times over.

## OLIVER

"What?"

"Nothing." I smile.

"Why do you keep staring at me?" Saylor puts the cup of coffee down, frowning.

"I can't look at my beautiful wife?"

"You're staring, not looking. You're making me feel self-conscious."

"Oh please. You look positively ravishing this morning. That glow on your cheeks... hmm, could that possibly have anything to do with the—" I raise my hand and count on my fingers silently. "—five times I made you come this morning?"

Saylor watches me through slits. "Don't get cocky now."

"Cocky? I'm not cocky. I'm a sex god."

Felix barks once before returning to his bone and I continue. "See, even the dog agrees."

Saylor rolls her eyes before picking up a piece of Danish pastry from her plate. The guesthouse is finally properly stocked with food and drinks. I'm not surprised after I almost bit Gilbert's head off for being his usual incompetent arse.

"So, do you feel like practicing with Rita this morning?"

"I didn't bring Rita." She eyes me with suspicion.

"Are you sure?"

I slide off the high chair and walk around Saylor. She turns to watch where I'm going. Even in one of my darkest hours, I remembered to pack Saylor's beloved guitar. After what I witnessed her do this morning with the scarf, I'm glad I had the foresight.

I hid the case in the foyer closet, hoping the opportunity would come naturally. I didn't want Saylor to feel pressured to keep practicing. As I retrieve it, I can't keep the grin off my lips.

"I can't believe you brought her." She eyes the case longingly, all the proof I need that I made the right call.

"I didn't bring the amps, but I ordered them yesterday. They should be here by the end of the day. I also brought my acoustic guitar, so you can practice with it if you want."

"How long are we going to stay here?" There's a peculiar tone to her question, and watching Saylor closely, I see guilt in her gaze. Shit, she did drop everything and her bandmates to come with me.

"If it were up to me, we would be on a flight back right now, but I can't leave Nana. Not yet, anyway. My father is a certified asshole, but he's still her son."

"I understand." Her gaze drops to her plate, prompting me to put the case down and breach the distance between us.

"Hey, everything will be okay, sugar. If you want to return to California, I'll understand."

Her face whips up so fast, it takes me by surprise.

"You want me to go back?"

"Hell no. But your life doesn't revolve around me. You have a career to think about."

Raising her right hand, she touches my cheek. "I'm not leaving you. We'll think of something. I'll stay here for as long as needed."

I move closer to kiss her, but a knock on the door stops me short. Saylor looks over my shoulder and asks, "Expecting company?"

"Are you guys done with your lovemaking? I have plans for you two, and the clock is ticking," Nana says from the other side of the door.

I cross the living room in two long strides, opening the door wide. Nana pushes me out her of way, her gaze zeroing in on Saylor.

"Finally. It's bloody freezing today."

Saylor stands up, bringing the lapels of her furry robe close together. At least she's wearing clothes underneath it.

"Why are you still wearing PJs? It's past noon already. I want to show you our town."

"I can get ready really quick."

Nana shoots me an appreciative look. "I'm glad you didn't choose one of those high-maintenance girls for a wife. We have enough of that nonsense already with your mother and Charlotte."

I give Saylor a long stare. "I hit the jackpot with that one."

My heart swells when my comment makes Saylor blush.

"Do you think Felix is going to be all right on his own?" she asks.

"I sure hope so."

"Are you still here, girly? Chop, chop. I'm not getting any younger, you know?"

Saylor runs to her room, closing the door behind her with a soft click. We didn't have the chance to move her stuff to my room yet, or vice versa. I don't care. As long as we're no longer sleeping in separate rooms, I'm happy.

"So, I take it things have gone back to normal between you two despite Saylor's amnesia?"

"Yes, at least I think so. The first month was rough, Nana, really rough. I honestly thought I would end up losing Saylor after all. If that had happened—" I get choked up and have to stop.

Nana is the only family member with whom I can be myself. Even when I tried my hardest to shut her out of my life like I did with everyone else, her support didn't waver. I'm glad she never gave up on me.

She pats my arm. "I understand, darling. I loved your grandfather very dearly, even though ours was an arranged marriage. Burying him twenty years ago was one of the hardest things I've ever done."

Saylor returns to the room wearing tight jeans and a thick sweater that hugs her curves perfectly. My cock twitches in my pants, despite my grandmother's presence. Jesus, I'm a deviant when it comes to my wife.

"I'm ready," she declares.

"Good." Nana claps her hands together. "Now if one of you could drag Charlotte out of her bed, I'd appreciate it."

"Bloody hell. Must she come?"

"Language, boy. I'm still your grandma. And yes, Charlotte

must come, even if she doesn't want to. I want to spend a nice winter's day out with all my grandchildren."

"I can get her going," Saylor offers.

"Oh no. Allow me this pleasure."

My lips curl into a grin. If I have to suffer Charlotte's presence, I'm getting some satisfaction out of it.

# CHAPTER 24
## SAYLOR

don't know what kind of stunt Oliver pulled with Charlotte, but she has fire spitting out of her mouth as she strides out of the main house. Oliver follows close behind, sporting a hint of mischief in his eyes. I notice also there's a bright red spot on his cheek that looks a lot like a handprint.

"You'd better put a leash on your husband, Saylor," the girl snaps at me right before getting into the car. Oliver's grandma is already inside waiting.

"What did you do to Charlotte?" I narrow my eyes at him.

"Just a little prank I used to pull when we were little."

"And that is?"

His grin expands, taking up his entire face. "I poured icy water over her head."

"What? That's mean!"

He shrugs. "That's what big brothers are supposed to do." He touches the sore spot on his face. "Although, she's learned how to fight back. I better remember to get the hell out of Dodge next time."

I point at him. "If you ever pull a stunt like that with me, expect more than a slap to the face."

"Ah, sugar, I would never do that to you." He moves closer

and whispers in my ear, "There's only one way I want to wake you, and that's by eating your sweet pussy."

Heat rushes to my face as an overwhelming need hits me hard. Holy fuck. How can this man turn me on with only a few naughty words?

Clearing my throat, I say, "Your grandma is waiting and I'm freezing my butt off. Come on."

Oliver opens the driver door and kicks Linus out, announcing he's driving. There's a moment of hesitation on the poor guy's part, but once Adeline says it's okay, he gives up his seat to Oliver. Since he's now driving, I take the front seat on the passenger side. It's weird on this side, like something's missing.

"I don't know how you can drive so well in Cali. I'd probably kill a few sheep if I attempted to drive on the wrong side of the road."

"You and your American mentality. Who said *we* drive on the wrong side of the road?"

"I'm sorry, wasn't the first car invented by a German? On what side of the road do they drive again?" I raise an eyebrow at him.

"Touché, sugar."

"Beautiful and smart. Jackpot, Ollie," Adeline says, making me blush again.

"Where to, Nana?"

"I think Saylor would love to see the Hatfield House. She'll probably find it cheerier than our home."

"Ugh, not that place again," Charlotte mumbles.

"I promise we'll hit the shops afterwards," Adeline continues.

"Bloody hell. Not the shops," Oliver groans, then turns to wink at me with a tiny smile on his lips.

The butterflies in my stomach make their presence known in a vicious manner. Why did I have to be so lucky and get savage insects instead of the pretty ones?

Adeline's promise seems to appease Oliver's sister, as she doesn't make any other remarks.

Hatfield House is one of the great stately homes of England, Adeline tells me. It's set in a large park—the Great Park—and an earlier building on the site was the Royal Palace of Hatfield. Only part of it still exists, a short distance from the present house. Adeline speaks animatedly about the history of the place, as if she had been there during the time Queen Elizabeth I resided in it. Once we arrive, Adeline insists we take the brief tour of the old royal palace.

"Nana, you're killing me here," Charlotte groans.

This time, the matriarch chooses to ignore her grandchild.

The 'brief tour' takes more than an hour, and we don't even cover the entire thing. I try to show interest whenever Adeline makes a comment, but the lack of sleep from last night is finally catching up with me, making it difficult to concentrate. When she turns away, I fail to suppress a yawn and Oliver catches it.

"Tired, sugar?"

"Yes. Someone didn't let me sleep last night."

"Oh really?" He wraps both his arms around my waist, pulling me closer. "Expect to not sleep for the next few nights. We have to catch up."

I feel it again, that tug in my chest as my heart goes on manic mode. I can't believe it took me over a month to finally see the truth hidden inside of me. I should've known from the start that falling in love with Oliver was inevitable. He's my person, even if I don't remember parts of our history.

"We don't need to catch up only after dark, you know."

His eyebrows shot to the heavens. "What are you proposing, sugar? Do you want to find a family restroom?"

"How come I have the feeling we've done that before?"

Oliver answers me with a sweet yet toe-curling kiss. It only lasts a few seconds, though that's because Charlotte makes gagging sounds and tells us to get a room. With cheeks aflame, I step back, looking at everything but Adeline or Oliver's sister.

We head to the exit, stepping out into the cold, gloomy weather once more. Charlotte is already walking ahead. I lag behind, throwing a long glance in the garden's direction. Even under the gray sky it looks breathtaking. From where I stand, I can see the mini maze box and beautiful topiary.

Oliver must've caught me staring, as he says, "We'll come back here another day. Charlotte will have our heads if we delay her shopping another second."

"All right. I'm getting kind of hungry anyway, and the garden looks massive."

"I reckon it's probably close to forty acres."

"Forty?"

"Hey, we're talking about the Tudors here. We have to take a picture in front of Queen Elizabeth's Oak. It's a must." His eyes twinkle and I pinch his arm, not doing any harm through the thick woolen jacket he's wearing. I know he's mocking me somehow.

I didn't realize that when Adeline said shopping, she meant the catered-for-tourists shopping area. The Stable Yard Shops surround a super cool fountain topped by a pineapple—the symbol for hospitality, I'm told. One shop that catches my eye particularly is Heritage Brides. I veer in its direction for no reason. I guess I'm curious. The store is based in the Harness Room at the Stable Yard of Hatfield House. The ancient barn has been turned into a vintage woodland wonderland. From a quick glance, I can tell they stock the finest wedding dresses and accessories.

A sales assistant approaches me and asks If I need any help. She's not super cheery, nor overly arrogant, and I give the usual bullshit excuse she must be tired of hearing that 'I'm just look-ing.' She keeps hovering nearby, though, and that begins to unnerve me. Does she think I'm going to steal a freaking wedding gown?

I leave the store after a minute, finding Oliver waiting for me with his hands tucked inside his coat.

"Did you find anything you like, sugar?" He's grinning like a fool.

"Ha-ha. No."

"Excuse me," someone says behind me. I turn to find the shopgirl not too far away.

"What?" I say, irritated. Does she want to check my purse?

"Uh, I'm sorry to bother you. Are you Saylor Blue from Wreck of the Day?"

The words vanish from my vocabulary as my jaw drops. I didn't expect to be recognized in freaking England.

"Yes, the one and only." Oliver wraps his arm over my shoulder.

Shopgirl spares only a glance in Oliver's direction before she returns her attention to me.

"Would you mind terribly signing an autograph for me?" She extends a piece of paper and pen in my direction.

"Uh, sure," I say, feeling a little guilty for my earlier outburst.

"It's for my younger sister. We both love your songs, but she's truly a superfan."

"Oh, what's her name?"

"Caroline. She's driven her nurses bonkers by insisting to play your songs nonstop."

"Nurses?"

Sadness takes over the woman's face. "Yes. She's been in hospital for a couple of months now. She has leukemia."

"I'm so sorry to hear that."

"It sucks, but this will sure cheer her up." The girl waves my autograph before thanking me and returning to the shop.

I'm still staring at the store, reeling, when Oliver breaks the tension by being a goof.

"Bloody hell. I must be losing my mojo. She didn't even ask for my autograph."

"Good. Someone needs to bring your ego down a notch."

He watches me through slits and I wait for his smartass reply.

Instead he looks over my shoulder and says, "Come on. Nana and Charlotte have already headed to the restaurant."

"That's it? No wiseass remarks from you?"

"Nope."

"You're definitely losing your mojo."

He snakes his arm around my shoulder, pulling me closer so he can whisper in my ear. "Let's see if you still think that later today."

The promise in his words turns my legs to mush. I ought to stop baiting him like that, unless I want to combust on the spot.

The restaurant is busy, but not packed to the gills. It seems we missed the lunch hour rush only to arrive in time for tea. My internal clock is a mess anyway, so I don't care what type of food I eat, so long as I fill my belly.

The décor is a mix of streamline wood and metal furniture. Long tables take up the middle while smaller ones line the walls. Modern light fixtures hang from the ceiling, giving the place a sleek industrial look. Big windows allow the light to pour in, even though the sun has yet to make an appearance today.

Adeline and Charlotte are sitting at one of the smaller tables by a window. When we join them, Charlotte doesn't glance from the menu in her hands; either she's still pissed at Oliver for his earlier prank, or the situation with her father is also affecting her deeply. My gaze immediately switches to Oliver. So far, he hasn't shown any sign that he's on the verge of going back to that dark spot I found him in last night. I'd like to say I'm the reason, but in all honesty, I think he's hiding his turmoil from me.

I reach for his hand under the table, lacing our fingers together. He looks at me with such adoration in his gaze that it's hard not to swoon. He's so beautiful, and when he smiles, I just want to hold him tight and never let him go. My vision blurs as I catch an image of another time: Oliver standing in front of me, holding a diamond ring between his fingers. The memory is gone as fast as it came.

"Sugar, what's the matter?" He watches me like a hawk, a big frown marring his forehead.

"I-I… it's nothing." I break eye contact. For whatever reason, I don't want to share what just happened with the rest of the table. No, I want to tell Oliver when we're alone.

He brings our hands to his lips and kisses my knuckles.

Charlotte finally puts her menu down, raising her hand to call a waiter's attention. She drops her arm with a jerky movement, making a strangled sound. We all notice her strange reaction, her gaze fixated on a point behind me. Oliver and I turn to see what warranted such a strong reaction from her, and we find a young couple at the entrance of the restaurant.

"Do you know them?" I ask.

"Isn't that Joseph Whitman the Third?" Adeline asks.

"Yes," Charlotte hisses.

"Your ex-boyfriend?" Oliver watches Charlotte closely.

She only nods this time before standing abruptly and announcing she has to use the restroom.

"Nana, do you know why Charlotte and that preppy boy broke up?"

"I'm afraid I don't, honey. But to be completely honest, I wasn't too upset about it, unlike your mother. I never liked that boy."

The *boy* in question stops by our table to greet Adeline.

"Mrs. Best, what a surprise to see you here. I've heard about your son. I'm so sorry."

"No need to say sorry. My son is still very much alive."

Adeline's sharp response don't seem to affect Charlotte's ex.

"Naturally. Didn't I just see Charlotte walk away a second ago? I would love to say hello."

"Shouldn't you be at Oxford?" Oliver butts in, not even attempting to disguise his contempt toward the man.

The guy looks down at Oliver as if he were an insignificant gnat. I want to punch his throat. Who the fuck does he think he is?

"How would you know about the schedule of such a prestigious school? Didn't you exchange a proper education for showbiz?"

His tone drips with contempt. I can't believe Charlotte dated that idiot. Just a minute in his presence and I already want to kill the guy.

"How is the family business going? I just read in the papers about the closing of half a dozen Whitman stores throughout the country."

Joseph's mask finally cracks, his face turning a deep red as he stares daggers at Oliver. "Not that you would know anything about it, but this is all part of a strategic maneuver. The business is as good as ever."

He spins on his heel, dragging his date with him. *Good riddance.* Charlotte comes back a couple of minutes later.

"What did he want?" she asks as she sits back down.

"Nothing, just to annoy everyone with his presence."

"Are you okay, Charlotte?" I ask.

She massages her temples and glances down. "No. I have a bloody headache. Do you mind if we just go home?"

Adeline turns to stare at her granddaughter properly, narrowing her eyes. "Yes, we can go now. I'm finding myself quite weary as well."

# CHAPTER 25
## OLIVER

t was fucking hard to control my temper back in the restaurant. It was the first time I'd met Charlotte's ex in person, but I've heard about him and his family. I have to ask, what the fuck was she thinking? I'm an arsehole and never made any attempt to hide it, but that guy is in another league. He's deceitful, I could tell just by looking at his smug face.

My intuition tells me something bad went down with Charlotte and that wanker. It had to be serious enough to make her change her mind about attending Oxford. She won't tell me, though. I made sure she would never come to me with her problems. Add that to the list of things I regret in life.

I'm jittery when I walk into the guesthouse, making a beeline for the little minibar in the living room. I tried my best to suppress the shit storm brewing inside of me for Saylor's sake, but I just can't keep doing it stone-cold sober.

I feel Saylor's presence behind me as I break the seal of the brand-new bottle of whiskey. I pause before turning around, clutching the empty glass hard until my knuckles turn white.

"Oliver, talk to me."

"I'm tired of talking."

"So, you'd rather get drunk?"

"It helps, sugar." *God, I sound so pathetic.*

She stops next to me, taking the bottle. "Look at me."

I do as she asks, tired of keeping up the charade any longer. "I'm fucked up, sugar. Can't you understand?"

"I'm fucked up too. So what?"

"I can't stay here, in this town, in this house. It's messing with my head."

"They we won't. Adeline will understand."

"You wouldn't think I'm a coward for running away?"

"Do you think I'm coward for not wanting to stay at my mother's place?"

"Of course not." I don't say it out loud, but it's a completely different situation. Saylor had been the victim. I'm the villain, and nothing is ever going to change that.

"If being here hurts you, then I say we leave right now. I want to restart our lives together, Ollie." She touches my face so tenderly that I want to bottle the feeling her touch elicits for when she's not around.

I capture her hand to place a kiss on her open palm. "Me too, sugar."

"I have to tell you something."

The change of subject subterfuge is obvious, but I don't care. When the small smile blossoms on her lips, it makes it easy to forget about all the shit in my life.

"Oh yeah? What?" I pull her flush against my body, suddenly thinking about other ideas on how to feel better.

"I remembered something today."

The air whooshes out of my lungs like a strong gale. I can't remember how to draw it back in. "What?"

"It was just a flash, gone too quickly for me to really hold on to it. I think I got a glimpse of when you proposed to me."

"For real?" I almost can't contain the excitement in my voice.

"Yeah."

I crush her against my body as I claim her mouth, and she matches my urgency with the same ferocity. No, I take that back —she's the one in charge. Like a boss, she pushes me against the edge of the counter, looking wild. And I love it. She drops to her knees, her gaze glued to mine. Using both hands—something she's been doing more and more often without realizing—she unzips my jeans and frees my erection. I brace against the counter, watching my beautiful wife through a red-hot, lust-infused gaze. Her pink tongue darts out, licking the drop of precum from the tip.

"Saylor…." I close my eyes as a shiver runs down my spine. Fuck. I had forgotten how good her warm tongue feels on my cock.

"What is it, Ollie?"

"Don't stop what you're doing."

"Do you like when I do this?" She licks my entire length this time, starting from the base and lazily drawing her tongue back to the top.

"Fuck yeah."

She repeats the motion, just as slow as before. It's the best kind of torture.

"You have to remind me what you like."

She watches me through her thick eyelashes with a teasing grin on her lips. She knows exactly how do drive me insane, but all right. I'll play the game.

"I want your warm lips wrapped around my cock. I want you to suck me hard as I fuck your mouth."

"Bossy, aren't you?"

"I know what I want."

"And do you always get what you want?" She raises an eyebrow.

"I got you. Do you need more proof than that?"

"Was I hard to get, Ollie boy?" She replaces her tongue with her hand, pumping my cock up and down in a delicious rhythm.

"Very much so." I almost can't get the words out.

She brings my entire length into her mouth, sucking a little as she does.

"Fuck me," I say.

My nut sac tightens as a wave of pleasure curls around my spine. I have to clench my ass cheeks together to avoid coming prematurely.

Saylor is committed now, no more teasing on her part. I don't know what drives me wilder, her expert mouth milking my cock or the delicious sounds she's making in the back of her throat. I don't think I can avoid the inevitable for much longer. I begin to pump my hips, literally fucking her mouth like I said I would. She takes everything I have without complaint, and a few seconds later I surrender to the ecstasy, grunting her name like a caveman as I come.

She drinks every single drop of my release, only stopping when there's nothing left.

Sagging against the counter, I open my eyes again and glance at her. Her lips are swollen and red, matching the flush of her cheeks. It's the most beautiful sight I've ever seen.

I lift her, then sweep her off her feet.

"Oliver, what are you doing?"

"What do you think, sugar? I gotta return the favor."

I enter the first room I come to and drop her on the middle of the mattress, wasting no time getting rid of her skintight jeans and panties. Her desire is already evident, and when my tongue finds her sweet spot, I groan. She tastes like peaches, smooth on my tongue, sweet in the back of my throat. Fuck, I could feast on her all the day long.

Using the entire arsenal I have at my disposal—tongue, fingers, and teeth—I have her begging for mercy within minutes. Her fingers are in my hair, pulling the short strands until it hurts. But it's a good kind of hurt.

I'm already hard again, so when Saylor screams my name from the top of her lungs, I crawl over her until my cock is exactly where it needs to be, at the entrance of her sweet pussy.

She pulls my face to hers for a kiss at the same time her legs wrap around my waist, guiding me in. I try to keep the pace slow, but everything seems overcharged with raw desire. We both come again simultaneously only a few minutes later. We're finally in sync again and it feels as amazing as it used to be.

# CHAPTER 26
## SAYLOR

The amps arrived yesterday while we were gone, but this morning, when I couldn't sleep and tiptoed to the living room, I left them untouched. Oliver is sleeping like the dead, and I want him to have his rest. Instead, I grab his acoustic guitar, bundle myself in warm layers, and venture out into the freezing morning. Dawn is still an hour away at least, and heavy mist surrounds the property. Spooky, but I feel safe with Felix next to me.

I sit on the bench in front of the house with the guitar propped on my lap. Closing my eyes, I take a deep breath. Frigid air fills my lungs, but it's clean and crispy, and it invigorates me with an energy I can't describe. It's a pity Oliver can't bear to be in this place; it's so beautiful and peaceful, especially this early in the morning.

The only problem with playing outside is cold, stiff fingers. I open and shut my hands, taking special note of how the left feels stronger now. I've almost completely recovered sensitivity, and there's only a little numbness left.

I try a few chords on the guitar, adjusting the strings as I go until I get to the sound I want. Then I play the new song I wrote for Oliver. It's a ballad, and it does something to my heart.

There's ache mixed with hope there. The sound is off; I can't quite get the notes right yet. It's been too long since I played that it's almost like I have to relearn how to do it.

A month ago I would've been frustrated beyond reason. Not now. I don't let my handicap get to me. I'll keep pushing through until I'm back at the top of my game. I play the song a few more times before I decide on another challenge—my duet with Oliver. I still haven't listened to the entire song, but I did download the music sheet and memorize it. If I can't bring myself to listen to the recorded version, then I'll just have to sing it.

Ignoring that the guitar intro sounds nothing like it should, I plow through. My heart is hammering inside my chest, and when I sing the first verse, my voice sounds choked. Felix whines next to me, as if he can feel the pain in my voice. Instead of fighting the feeling, I let it take over. I've never been moved so much by a song. The parts that belong to Oliver are even harder to sing as I imagine his beautiful voice giving life to the verses.

Then I actually hear him sing. At first, I think I'm imagining things, until Felix barks twice.

I stop and turn to the front door, finding Oliver leaning against the frame.

"Why did you stop?"

"How long have been standing there?"

"A minute or so." He joins me on the bench, sitting next to me. "Shall we continue?"

Heat rushes to my cheeks. It's one thing to play awfully by myself, but I'm embarrassed to sound so terrible in front of him.

"The guitar sounds nothing like it should."

"So what? Come on, sugar. There's no one around to judge. It's just you and me."

"You and me against the world."

He smiles, melting my heart and my hesitation. Before I resume playing, I lean over and kiss him. I just can't help myself.

With his lips still glued to mine, he says, "Nice evasion tactic, but you won't distract me so easily."

"Stop being so irresistible, then."

"Impossible."

I move away before it really becomes impossible to stop kissing the man.

"From the top?"

"Yes."

My fingers are practically frozen so I rub my hands together. Oliver captures them between his, bringing them closer to his mouth to blow hot air on them. Once they don't feel stiff as a board any longer, I try the guitar again. The intro still isn't right, but it sounds a little better than before. As I progress through the song, my anxiety lessens. When Oliver joins me, it feels like this moment is the final piece that makes us whole.

The song is over too soon, but the energy it created remains. I lock gazes with Oliver and know he's feeling the significance of this moment too.

"I love you." Truer words have never left my lips.

"I love you, sugar. I always will."

His hand finds the back of my head to guide me to his waiting lips. The guitar is suddenly gone from my lap, and in the next second, Oliver pulls me onto his. Cold lips suddenly turn fiery hot even though we're in no hurry this time. My tongue dances with his sinfully slow, which proves to be even sexier than the frenzied kisses we shared in the last couple of days. I taste complete happiness, and it's the most intoxicating flavor in the world.

Oliver stands, carrying me without breaking the kiss. Heat has already pulled between my legs, anticipation leaving me dizzy. I'm high on his touch, wanting his mouth everywhere on my body.

The noise of a car approaching interrupts our glorious moment. Headlights break into our bubble of happiness. Without putting me down, Oliver turns around. Felix begins to pace in front of us, barking as if he's pissed about the interruption too. Mercifully, the headlights are turned off once the car parks in front of us.

Charlotte emerges, and it's only when she stops in front of us that I see her tear-streaked face.

"Ollie, Father is dead."

## OLIVER

I put Saylor down and ask Charlotte to repeat the news. She does, and yet my brain can't seem to grasp the meaning of her words. It takes me a minute or two to recover from the shock, and then I don't know what I should be feeling. Contradicting emotions battle within my chest: sadness, relief, even happiness. But the most overwhelming is a sense of failure. I failed to be the son my father wanted me to be. He made that crystal clear the last time we spoke, and that's the final memory that will trump all others. Not that I had a great deal of pleasant moments to remember with the man.

"Ollie, can I do something?" Saylor touches my arm, concern etched on her pretty face.

"I need to see Nana."

"Of course."

"She was talking with Dad's doctor when I left. Mum's locked herself in her room and won't speak with anyone."

"Maybe I can try," Saylor offers, but both Charlotte and I know it's no use.

"Thanks, sugar, but that's okay. Mother has a penchant for the theatrics. She'll get over it soon."

Saylor frowns and I realize my comment was a little insensitive. She can't possibly know that my parents' marriage was a loveless one.

I pull her to me to kiss her forehead. "Let's change and head to the main house."

"Can I wait here with you? I-I can't be in that house by myself right now." Charlotte hugs herself, reminding me of when she was just a little girl and found out her brother had died. I couldn't offer comfort to her then, not when I was so consumed by guilt.

I let go of Saylor and walk toward my sister, pulling her into a tight hug. She buries her face in my chest and starts to tremble. "It's going to be okay, Char."

Through sobs, she says, "I can't believe he's gone. I didn't even have the chance to talk to him. Why didn't he want to see me?"

I keep my mouth shut. I'll never tell Charlotte what our hateful father said in that room. She doesn't need to know her own father didn't give a shit about her.

*Fuck that man. I'm glad he's dead.*

# CHAPTER 27
## SAYLOR

Everything happened in a blur following the news of Oliver's dad's passing. He tried his best to maintain a detached approach, taking on the most practical tasks of organizing the funeral and dealing with the family's lawyer. Charlotte didn't care with pretense, and she let the world know how badly she was hurting. I couldn't be certain, but it seemed the man had only been hateful toward Oliver. That made me resent him even more.

Call me a bitch, but I couldn't empathize with Charlotte's pain. For starters, my own father was garbage, so I couldn't relate. And then there was the fact that the man treated Oliver horribly. So yeah, good riddance.

Thanks to my strong feelings toward Dr. Frank Best, I was stuck in limbo. I didn't know what to say to Charlotte or Adeline that wouldn't sound fake. My only solace was that Oliver didn't shut me out completely. At night, he let me soothe away the stress and pain he was trying so hard to hide. We made love until our bodies couldn't take anymore, until we were utterly spent.

Things only improved when Liv and Sebastian arrived for the funeral. I was glad to have my best friend with me, and

Sebastian's presence did wonders for Oliver.

The day of the funeral finally arrives, which means we're only a day away from leaving all of this behind. I never yearned more to escape from a place than I do now.

Upon Lydia's insistence, the wake is to be held at the family's property. This is the second time I've attend a funeral—the first was for Sebastian's parents. The difference is glaring. Here, there isn't a single person weeping in silence, not even Charlotte. It's like no one cares that Dr. Best is dead. Charlotte is more withdrawn than ever, but I feel that has more to do with the presence of her ex than anything else. When he tried to offer his condolences, she stiffened as if his proximity caused her harm. Something about her reaction resonated with me, and I'm making sure to keep an eye on the guy from now on.

The room where the wake is being held could be called a ballroom. It probably *is* a ballroom. It's spacious with tall windows and a high ceiling, yet I feel smothered. It's like the air around me is oily and it sticks to my skin.

The open casket sits on a dais, a small podium with a mic in front of it. Fancy chairs have been set into rows, leaving an aisle in the middle. Flower arrangements frame the seating area but do nothing to cheer the place up.

Oliver sits next to me stiff as a board, his hand clutching mine in an iron grip. In his other hand, he holds a piece of folded paper, the speech he's been asked to give by his mother. The family lawyer addresses the crowd first, saying all the right things about Dr. Best before he calls Oliver up. My stomach is in knots. What could Oliver possibly say about a man who denounced his own son? Oliver notices my stare and winks at me before standing. He throws a quick glance in the open casket's direction, then turns to the assembly.

His face is stoic and devoid of emotion. He looks like a god of death wearing his dark suit and somber expression. Staring down at the paper in his hand, he takes a deep breath before facing the room again. He opens his mouth but no sound comes forth. His eyes narrow instead and it seems his face has gone even paler. A murmur behind me has me turning on my seat. Standing in the middle of the aisle is a young man with light brown hair and a face almost as striking as Oliver's.

"This is a private event," Oliver addresses the newcomer.

"Ollie, don't you recognize me? It's me, Harry."

*What? Harry? The supposed dead brother?*

A second goes by before Oliver's mother lets out a shriek and collapses on her chair. The lawyer catches her in his arms. The murmurs become louder. Oliver holds on to the podium as if he too needs support to remain upright.

Someone grabs my wrist tight. It's Adeline. I had forgotten I was sitting next to her. Her face is ashen.

"Are you okay?" I whisper.

"I need to go to my room."

I'm torn between helping the elderly lady or going to Oliver. Liv comes to the rescue and says she'll take Adeline, who's in too much of a daze to refuse.

Oliver is still frozen when I touch his hand. "Ollie?"

Two large guys wearing dark suits emerge from out of nowhere and grab the intruder by his arms. I hadn't realized there was security here. They're ready to drag the man out when Oliver tells them to stop.

Ignoring me, he strides down the aisle, stopping in front of the man.

"How can that be? They told me you were dead."

The man closes his eyes for a brief second before looking at Oliver again. "It's a long story."

"How dare you interrupt this private and difficult moment, trying to pull a scheme." The lawyer strides toward the group, fury twisting his face. "Take this con artist out of here."

"I'm not lying. Ollie, tell them."

Oliver stares at the stranger for what feels like an eternity before he finally says, "I would like to have a word with him in private."

"You can't be serious. Harry is dead, Oliver. And you just lost your father. You're not thinking straight."

"I said I would like to hear what he has to say, so back the fuck off!"

I wince, even if his outburst wasn't aimed at me. The security guys, realizing Oliver is the new boss here, release the young man's arms and back away.

"Let's talk in Dad's old office," Oliver says, and it doesn't escape my notice that he's already accepted this stranger as Harry.

I'm hopeful and at the same time scared. It would be beyond miraculous if Harry had been indeed alive all these years. But what kept him from coming forward until now?

I'm terrified of what the truth will do to Oliver's mind.

# CHAPTER 28
## OLIVER

don't know what to think as I stare at the man in front of me. My brain is shouting that he can't possibly be my brother. He's dead—that's what everyone told me. Though the details of what happened to Harry are hazy in my memory; I was so stricken with grief and guilty that it was hard for me grasp the meaning of the explanation given to me then.

Despite his animosity toward the newcomer, I asked Charles Cowell, the family lawyer, to be present during this meeting, not trusting myself to ask intelligent questions. I keep staring at the man, trying to find vestiges of my younger brother in him. There's a picture of Harry on the desk, and my gaze bounces from the frame to the guy nonstop. There's a resemblance, I can't deny that, but I'm afraid to believe the story only to have my hopes crushed if this guy proves to be a con artist like our lawyer believes.

"What makes you think you are the deceased son of Dr. Frank Best?" Charles starts.

"I'm Harry Best. I'm not lying."

The lawyer laughs without humor, then throws a glance in my direction that says he's not buying this bullshit.

"If you are my brother, where have you been all these years?" I ask.

"I don't remember much about the day I disappeared. I vaguely recall you scowling at me, then me running away. That's when Elliot Jenkins hit me with his car. That part of the story I was told."

"Wait a second. Isn't there a Jenkins living nearby?" I turn to Charles.

"Yes, ten minutes from here."

"Yes. We've been neighbors all this time," Harry adds.

*Bloody hell. I'm already thinking of him as if he's my brother.*

I glare at him. "If Elliot Jenkins hit you and you survived, why didn't he contact us?"

I'm afraid to know the answer. What if Harry had been held against his will? Bile rises in my throat at the thought.

"He panicked. He had been drinking that day and would've lost his doctor's license if he'd come forward. He brought me to his place and took care of me. I survived. Later, his wife got attached to me. She had just lost her only son to a terrible disease, so they kept me and raised me as if I were their son. They convinced me that all my previous memories had been a figment of my imagination. I knew it wasn't so, but I figured I would be doing everyone a favor if I just disappeared forever."

Guilt eats at my insides. If what this man is saying is the truth, I'm still responsible for this mess.

"I didn't mean to snap at you that day," I say.

He gives me a rueful smile and I see it then, the six-year-old Harry in that expression. I don't want to believe it—it's almost too convenient to be true—and yet I can't stop the hope that surges within my chest.

"I know that now, but to the mind of a six-year-old who idolized his brother, it felt like I wasn't wanted. But it wasn't only because of you that I chose to stay with the Jenkinses." He pauses, throwing a quick glance at the lawyer. "They were the opposite of Mum and Dad. They doted on me, paid attention. They were the loving and devoted parents I always wished for."

Charles scoffs. "Oh, that's rich. I've never heard so much horseshit in my entire life, and I'm a lawyer."

"I know it's hard to believe," Harry continues.

"So, the Jenkinses didn't keep you as a prisoner?" I ask.

"No. It took me months to recover. When I was finally able to ask about you, Mum, and Dad, the Jenkinses told me I was confused, that I must have hit my head. I planned to run away, but like I said before, I liked living with them and in my mind, if the family I was supposedly imagining really existed, they would be looking for me."

"You had a funeral," I choke out.

"I know. I visited my headstone not too long ago."

"If you really are Harry Best, then you won't mind submitting material for a DNA test," Charles cuts in.

"Of course not. I'm telling the truth. What kind of an idiot would claim to be someone they aren't in this day and age when it's so easy to prove otherwise?"

"Oh, no test is foolproof." The lawyer leans forward, leveling Harry with a hard stare.

"You do realize you've accused the Jenkinses of kidnapping. They'll go to jail for it," I tell him.

"That's why I never came forward until now. They're both gone. Mum—I mean Mrs. Jenkins died three years ago. Mr. Jenkins died before Christmas."

I rub my face as I try to process a story that has every single red flag possible. But what if this stranger is telling the truth? What if he is indeed Harry?

♡ ♡ ♡

## SAYLOR

My mind is reeling as I step into Adeline's room. I wish Oliver had asked me join him at the meeting with the potential Harry. His grandma is lying on her bed, and Liv is adjusting the pillow for her. As I approach them, Adeline's keen eyes lock with mine.

"Did you talk to him?"

"Oliver? Not really. He locked himself in with the lawyer and the man who claims to be Harry."

"You don't believe he's my grandson?"

"I don't know what I think. There's nothing I want more than for Oliver to get his brother back, but I'm just too jaded. The timing is a little too convenient."

"Yes, I have to agree with you."

"How did Harry die, if you don't mind me asking?"

Adeline's gaze seems to turn inward as she stares ahead. "We don't know all the details. He just vanished."

"Vanished? I had always been under the impression that Harry died after being hit by a car. At least that's the story Bas told me." Liv moves to stand next to me.

Adeline shakes her head. "The police found Harry's jacket soaked in blood tossed to the side of the road. They believe he was hit by a car, and the person responsible got rid of the body to not be implicated in the crime."

A shudder runs down my spine. "So, it's possible the man is telling the truth."

"Yes. It's possible," Adeline replies before her face scrunches up.

"What is it?" I grab her ice-cold hand.

"My nerves are fried, darling. I'm an old lady. It's too much excitement for one day."

"Can I get you anything?"

She looks at me, her eyebrows furrowing. "I want you to stay close to your husband. Oliver is in a very fragile state, and Harry's death has always been his weakness. It won't take much for a con artist to dupe him. I want to believe the man downstairs is my grandson, but I wasn't born yesterday."

"Bas and I can stay longer too," Liv says.

"That would be much appreciated. The more Oliver is surrounded by people who truly love him, the safer he will be."

I can't help the feeling of foreboding Adeline's words bring. Despite the outcome of today's revelations, I see a bumpy road ahead for Oliver and me.

# CHAPTER 29
## SAYLOR

deline's words are still reverberating in my head as I run down the stairs. I've taken her advice to heart and, wanting it or not, Oliver has himself a clingy wife now. I don't want to ever see him in that awful state he was when I found him in the tree house again.

I don't care that he didn't ask me join him in the study while he interviewed his maybe brother. My plan is to burst into that room regardless, but when I reach the end of the stairs, I catch a scene that makes my already agitated mood turn into a hurricane.

Charlotte is backed into a corner by her ex-boyfriend, and he's all over her personal space.

*What the actual fuck.*

I've interacted enough with her to know something isn't right. Charlotte is a firecracker; she wouldn't tolerate that kind of behavior by anyone unless there's more to the story.

I make a beeline toward the duo, catching the end of Joseph's statement. "Come on, Char. Just a quickie for old time's sake. No one will notice we're gone."

Charlotte turns her head when her ex tries to kiss her, and something inside of me snaps. I grab the back of his jacket's collar and yank him off her. Taken by surprise, he doesn't offer any resistance. He actually almost falls on his ass. Too bad he managed to catch his balance at the last moment.

"Get your filthy hands off her, creep," I say.

"Who the fuck are you?" He glares at me.

"I'm Charlotte's sister, and unless you want to lose a limb, I advise you to take your sorry ass out of this house before I let my dog have his way with you. I doubt anyone will miss you."

"Oh, you're the 'popstar' Oliver married." The asshole actually uses air quotes. I almost laugh.

"Holy shit, did you just try to insult me? Honey, where I come from, we eat snobby assholes like you for breakfast."

"Do you even know who I am?"

I put my hand over my chest. "Wait? Are you next in line for the throne? No? Oh I see, you're just one of the has-been idiots still clinging to your family's name because that's the only thing you have left."

I have no idea what I'm saying; I'm just going with what Oliver said to the man the first time we had the displeasure of crossing paths with him. It seemed to piss him off before, and it's working again now. Joseph's face turns bright red and his eyes spark with fury. *Jackpot! He does have money issues.*

"You know nothing about me, bitch."

"I'm only going to say it one last time. Get. Out!"

He looks over my shoulder—at Charlotte, to be more precise —before he turns on his heel and stalks out the front door.

*Good riddance.*

"Thank you." She walks around me, looking paler than a sheet of paper.

"It was a pleasure. Are you okay?"

She nods. "Not this very second, but I will be. I…." She looks down. "I hate that I can't find my voice when he's around. You must think I'm pathetic."

"I don't think that at all. Sometimes talking about things helps."

She glances up again, her hazel eyes brighter than usual. "You have enough on your plate right now. Don't worry about me."

I know I won't get Charlotte to open up, so I change the subject to the other big issue in our hands.

"How are you handling the whole Harry thing?"

"Shit. I don't know what to think about that one. I don't remember him. I was too young when the accident happened."

"But do you think it's possible?"

Charlotte glances down the hallway where Oliver is presently locked with the man. "Yes, I think it's possible. No one would be crazy enough to claim to be someone they aren't when there's DNA testing now."

"True. I was headed that way. Do you want to join me?"

She takes a deep breath and glances at me again. "I really should, but I don't think I can handle more stressful situations right now. I'm going to rest for a little bit."

"Okay then. I'll come back later with more news."

Charlotte heads up the stairs and I down the corridor. Before I can knock on the door, it opens wide. The lawyer comes out, not looking happy at all. He pauses when he sees me and I take the opportunity to quiz the man.

"What happened?"

"In all my years as a lawyer, I've never heard so much bullshit in my life."

"So, you don't think that man is Harry?"

"Oh, I didn't say that. He could be your husband's brother, but the story he told us? Too suspicious. I don't buy it."

"Why?"

"You don't worry your pretty little head with it. Even if Harry has come back from the dead, you'll still get a good chunk of the Best's fortune."

*Did he just accuse me of being a gold digger?*

"I didn't marry Oliver for his money," I say through clenched teeth.

"Sure you didn't. I wasn't born yesterday, sweetheart."

*Oh that does it. I'm sick and tired of dealing with overentitled assholes.* I push the much larger man against the wall and pock my finger in his chest. "Don't ever call me 'sweetheart' again. I don't care about the Best's fortune. The sooner you get that into your thick head, the easier your life will be."

I step back because I can't stand to be that close to him.

"What's going on here?" Oliver asks, looking from me to the lawyer.

I smile sardonically. "Nothing. I'm just making things clear to your lawyer."

Oliver narrows his eyes, clenching his jaw hard as he stares at the man. "You have a job to do, Charles. Fucking go already."

The lawyer straightens his jacket and leaves without another word.

Once he's out of sight, Oliver touches my shoulder. "Are you okay, sugar?"

"Yes, I'm fine. Are you?"

He nods. "Considering everything, I am."

I watch his face closely for any signs of that darkness I hate, finding none. I look over his shoulder into the study but don't see anyone.

"Where's the maybe Harry?"

"Maybe Harry?" Oliver smirks.

"Uh, well, I don't know what to call him."

"He's gone already."

"Oh." I can't keep the disappointment out of my voice. "I was hoping I could meet him."

"In due time, sugar. I think it's best to only introduce him to you once the DNA results come back."

"You don't think he's telling the truth?"

"To be honest, I don't know."

# CHAPTER 30
## SAYLOR

The DNA results returned a week later. I wasn't surprised when it revealed the man raised by the Jenkinses was in fact Harry Best. The lawyer broke the news to the family. He also said that the PI he hired to look into the guy's past didn't reveal anything shady. His story checked out. The Jenkinses indeed had a son named Simon Jenkins, and the PI couldn't find any records that the child died. Because Oliver's mom didn't want the family's name dragged into a scandal, she decided not to involve the police. Matters would be handled privately.

"What are the next steps?" Oliver asks after a few seconds of silence.

"I'm afraid there's a lot of paperwork involved. There's the matter of inheritance. Your father had a will, but with the sudden return of Harry, things will become more complicated. He isn't mentioned in the will for obvious reasons, but he has grounds to contest it."

"Why would he contest it? Charlotte and I will split our share equally with him. Right, Char?"

The girl who had been looking out the window, distracted, turns to her brother. "Yeah, sure. Whatever."

"I'm awfully tired," Oliver's mom announces. "Charles, you take care of all the paperwork. I want to be done with this as quickly and painlessly as possible."

"You don't even sound excited to know your son is alive," Oliver says.

"How dare you speak to me in that judgmental tone. I buried my son, I dealt with the grief of his passing, and I moved on. That man is a stranger to me."

My jaw drops. *She did not just say that. What kind of mother says that?*

"You're a piece of work. No wonder Harry preferred to stay with the Jenkinses." Oliver's body shakes as he tries to keep his voice down.

She levels him with a glare. "Don't forget the part you played in his decision, son. I'm not the only one to blame."

Oliver winces as if he was physically hit, making me see red. I stand up as fury crackles though my veins. He might feel the need to show some restraint out of respect, but I sure don't. "You are a vile woman. You don't deserve the children you have."

"You insolent brat. I want you out of my house this instant." Her eyes flash with so much hate, it almost makes my knees buckle. But I stand my ground. I'm tired of witnessing her throwing barbs at Oliver for no good reason aside from being a fucking bitch.

"This is not your house," I say. I haven't forgotten that bit of information Adeline dropped when I first met her.

Oliver stands as well, placing himself between me and his mother. "Sugar, it's okay. She's not worth it."

I lock gazes with him, still frustrated as hell that I can't kick the shit out his mother. I would love to give her a taste of my knuckle sandwich. Oliver's eyes sparkle with pride and also raw desire.

*Holy shit. Is he turned on by this confrontation?*

Not saying another word, I turn on my heels and leave. I

need fresh air. Oliver follows me, but before I can walk out the front door, he drags me into the powder room, locking us inside.

"Oliver, what are you doing?"

"I'm celebrating, sugar." He grabs my face and kisses me long and hard.

Thoughts of escape and fresh air are forgotten. Who needs nature when I have Oliver Best instead? My hands find the button of his jeans, impatient all of a sudden. Then a vision of a similar moment invades my mind: Oliver and me, in another bathroom, kissing and touching like maniacs, frustration and desire mingling in my heart.

My hands stop, my lips freeze, and I take a step back. Oliver notices the sudden change in me immediately.

"Sugar, what's wrong?"

"We've done this before."

"You remembered something?"

"I-I think so."

"What exactly?"

"Us going at each other in a bathroom of sorts."

He curls his lips into a wicked grin. "Oh yeah. That was epic. You attacked me in a family restroom at LAX."

"I did what?"

"Ah, sugar. It's better if I show you what we did."

He kisses me again while his hands get busy with my jeans. Definitely not the best outfit to be wearing for impromptu hookups in small bathrooms. With his help, I shimmy out of them, getting naked from the waist down. Oliver's magical fingers are already on my pussy, teasing me beyond coherent thinking. I sit on the sink, opening my legs to grant him better access. He inserts one finger while his thumb applies pressure on my clit, but the hard edge of the marble sink is digging into my ass cheeks, preventing me from truly enjoying his ministrations.

"Ollie, as much as I'm loving this, this is not a very comfortable position for me."

"How can I make it better, sugar?"

"Your cock deep inside of me sounds like a terrific idea."

He frees his erection from the confines of his boxer shorts in the next second, burying it deep inside of me with a precise push. I have to bite his shoulder to muffle my cry of pleasure.

Oliver fucks me in that bathroom hard and fast, both of us coming within seconds of each other. And the best part is that the memory it brought forth stayed with me this time, vivid as ever.

I will remember us. Every single memory.

# CHAPTER 31
## SAYLOR

Oliver left soon after our hookup to visit his brother. I went back to the guesthouse for a shower and later decided to visit his grandma, since she missed the meeting with the lawyer. I doubt Oliver's mom bothered to tell Adeline the news.

I find her sitting up on the bed, reading the same book of poetry she's had by her side for the past week. The moment she looks at my face, she knows what I'm about to say.

"The DNA results are in?"

"Yes. It's him. Harry is alive."

Closing the book, she shuts her eyes for a brief moment. "Then I suppose I need to get my arse out of this bed and greet my grandson properly."

"Maybe Oliver can bring him here. You shouldn't tire yourself."

"We'll see. How did Ollie take the news?"

Heat rushes to my cheeks and I avert my gaze. "Uh, quite well, actually."

"Quite well, you say, huh? And that blushing?"

I cover my cheeks with my hands, hating how my face always betrays me.

"What blush?"

"Oh, darling, you don't need to feel embarrassed around me. I know all about the birds and the bees." She laughs. "I sure hope all this celebration will yield a little Best before I depart this world."

*Fuck a duck. Is she talking about babies now?* That hadn't even crossed my mind.

"You're not leaving us any time soon," I say, not willing to get into the baby talk. There's so much I want to do before I even begin to contemplate having a kid—getting my memories back, for instance.

"Yeah, yeah. So, have you met him yet?"

"No. Oliver didn't want me to meet him before the test came back. Understandable, of course. He went to see him now."

Now that we know without a doubt that Simon Jenkins is really Harry Best, a ball of anxiety unfurls in my stomach. There's so much I don't know about Oliver's past.

"You look concerned. Tell me what's on your mind, child."

"How was Oliver's relationship with Harry?"

"What you can expect from a relationship between two brothers. They loved each other, but due to the age gap, they fought a lot too. Four years is a big difference when you're young. As Oliver grew older, he didn't care much for Harry tagging along."

"They quarreled right before the accident. That's why Oliver carried so much guilt for so long."

"Yes. And my son and his wife didn't make things easier for him either. They blamed the boy too. I know it's not right to speak ill of the dead, but my son was a terrible father."

"When he asked to speak with Oliver, I thought he wanted to wish him happy birthday. Instead, he told Oliver he wished he had died instead of Harry."

I regret my words the moment I see the effect on Adeline's face. "He did what?"

"I'm sorry, I shouldn't have said anything."

With shaking hands, Adeline reaches for the glass of water on her nightstand. "That vile man. I would kill him if he wasn't dead already. I can't believe I raised that monster."

Once she finishes taking a few sips of water, Adeline continues. "Don't look at me with that guilt-ridden expression. I'm okay. Now, you wanted to know more about Oliver and Harry's relationship. Well, before Oliver got into his independent phase, he was quite close to Harry. You could say Harry was Ollie's shadow."

She pauses to lick her lips and looks off into the distance. "There was one instance, I remember it vividly like yesterday. Harry fell off the tree house and broke his pinkie. It didn't quite heal right because he kept messing with the cast. In consequence, he ended up with a crooked finger. The poor boy cried his eyes out because of it, saying all his friends from school would make fun of him. Do you know what Oliver did?"

She glances at me, a small smile tugging the corner of her lips.

"No."

"He broke his finger on purpose and asked the doctor to make sure it healed crooked as well."

"He did not."

I can't imagine anyone getting hurt on purpose like that. For Oliver to do it so his brother wouldn't feel inadequate speaks volumes to his character. My love for him expands in that moment, my heart overflowing.

"He sure did. That's the kind of person he is. So when he went dark after Harry died, I didn't let him shut me out like he did with everyone else. Someone in this family had to keep loving him even if he couldn't love himself."

My eyes prickle and I fight to keep the tears in check.

"I've never noticed that Oliver has a crooked pinkie."

"Oh, he doesn't have one. He was only eight, after all, so the doctor didn't do as he asked and Ollie's finger didn't heal crooked. By that time, Harry didn't even care anymore. The defect wasn't even that noticeable. You'd have to look closely to see."

Adeline tries to suppress a yawn and I take that as a sign to let her rest. On the way back to the guesthouse, I call Liv—who's already returned to Cali—and tell her the news. She's shocked but also happy for Oliver. I also call Tabatha once I get to the guesthouse. Felix jumps from the couch to greet me. He clearly wants to play, but I have to finish the call with Tabatha first, so I lock myself in the bedroom, keeping him out. *Sorry, dude.*

The first thing out of her mouth is to ask when I'll return home. I try to explain that I don't know yet, and to say she's pissed is an understatement.

"So let me get this straight. You're ditching the band so you can stay in England babysitting your husband? Oliver's brother is alive. Yay! I get that he wants to stay longer to reconnect with him, but I don't see why you have to stay as well."

"I'm sorry, Tabby. Things aren't that simple."

"It *is* that simple. You're not only ruining *your* career here, Saylor. Think about *us*."

I pinch the bridge of my nose, trying to keep the brewing headache at bay. I had truly believed Tabatha would understand my situation. Then an idea pops into my head.

"Why don't you guys come to the UK? I'm sure Allan can arrange for a couple of appearances and interviews."

Plus, it would also keep Oliver occupied. I don't want him to ditch all his dreams on account of his brother.

"I don't know, Blue."

"I finished a new song. These weeks here in England have been great for me, Tabby. I even started to remember things."

"You have?" Her tone changes, so I press on.

"Yes. And we could arrange studio time here as well."

"How is your hand? Does that mean you can play Rita again?"

"I'm not quite there yet, but I've been practicing daily."

"I'll talk to the girls. I'm itching to work on new songs. I don't like this lull. It makes me feel useless."

"Me too, Tabby."

I feel a thousand times better after I end the call.

"Sugar, are you home?" Oliver calls from the living room.

My heart does a somersault upon hearing his voice. The story Adeline told me comes to the forefront of my mind, making me want to cover Oliver in kisses and tell him how much I love him.

"Yes."

I open the door with tremendous eagerness, ready to jump into his arms, but the massive bouquet in his hands stops me.

"What are those?"

"Uh, I think they're called flowers." He walks in my direction, a cheeky smile on his lips.

"Ha-ha. What's the occasion?"

"Can't a guy bring his gorgeous wife flowers without a reason?"

"Nope. It usually comes attached with an 'I'm sorry I screwed up.'" I narrow my eyes at him. "You didn't do anything stupid, did you?"

My tone is light, but the question isn't. I don't know yet if I should be worried that Oliver will make a hasty decision when it comes to Harry. I hate not knowing everything. Perhaps if I had my memories, I wouldn't feel so out of my depth. I'm in love with my husband, but he's still a mystery to me.

Oliver hands me the flowers and I hide my face in them as if I'm smelling their scent. In reality, I'm trying to hide the guilt that might be showing on my face. I feel like I'm betraying his trust for even having these thoughts.

"They're gorgeous. Thank you."

I go in search of a vase to put them in, and while I have my back to Oliver, I broach the subject that's giving me so much anxiety.

"How was the meeting with your brother?"

"It was good but awkward. I mean, he's my brother, there's no doubt now, but he's still a stranger, you know?"

"Yes, I can imagine."

"I've invited him for dinner tonight. I've already told Mum and Charlotte."

"That's good. Do you think your grandma will be up to it? I saw her earlier, and she looks frail."

"But she's okay, right? Shit, I've been a terrible grandson."

I turn to find Oliver looking worried sick. *Shit.* He hasn't visited his grandmother that much in the past week, but I didn't mean to make him feel that bad.

"Other than fatigued, she looks okay. You should go say hello to her today. She misses you."

"Yes, I will. But first." Oliver reaches for me, pulling me close. "I want to continue our celebration." He kisses me tenderly at first, making me melt against his body.

The brush of his tongue against mine rekindles a fire in the pit of my stomach, and I'm panting and moaning in a split second. With a groan, Oliver lifts me, the skirt I'm wearing bunching around my waist. Oh yeah, I decided to only wear skirts from now on. He places me on the kitchen counter, his hips now exactly in the right spot. Dry humping never felt more maddening. I want to strip off all of our layers. Oliver's hand finds my core, and through the panties and tights I'm wearing, he presses his thumb against my clit.

"You realize this is a very similar position to the one from earlier today."

"Oh yeah, and it worked so well then."

Felix barks twice, reminding us that we aren't alone.

"We can't do this in front of him," I say.

"He's a bloody dog, sugar."

"I don't care. It feels wrong."

"Oh fine."

Oliver lifts me off the counter, and I wrap my legs around his waist to keep me from falling. With long strides, he crosses the short distance to our room, closing the door with his foot.

"Alone at last."

"Shut up and kiss me."

He does as he sets me on the edge of the mattress before kneeling in front of me. His mouth leaves mine to place kisses down my neck while his hands are busy with my breasts. It's only been a few hours since we last had sex, but I'm panting and moaning for this man as if I haven't seen him in ages.

He leans back to peel off my tights and underwear, leaving me completely bare to him once more. His apt fingers return to my pussy, stroking and making lazy circles that drive me insane. Still kissing him, I make quick work of his fly, using both hands this time. His rock-hard cock springs free from his boxers, only to be trapped again by my fingers. I pump him at the same pace that his fingers work me, but I want more than a simple hand job. I guide his head to my entrance, shoving his hand out of the way.

"So bossy today."

"I'm having withdrawals. I need another hit now."

"Your wish is my command." He sheaths himself inside of me fast, eliciting a sharp moan from me.

Wrapping my arms around his neck, I fall backward, bringing Oliver with me. He runs his hand down my leg, curling behind my knee to bring it over his shoulder. This is a win position for us, I realize; he hits me exactly in the right spot like this. Our grunts become louder and uneven, but still in sync. Our lovemaking takes longer this time, both of us wanting to prolong the sweet torture. But everything good in life must come to an end, and together we come in a cacophony of moans and shouts.

I tremble in his arms while the last tremors of ecstasy run through my body. Resting my cheek on his shoulder, I take a deep breath, inhaling Oliver's intoxicating scent. My internal walls clench around his cock, making him chuckle.

"Give me a minute, sugar, and we can have another round."

Pushing back, I lock gazes with him. "I love you, Ollie. More than I thought I could love someone."

"I love you too, sugar." He tucks a loose strand of hair behind my ear.

"What's going to happen next? I mean with Harry and all."

I don't need to add anything for Oliver to get my meaning. We can't stay here forever.

"I was thinking about inviting Harry to spend some time with us in Cali."

My stomach clenches painfully as anxiety returns. My mind and heart rebel against the idea of Harry in California with us, invading our life there. It's a crazy thought considering Charlotte lives there too. It makes sense for him to go.

"I didn't know how long you wanted to stay here, so I suggested to Tabatha that the band come to the UK. We can maybe appear on some TV shows or even record a couple new songs."

Oliver's eyes twinkle at the same time his face splits into a toothy grin. "You did? That's bloody brilliant."

He crushes me against his chest, happy as he can be.

So how come all I want to do is cry?

# CHAPTER 32
## SAYLOR

inner. I've never dreaded a situation that involved food so much in my life. We're in the living room, lounging in front of the fireplace, waiting on pins and needles for the guest of honor to arrive. Oliver's mom is getting loaded, already acting like a crazy drunk lady. I've lost count of how many martinis she's had. At least she seems to have forgotten our earlier argument. I still loathe her as intensely as before, though.

The doorbell rings, making Oliver jump from his spot on the couch next to me. He beats Gilbert to the door, and from where I stand, I can hear his animated voice greet his brother. I suppress my apprehension, putting a bright smile on my face to welcome Harry.

"Saylor, let me introduce you to my brother."

I extend my hand to shake his, getting chills when we touch. The skin on my arms breaks into goose bumps. The contact is brief, but the weird sensation lingers. My smile wilts a bit as I take a step back. I hope no one noticed my reaction to Harry, especially Oliver. The last thing I want is for him to think I don't like his brother.

"What a pleasure to meet Oliver's better half. He hasn't stopped gushing about you since we reconnected."

"Oh, we've talked about me?" I glance at Ollie, the surprise in my tone sincere.

"Of course, sugar." He throws an arm around my shoulder, pulling me closer to kiss my temple. "Why the surprise?"

"I thought you guys were catching up."

"We did that too," Harry answers with a smile that looks genuine.

The feeling of foreboding dispels a bit. Harry seems like a nice guy. I have no reason to worry. Maybe my anxiety is nothing more than misplaced jealousy. Truth be told, I don't want to share Oliver with anyone, not even his brother. It's selfish, I know, but I just started rediscovering us. Harry feels like an intruder.

They move along and when Harry stops in front of his mother, the lady has trouble standing upright. She runs her hands down her pencil skirt, swaying on the spot. Good grief, she's pathetic. I don't get why she's nervous. She made it clear earlier that she doesn't give a damn about her son.

"Good evening, Harry," she says, still trying to maintain some dignity.

"Mum, you look exactly how I remember."

"I do?"

"May I give you a hug?" He opens his arms wide, expectantly. If she doesn't hug the guy, I'm going to kick her ass.

But Harry's question seems to catch her by surprise. Maybe if she hadn't been sloshed, she would've refused, but she accepts the hug and even pats Harry's back as well. It's the most affection I've seen her demonstrate since I met her.

Charlotte is way less awkward when it's her turn to greet her long-lost brother. She hugs him tight, eyes filled with tears when they come apart.

"Ah, Char. Don't cry," he says.

"I'm sorry. I swore I wasn't going to." She wipes at a lone tear that escaped.

"Where's Grandma?" Harry asks as he looks around the room.

"She hasn't been feeling well since Dad's funeral. She's very sorry she couldn't join us for dinner, but she wants to see you tomorrow, if you don't have any other plans."

"No. My schedule is wide open."

"You don't go to school?" I ask, curious, but somehow it seems the wrong question to ask.

Oliver's eyebrows furrow and Harry's cheeks turn bright red.

"Uh, I had to drop out of school when Mr. Jenkins got sick. We couldn't afford a caregiver."

"I'm so sorry."

Gilbert comes into the room to announce dinner is served. I'll never get used to the level of formality in this house.

When it comes to the seating arrangements, I find myself opposite Harry, with Oliver next to me. Throughout dinner, I keep staring at the man, looking for any resemblance between him and Oliver but finding none. It's no big deal, really—Charlotte looks nothing like Ollie either.

At one point, my gaze drops to Harry's hands. Adeline never specified which pinkie Harry had broken, but from where I stand, both look perfect.

*Saylor, stop looking for trouble where there is none. Adeline did say you could barely see the defect.*

Oliver and Charlotte keep Harry engaged, showering him with questions. None of them ask the things I'm burning with curiosity to know, though. I bite my tongue for as long as I can, but restraint was never my forte. When there's a lull in the conversation, I open my big mouth.

"Forgive my asking, but what happened to the real Simon Jenkins?"

"Sugar." Oliver covers my hand with his, but his tone is one of reproach.

I bite my lower lip, glancing down. Maybe my question was a little out of line.

"Dad—I mean Mr. Jenkins told me Simon had a chronic disease with a short life expectancy. That's all I know."

"There are no records of Simon's death, right? That's why you could take his identity," Charlotte says.

"That's correct."

"So, did they just bury their son in a shallow grave?" I blurt out, sticking my foot in my mouth again.

Oliver squeezes my leg, and this time it's not a prelude for sex.

"I don't know. It didn't occur to me to ask. He only told me the truth towards the end and… well, it was a hard situation."

"Creepy." Charlotte shudders.

"What are your plans, Harry? Are you going back to school?" I ask.

I hope he says yes, but Oliver answers before Harry has the chance. "I've actually already invited him to come to Cali with us. Perhaps he can help with Renegades."

Irritation simmers low in my gut. This is the first time I'm hearing about the Renegades idea. I hate it.

"Have you spoken to Allan and Sebastian about it?" I ask, trying my best to keep the irritation out of my voice.

"No. It just occurred to me."

I clench my jaw and stab a piece of potato with a little too much force.

"You don't think it's a good idea," Oliver continues, clearly displeased with my reaction.

"I didn't say that. But you have to remember that you have partners. Besides, what does Harry know about showbiz?" I throw Harry an apologetic glance. "No offense."

"None taken. Please don't argue on my account. Ollie, that's a great offer, but I'm going to side with Saylor here. I know nothing about showbiz. I'll be glad to just play tourist while I'm in California."

*Thank God someone here is sensible.* But Harry's defense of my argument doesn't do anything to mollify Oliver, I can still sense the tension radiating from his body. I foresee a fight in our future. My mood is also sour now, but I don't regret speaking my mind.

Our main dishes are taken away, and a minute later, dessert is served—chocolate lava cake with vanilla ice cream. At least something positive about the evening. There's really nothing better than gooey chocolate and ice cream.

Harry looks down at this plate and scrunches his nose.

"What's the matter? You don't like chocolate cake?" I ask.

He glances up. "Uh, as a matter of fact, I can't stand chocolate."

A sudden silence takes over the room. You could hear a pin drop.

"You're joking, right?" Oliver asks.

"Uh, no. Don't you remember that, Ollie?"

"Remember what? You were practically addicted to chocolate. It was so bad Mum took you to see a doctor," Oliver replies.

"That's true," the woman mumbles, the first time she's spoken since we sat down.

I catch something odd in Harry's eyes. A flash of surprise, followed by… anger? It's gone too quickly for me to be certain. Maybe I read it wrong. Why would he be angry?

"Strange," he says. "I must have gotten an aversion for the stuff after my accident."

Oliver makes a strangled sound in the back of this throat, making me glance his way. "What's wrong?"

He looks at me and smiles tightly. "Nothing, sugar."

He's lying. I want to call him on his bullshit, then decide we've already bickered enough for one evening.

# CHAPTER 33
## SAYLOR

Two days after the dinner, Adeline calls the guesthouse early in the morning. First, it's the house phone that rings nonstop, but it's easy to ignore that since it's all the way in the living room. Felix barks at it until it stops ringing.

Then Oliver's phone starts.

Curled around my body, he stirs in his sleep, pulling me even closer to his morning wood. There hasn't been a day since we started sleeping in the same bed that this hasn't occurred, but it seems we won't be able to care of it today.

"Ollie, your phone is ringing."

"Let it ring." He buries his nose in my hair.

"It might be important. Whoever's calling is being very persistent."

With a groan, he rolls onto his back, reaching for the phone on the nightstand.

"Hello?"

I can't hear the other person, but a few seconds later, Oliver says, "Nana? Is everything okay?"

There's another pause. Wide awake and worried sick, I sit up in bed, watching Oliver with rapt attention.

"Okay, yeah. I can do that."

"What is it, Ollie?"

He raises his index finger to ask me to hold on, focused on the conversation.

"Okay, Nana. I'll see you soon."

He ends the call, turning to me as he does so.

"What, Oliver? You're freaking me out. Is Adeline okay?"

"More than okay. She's feeling so well, she wants to go to the green market to buy fresh produce. She decided to invite Harry to come over for lunch. She's cooking one of her old recipes."

"She's really up for all that?"

"If she says she is, we won't be able to talk her out of it."

"Okay, then we better get ready." I untangle myself from the warm sheets, throwing my legs to the side of bed. Once up, the room begins to spin as a dizzy spell hits me out of nowhere. Stumbling, I fall back on the bed.

Oliver is next to me in an instant. "What's the matter?"

I shake my head. "Nothing. I think I stood too fast."

Pinching my chin between his forefinger and thumb, Oliver turns my face to his. "You're not getting migraines again, are you?"

Oh, I see where the troubled gaze is coming from now. I grab his hand and place a quick kiss on his open palm. "Don't worry. No migraines for this girl. This was nothing. Like I said, I stood too fast. I'm okay now."

"Sugar, I want you to tell me if you're not feeling one hundred percent, okay?"

I lean forward and kiss him. His worry is breaking my heart. I've kept the truth of my condition from him for a long time and he hasn't forgotten about it. I don't know why I was so stupid before.

The kiss is sweet but short. When it ends, I'm dizzy for entirely different reasons. Oliver's gaze drops to my mouth, his thumb making lazy circles over my hip bone.

"We really should get going," I say, almost breathless.

His hand moves up my side to graze the underside of my breast. "She won't kill us if we're five minutes late."

"Five minutes?"

Oliver grabs my hand and places it on his erection. "Feel this, sugar? It won't take long."

"You always wake up like that." Despite my words, I curl my fingers around his cock anyway.

"It's all your fault." His finger flicks my nipple, causing a zing of pleasure to travel down to my core. I won't win this fight. I don't want to win this fight.

I let go of his erection to push him back on the mattress. Before he can say anything, I climb on top of him, effectively impaling myself on his cock. The beauty and practicality of sleeping naked.

"Ah, sugar. I love when you take the lead."

"You said five minutes. Let's see if you were telling the truth." I move at a faster pace than usual. Not because we have an appointment, but because I'm too horny for my own good. I don't want to take it slow.

We both come within three minutes, a record for us. Most women would be pissed at that, but that's because they aren't married to a god of sex like I am.

I fall on top of him, thoroughly satisfied, and kiss his chest. He wraps his arms around my back, keeping me in place while he's still hard inside of me. Oliver will be good to go in another minute or so. Too bad we don't have time for a second round.

"We really should get moving," I say.

"I know. Let me enjoy this for a few more seconds."

"Will we ever get tired of each other?"

"Never. You'll be giving me raging boners until I'm ninety."

"Only ninety, huh? What happens after that?"

"Don't know. I never thought I would live past ninety."

I raise my chin and peer up at him from under my lashes. "You promise to still be turned on when I suck your shriveled ninety-year-old balls?"

Oliver bursts out laughing, shaking me in the process. "The pictures you paint in my head, sugar."

♡ ♡ ♡

Adeline is waiting for us in front of the house, pacing back and forth impatiently.

"There you are. What took you so long?"

"Uh, we got ready as soon as we could," I say.

"Right. And you're both glowing for no good reason."

Oliver chuckles while my face bursts into flames.

"Let's go, get in the car. At this hour, all the good vegetables will be gone."

This time, Oliver doesn't ask to drive, preferring to sit in the back next to me. His hand is covering my knee casually, but the lazy circles he's making with his fingers are turning me on again. For fuck's sake, his grandma's sitting next to me. It seems like my hormones have gone haywire. I'm hornier than I've ever been all of a sudden.

Adeline takes the lead in the green market, walking ahead of us with purpose. She does feel better, removing one item from the list of things I have to worry about. Oliver is in charge of the shopping trolley, which soon gets filled with all kinds of vegetables and fruits. Adeline stops at a shop with the most luscious-looking berries and my mouth waters. She selects a handful of strawberry baskets and their aroma fills my nose as I pass them to Ollie.

"Oh blimey. It seems I didn't bring enough cash with me. Ollie, do you mind paying for this?"

"Sure, Nana." He pulls his wallet from his back pocket and stares at it for a beat. "Oh, this is embarrassing. I have no cash."

"What do you mean? I saw at least three hundred pounds in it yesterday when I took cash out to pay for the pizza," I say.

"I gave it to Harry when I saw him later and forgot about it."

"You gave it to Harry? Why?"

"Because he asked me."

Oliver's explanation seems like the most normal thing in the world to him. To me, it's just super odd. Why is Harry hitting him up for money already? I glance at Adeline and it seems she shares my sentiment, her eyes narrowed in Ollie's direction.

"I have some cash on me," I say, realizing the shop owner is still waiting for payment.

"Anywhere else you want to hit, Nana? I can look for an ATM," Oliver offers.

"No, I'm good. I got everything. Now tell me, why is Harry asking you for money? Is he in some kind of trouble?"

Oliver rubs the back of his neck. "I don't know. He just asked to borrow some cash and I gave it to him. No big deal."

Adeline makes a disapproving noise in the back of her throat. I keep my mouth shut this time, but the ball of anxiety returns to my stomach with a vengeance.

# CHAPTER 34
## OLIVER

Saylor and Charlotte are helping Nana in the kitchen when Harry arrives. Mum is MIA, and no one really cares if she decides to skip lunch altogether. Gilbert gets to the door before I can and he's already taking care of Harry's coat. From where I stand down the foyer, I notice it's not the same one he's been wearing since I met him. His clothes also fit better and look brand new. Maybe that's why he asked for the money.

I had almost let Nana's and Saylor's disapproving opinions get to me. They think I didn't notice the glance they traded at the market. I don't know why they think it's so wrong for me to give money to my brother; he'll inherit a third of the Best fortune anyway.

"Looking good, brother. New clothes?"

Harry looks down, patting his jeans. "Yeah. I figured I should start dressing like a Best now."

I roll my eyes. "Whatever that means."

"Oh you know, clothes that don't come from secondhand stores and smell like piss."

"How bad was the Jenkinses' financial situation? I thought they had money."

Harry shakes his head. "They'd been living off appearances for years. I'm afraid to look at how much money they owe the bank."

"Well, it's not your problem now."

"I don't know. I get what you're saying, but in a way, the Jenkinses were my parents. They raised me. I'd hate it if the bank took their house to pay their debt."

"How much do you think is the estate worth?"

"I'm really terrible with numbers, but I think around two million pounds."

"That much?"

Harry shrugs and looks in the kitchen's direction. "That's my guess. I could be way off."

I pat his back. "Let's call the bank tomorrow and find out. Maybe we can negotiate with them and buy the property."

"Really? That would be brilliant."

His eyes shine with excitement, reminding me of his younger self. The guilt squeezing my heart lessens a bit. I'll do anything in my power to prove to him that he matters.

"Come on. Nana's dying to see you."

"What's that delicious smell?"

"Oh, she's cooking one of her special recipes."

"Nana's cooking? I thought she was ill."

"Well, she's not anymore." I open the door that leads to the kitchen, my eyes immediately zeroing in on Saylor.

My heart skips a beat as it always does when I look at her, even if at the moment I'm a bit irritated with her. I don't think she's embraced Harry's return completely. It's like she doesn't trust him for some reason.

I should talk to her. Lack of proper communication almost tore us apart before. I won't let it happen again.

Nana turns around with a wooden spoon in her hand. She's smiling brightly at me, but when her gaze switches to Harry at my side, I notice her radiance dims a bit. She puts the spoon down and comes to us, her eyes glued on Harry. She stops in front of him, not hiding the fact that she's totally scrutinizing his face.

"You look so different," she finally says.

"Of course he does, Nana. He's not six anymore," Charlotte replies.

"No, it's something else." She narrows her gaze, making Harry squirm where he stands.

"You still look the same, Nana," he says.

"Pfff." She waves him off. "Impossible. The years have not been kind to me. So, Charlotte tells me you no longer like chocolate."

"That's true."

"What did the Jenkinses do to you, some kind of high-tech brainwashing?"

"Nana!" I say. *Jesus, she's worse than Saylor.*

She switches her attention to me. "Oh, will you relax? I'm just teasing. Come, Harry. I have a task for you. Are you good with knives?"

He shrugs and looks at me. "I guess?"

Nana scoffs. "You guess? You're either good or you're not. I need you to cut some onions for me. The girls refused."

Harry wrinkles his nose when Nana turns, looking at me for help.

I laugh and shake my head. "Hey, don't look at me. She's been pulling this crap with me for years. Now it's your turn."

Nana has everything set up already on the kitchen island: a big knife, the cutting board, and a bowl filled with onions.

"Sweet Lord. You want me to cut all these onions? What are you making, Nana?"

She grabs his hand and sprawls it across the cutting board next to the knife. "Something delicious. Now off to work."

"Welcome back, brother," Charlotte says, trying and failing to suppress a giggle.

Nana drops her gaze to Harry's hand, seeming to freeze for a couple beats.

"Nana?"

She snaps out of her trance and looks up at me. "Yes, dear?"

"Uh, Harry needs his hand if he's to cut all those onions."

"Oh, right. I'm sorry."

She lets go of him and takes a step back. I'm not sure what just happened, but it seems to me that her face has gone a little paler. Maybe we shouldn't have let her exhaust herself like that. I feel a sharp pang in my chest when I think she might not stay with us that much longer. It's the way of life, and Nana's lived a long one, but I'm not ready to say goodbye yet.

# CHAPTER 35
## SAYLOR

Allan has worked his magic and he and the girls are arriving tomorrow. They'll stay a couple of weeks, and hopefully by that time we'll be ready to return to California.

I'm in a good mood despite the shitty weekend. Oliver decided last minute to travel with Harry, a trip only for the lads, so I was bored out of my mind. I thought that maybe I could hang out with Charlotte, but I discovered she'd gone off to London earlier.

Abandoned by everyone, I took the alone time to practice with Rita, trying to keep the worry at bay. It worked while I was at it, but the nights were sleepless. I didn't like the idea of Oliver alone with Harry. I got a strange vibe during Adeline's lunch. Her reaction to her grandson was peculiar to say the least, and when I asked her about it later, she was evasive.

I've been practicing Rita for the past hour, trying to nail down one of my easiest songs. The amps are at the lowest volume possible. Felix isn't a fan of my guitar riffs, or maybe I suck so hard that not even the dog can stand it.

I hear the sound of tires against gravel outside and drop everything to run to the window. It's Oliver's car.

I burst outside to greet my husband properly, jumping into his arms and showering him with kisses. He has to take a few steps back to keep his balance.

Laughing, he says, "Hello, sugar. Miss me?"

"So fucking much." I kiss him passionately, savoring the taste of him.

Oliver walks into the house with me still clutched to his frame, not breaking the kiss until Felix decides to join me in welcoming him. The dog barks and jumps around us, and Oliver drops me back on my feet to kneel in front of Felix.

"I've missed you too, mate." He scratches behind the dog's ear.

"So, how was the weekend?"

"It was brilliant. We had a lot of fun in Dublin."

"I thought you'd get back earlier."

"We did, but we had an appointment with the bank in London."

"Appointment? What for?"

"I'm going to buy the Jenkinses' property."

And just like that, my mood turns sour. "Why?"

"Because Harry lived there his entire life and it means something to him."

"That's fine, but I don't see why you're the one who has to buy it. Can't he buy the property with his inheritance money?"

"We don't know how long it'll take for him to have access to it. And the bank was ready to put the house up for auction. We had to move fast. I have the money. It's no big deal."

"How much is the property?"

"Two million."

I blink a couple of times, trying to process what he just said. Then I get real mad. "Are you out of your mind?"

"Why are you angry? I have plenty of money. So what if I want to spend a little to make my brother happy?"

"A little? Two million pounds isn't pocket change, Oliver. I see what's going on here. You still feel guilty for something you shouldn't, and now you're trying to make up for it by making ridiculous grand gestures."

"You wouldn't be saying that if the grand gesture was for you!"

I wince involuntarily, taking a step back. My vision blurs, but hell if I'm going to cry in front of him.

"I would never have allowed you to buy me something that expensive," I say through clenched teeth. "That's the biggest difference between me and your brother."

"What are you saying, Saylor? Do you think Harry's taking advantage of me?"

I should keep my mouth shut, but I'm beyond the point of reason.

"To be completely honest, yes. First it was only a couple hundred pounds, and now we're talking millions. You've just met him."

"He's my brother!"

"He hasn't been your brother for thirteen years!" I shout, hot tears rolling down my cheeks.

I hate that Oliver's taking Harry's side, that he can't see what's right in front of him.

"Harry warned me about this. He said you'd be angry. How foolish I was to tell him otherwise."

There are so many things I want to say to that comment, but I keep them all bottled inside. I turn on my heels, grabbing my coat, and burst out of the house. Felix follows me, but Oliver doesn't. Which is fine; I didn't make a dramatic exit in the hopes he would come running. I need time alone to cool down. I don't want to say things that will only make matters worse. Words can't be unsaid.

Without thinking, I veer toward the tree house. It seems that spot's become mine too. Out in the cold, my wet cheeks almost freeze. I try to wipe them off but it doesn't help. Before long, I stop in front of the tree house and look up. *Maybe it's warmer up there.* Decision made, I start the climb, but when I'm halfway there, light-headedness takes over. I hold tightly to the pegs as the world around me starts to spin. Closing my eyes doesn't help, and before I know it, my body becomes boneless. Then nothing.

♡ ♡ ♡

## OLIVER

What the fuck just happened here? I keep staring at the front door minutes after Saylor burst out of it. We've never had such an ugly argument before, not even when she was hiding stuff from me. Rubbing my face, I walk to the bar, needing a drink to calm down.

Maybe I should've talked to her about buying the Jenkinses' property first. She's my wife, after all. I just got so caught up in Harry's excitement that it didn't even occur to me to check with her. It is a lot of money, but I already promised Harry I'd get the property for him.

The anger leaves my body as the whiskey flows down my throat. After the second glass, I'm thoroughly aware of how much of an asshole I was to her. Putting the glass down, I make a beeline to the door. I need to apologize to Saylor.

I hear Felix before I even head out. The dog's running back to the house, but there's no sign of Saylor.

"What is it, boy?"

He barks and circles me, but it isn't the usual happy greeting. Something's off.

"Where's Saylor?"

Felix takes off in the same direction he came from, and I have to run to keep up with him. He disappears through the cluster of trees that surrounds the property, taking the path that leads to the tree house. Moments later, he stops next to Saylor's sprawled form on the ground.

I feel the ground vanish beneath my feet. "No!"

Running the rest of the distance, I skid to a halt, kneeling next to her. I touch her face with shaking hands, her skin cold to the touch.

"Sugar, talk to me." I pull her onto my lap, laying my face against her chest to make sure she's breathing."

"Ollie?"

"Saylor, oh thank God. You're not dead."

"What happened?"

"I don't know. I found you on the ground. Did you fall?"

She sits up, rubbing the back of her head. "I think I did. I was climbing up the tree when everything went dark."

I touch the spot she just rubbed, trying to see if she has a bump. I find nothing.

"You fainted. That's it, we're calling Doctor Laurent. Maybe he can recommend a specialist in London."

"I'm fine, Ollie. I haven't had any migraines."

"Sugar, please. Don't fight me on this. I can't bear the thought of something happening to you."

"Okay, fine. Perhaps the family doctor can come by."

I would rather she saw a specialist, but seeing any doctor is better than nothing.

"I'm freezing. Can we go home now?" she asks.

I help her stand, pulling her into a tight embrace. "I'm so sorry, sugar. I didn't mean to snap at you."

"I'm sorry too."

"I don't want us to fight about my brother."

"I don't want to fight either."

I stop to look at her face, searching for signs that she might be getting sick again. Her eyes are red and puffy. I made her cry. I feel like such an asshole.

Touching her cheek with the back of my hand, I say, "You're my whole life, sugar. You'll always come first. Never doubt that."

# CHAPTER 36
## OLIVER

We head to London the next day to meet Allan and the band. I had invited Harry to ride with us before my argument with Saylor, but I'm relieved he had other plans and will meet us in London later. After yesterday's fight, it's best if Harry isn't around. I can see now that I haven't been handling this new situation well. Truth is, I've kept Saylor at arm's length as I tried to rebuild my relationship with my brother. I forgot for a moment that my relationship with her is also new and fragile.

We talked about it last night after our make-up sex marathon. No shouting, no accusations, just two adults having a sensible discussion about serious shit. It took me a while to accept that my last decision wasn't remotely smart. I've decided to speak with Charles about it, ask him to find a way for Harry to buy the Jenkinses' property himself.

I think Saylor and I are good. I want to believe we are, anyway. The last thing I want is to fight with her over money.

The first stop is my apartment in SoHo. I figured I would fly back to the UK often, so I've kept it. It's smaller than the house in Hermosa Beach, but big enough for two people.

"Welcome home, sugar." I open the front door, allowing her to enter first.

Saylor's never been here before, and I made sure to tell her that. All memories we make here will be brand new, not replacements. Her steps are deliberately slow as she takes in the dark living room. Nothing soft or cheery about it; it's a bachelor pad through and through.

She reaches the black leather couch, running her hands over the butter-soft surface before glancing my way. "This is nice."

"Let me show you the bedroom. It's even nicer."

She raises an eyebrow at me. "Oh, you don't say."

Chuckling, I take her hand and bring her to the master suite, where the focal point is the brand-new bed I bought online a couple of days ago. This place has been a revolving door, a center of debauchery really. God only knows how many women slept in my old bed. I wanted something that would be ours alone.

Saylor sits on the edge, bouncing on it as one does when shopping for a mattress. When she reaches for something on the corner, I realize it's the store tag. The fool who installed the bed forgot to remove it.

"So, did you go shopping for house goods without me?" She smirks.

"I wanted to surprise you. It was all done online."

"Uh-huh." She lies down on the bed, crossing her hands over her stomach. "I've never shopped for a mattress online, but this one feels divine."

Closing her eyes, she sinks further into the bed, burying herself in the soft pillows that take up most of the top section. I join her in the next second, hovering above her body, my forearms braced on each side of her head, effectively caging her in.

"You know what else feels divine?" I settle my nose in the crook of her neck, inhaling Saylor's sweet scent.

"What?" she whispers softly, arching her back.

"My cock buried deep inside your sweet pussy." I capture her earlobe between my teeth, tugging it slightly.

Her soft moan of pleasure makes my cock twitch inside my pants. I make sure she knows exactly how she's making me feel, thrusting my hips against hers. Her arms go around my neck as she opens her legs to better accommodate me.

"This feels so nice. Do you think we can keep our clothes on for just a little bit?"

"What are you saying, sugar? Do you want to dry hump?"

"Yes. Is that crazy?"

"Nope, that's kind of hot. I don't think I've ever done it before."

"What? Are you saying all of your make-out sessions led to sex?"

"Pretty much." I chuckle.

"How old were you when you lost your virginity?"

"Thirteen?"

"Oh my God. You were such a perv!"

"I was seduced by an older lady. It was a very Mrs. Robinson situation."

"What?"

"I'm just kidding. She was fifteen."

Saylor's expression relaxes, but now she's made me curious. "How about you?"

"I was a late bloomer. I didn't trade in my V-card until I was a senior in high school."

I thrust my hips again, making a little circle motion this time. "It's okay, sugar. I won't hold your lack of experience against you. I'll teach you some moves."

"Teach me—"

Her eyes narrow and I know she has some sassy reply on the tip of her tongue, but I silence her with a kiss. Then all I hear is her sweet moans, urging me to go on.

Dry humping might not compare to the real deal, but I wish I'd discovered it sooner.

♡ ♡ ♡

The girls and Allan are staying at a boutique hotel in SoHo. We meet them for drinks there at the rooftop bar. There's a visible change in Saylor when she reunites with her friends. Not that she was sad before, but she shines like a beacon now that she's surrounded by her bandmates. Something stirs inside my chest, an ache that wasn't there before. They were apart because of me, because Saylor chose to stay and support me through my hard time. It's high time I get my act together.

I make the decision then—we're going home as soon as Wreck of the Day is done with this last-minute promotional trip.

Allan has secured a large table that can accommodate all of us. After all the hugs and hellos, I lean back in my seat, throwing an arm around Saylor's shoulder to bring her closer to me. Everyone's eyes turn to us.

"So, the lovebirds are back," Remi says with clear pleasure.

"We sure are." I kiss Saylor's cheek.

"I knew it was only a matter of time. I'm so excited to be here. It's my first time in London," Remi exclaims.

Not counting Saylor, Remi is my favorite of the bunch. Not that I don't like Tabatha or Sticks, but Remi is just so full of joy all the time. Plus, she was the biggest cheerleader for my relationship with Saylor from the start.

The drinks keep flowing and we order appetizers as Allan fills us in on the schedule for the next couple of days. The girls have a couple of interviews lined up, plus studio time. Allan could've gotten them a TV interview with a studio performance, but I knew Saylor wasn't ready for that.

I haven't felt this relaxed since I came here. I'm thoroughly enjoying myself when my phone vibrates, Harry's number flashing on the screen.

"Hello?"

"Oliver, where are you?"

"I'm out with Saylor and the Renegades crew."

"Oh, I thought I was supposed to meet you at your place. I'm standing in front of your building now."

"I texted you. You didn't get my message?"

"No." His answer is blunt, and I get the feeling he's pissed.

"No worries, mate. I'll give you the address. Hop in a cab. We're in SoHo, not too far from my place."

"I don't have money for a cab," he says through clenched teeth.

His reply gives me pause. I gave him over three hundred quid the other day. Perhaps I need to have a talk with him about money management; it's obvious the Jenkinses weren't financially savvy.

"I'll pay for your bloody cab. I'll text you the address. See you soon."

I end the call before Harry can say anything else.

"Problems?" Allan asks.

I finish my drink before I reply, feeling the weight of Saylor's gaze on my face.

"No, mate. It's all good. Just miscommunication."

"Was that Harry?" Saylor asks.

"Yes. He didn't get my message that we were coming here. He went to my place instead."

"I don't know how you didn't have a nervous breakdown when Harry came in announcing he was alive. That's stuff doesn't happen in real life," Remi says.

"Oh, I don't know. You'd be surprised by the number of unbelievable things that happen to regular folks," Sticks replies, and I think it's the first time she's opened her mouth this evening.

Allan turns to her, not hiding the fact that the pretty brunette has captured his attention. I guess the alcohol's lowered his restraint.

"You got any stories, Elisa?"

"What? Did you just call her Elisa? No one calls Sticks by her first name," Remi says.

Sticks, for once, doesn't look away. Instead, she stares at Allan. "Nope. No stories. But I bet you have some, Allan."

Neither of them speaks or breaks eye contact. It's like they're lost in their own world. Jesus, when did their relationship turn this charged? I'm getting hit with secondhand sexual tension. They need to get a room and take care of that. Or better yet, maybe Saylor and I can get a room.

My phone pinging reminds me that I can't do that right now. Harry just said he's here and will be up soon. I guess he found money to pay for the cab after all. I stand and walk to the entrance of the bar, wanting to speak with him first before I introduce him to the rest of the crew, clear the air around us.

He's already at the door when I cross the busy open area, wearing clothes that I know cost a pretty penny. No wonder he has no money left. I'm irritated once again. He's an heir, but he hasn't received his share of the inheritance yet. Plus, I don't think he'll get a lot in cash. Most of the estate is properties. All the money I've been giving him is my own, earned with my work.

"So, where is everyone?" is the first thing that comes out of his mouth.

"Hello to you too, brother. They're at table over there. I didn't want you to have to look for us. What do you want to drink?" I start walking toward the bar. It's packed, but I manage to find an opening to squeeze through and flag the bartender. It's a bird, so getting her attention is almost effortless. She recognizes me on the spot.

"Oh wow. Oliver Best, Britain's most infamous bad boy, is in the house. What an honor."

"Hello, darling. How are you this evening?"

She leans forward, squeezing her boobs together and making sure I have a great view of her rack. "Now that you're here, much better."

I turn to Harry, ignoring her. "What would you like to drink?"

"Do you have Cristal?"

The woman freezes, then blinks a couple times. I also stare at Harry, thinking he's lost his mind. Only douchebags would think to order that in a bar. What's wrong with hard liquor?

"Oh, I don't think so. But I can check."

"Never mind. Just give me the most expensive whiskey you have, neat."

"All right, and you?" She turns to me.

"Same."

Once the bartender turns away, I glance at Harry, noticing the Rolex on his wrist.

"New watch?" I ask.

"I've always wanted one. They're pricey, but I guess I shouldn't be thinking like that anymore, huh?"

"No. On the contrary, you should always be cautious about money."

"Why? I'm wealthy now. Counting pennies is beneath me."

The bartender returns, placing our drinks in front of us. In good time too, because I'm about to lose my cool with Harry. Something I definitely don't want to do. The last time it happened, I thought I'd killed him.

I practically chug my drink before I feel ready to have a serious talk with my brother. We probably shouldn't be doing this now, but the longer I postpone it, the worse Harry's spending habits are going to get.

"I've been meaning to speak with you about the Jenkinses' property."

"What about? Did you already put in an offer?"

"No. I spoke with Charles Cowley instead. He's the executor of our father's will. I asked him to see if he could find a way for you to buy the property with your inheritance money."

Harry stares at me without blinking, but I notice his jaw

clench. After a few seconds of silence, he says, "I thought you were going to buy me that property. I thought it was a gift."

"I never said it was a gift."

Harry faces the bar and takes a sip of his drink. He's not happy about it, which nags at me. Saylor's words come to the forefront of my mind, that she never would've allowed me to spend so much money on a gift for her. That much is true. Yet Harry expects me to do so.

"I guess you didn't, I just thought…. Never mind. I suppose that means you're not going to give me any more money, right?"

"Not if you're going to blow it on silly things like expensive watches and clothes."

His stare is filled with disdain. "Oh, I don't see you shopping at secondhand stores." The venom in his words shocks me. Saylor's right, I don't know my brother at all.

"I worked for my money."

"I suppose you did. I'm sorry. I don't mean to sound like a spoiled brat. I guess I've lived so long not having anything that I got carried away. I won't be able to pay for anything tonight, though."

"No worries. I got you covered."

"Shall we join the group? I'm kind of excited to meet the rest of the band. They're hot."

"Sure. Let me pay the tab first. We have a different one at the table."

I signal the bartender and she comes running with a big smile plastered on her face.

"May I have the bill, please?"

She pouts, trying to play the seductive role. "Leaving me so soon?"

"Yes. I miss my wife already." I smirk.

Her eyes are as round as saucers. "So you're still married? I thought your wife died."

The amusement drops from my lips, the careless comment pissing me off. "No, she's not dead."

"I'm so sorry. I didn't mean to upset you. I don't keep up with tabloids much."

She runs my card and I sign the receipt, but leave no tip. It's vindictive, and I don't fucking care.

"She didn't mean to harass you, Ollie." Harry comes to her defense as I stride away from the bar.

"She thought I had lost my wife and was already coming on to me. That's disgusting."

"I'm sure you can get any woman you want. Why marry?"

I stop in my tracks and turn to Harry, leveling him with a glare. "I don't want any woman. I want Saylor. She's the only one for me. That's why I married her."

"So, you would never cheat on her?"

My nostrils flare and my hands turn into fists at my sides. I'm angry beyond reason. How can Harry ask me that question after we spent a weekend talking about Saylor, about how devastated I was to almost lose her?

"No. I would never cheat on her."

"Okay, okay. No need to go mental." He raises his hands in surrender.

From where we stand, we can see our table, so Harry walks ahead of me. I stay rooted to the spot, frozen for a few seconds as I try to reconcile the sweet boy I remember Harry to be with the callous man in front of me.

If Harry turns out to be someone with questionable morals, will I still want him around?

# CHAPTER 37
## SAYLOR

The moment Oliver returns with Harry in tow, I know something's wrong. The usual state of excitement Oliver has when his brother is around is absent tonight. In its place, I catch weariness. What happened?

Harry acts charming, even a little flirtatious, sitting between Remi and Sticks. Remi, as usual, monopolizes the conversation, but from time to time, Harry veers his question toward Sticks. Oliver doesn't seem to notice his brother's interaction, but Allan watches Harry through narrowed eyes. Every time the young man leans closer to Sticks to be heard over the loud music, Allan tenses as if he's preparing to pounce.

Tabatha watches the drama unfold with a smirk. Maybe there's more going on between Allan and Sticks, and she's finding the little drama entertaining. I would probably share her sentiment if I didn't already have an ill disposition toward Harry. I wish I had more to go on than just a mere hunch. I don't want any of the girls getting embroiled with him.

I tear my gaze from the group and touch Oliver's arm. "Hey, are you okay?"

"Of course, sugar. Why do you ask?"

"You've been awfully quiet since Harry arrived. Did something happen?"

Oliver smiles tightly before kissing me quickly. "Nothing happened, sugar. It's all good."

*Then how come he can't hold my gaze?* I bite my tongue and refrain from asking Oliver any more questions. We've fought enough about Harry, and I don't want to do so in front of our friends.

I'm ready to call it a night when Allan glances at his phone, then addresses the group. "I just got a text from one of your old buddies, Ollie."

"Who?"

"Anthony Bowman."

"Shut the fuck up." Oliver leans forward, the sudden change in his mood almost electric.

"Uh, who's Anthony Bowman?" I ask.

"He used to be in Boys Future, sugar."

"Oh, I was under the impression you didn't like your bandmates that much."

"It was only Tweedledum and Tweedledee who were wankers. Anthony was all right. He kept to himself, never got into trouble."

"He sounds nice," I say.

"He sounds boring." Harry grimaces to match his opinion.

"I would love to meet him," I continue, giving Harry the stink-eye.

"What did the message say?" Oliver asks.

"He's asking if we'd like to attend the opening of a new club."

"Oh, that sounds fun." Remi's already on board.

Oliver looks at me. "What do you say, sugar?"

I shrug. "Sure, why not? It's not like we have to be up early tomorrow or anything."

He smirks. "You're so cute when you use sarcasm."

"So, are we going?" Remi's literally bouncing in her chair.

I roll my eyes. "Yes, we're going, Remi."

She throws both arms up in the air. "Yay! Partay!"

We split into cabs, and it doesn't escape my notice that Harry joins Allan, Sticks, and Remi while Tabatha comes with us.

"So, how are things going with you and your brother?" she asks as soon as the cab starts moving.

"Good, it's going good." Oliver doesn't hold her stare long, looking out the window instead.

Tabatha leans closer to whisper, "What's eating him?"

"I don't know."

We both turn to stare at Oliver, who seems oblivious to our scrutiny. I bet that dingleberry did something to upset him. I wish I could unleash the Saylor fury on him just like I did with Oliver's mother, but unfortunately I have to be very careful with that porcelain child. I hate it.

"This trip is good and all, but we have commitments back home that can't be postponed anymore, Blue. When are you coming back?" Tabatha speaks loud enough that it's impossible for Oliver not to hear her.

I open my mouth to reply, but he beats me to it. "We're coming home with you guys."

"We are?" His answer surprises the hell out of me.

"Yes. I don't need to stay here to wait until Charles figures out my father's will. I'll come back here if needed."

"Thank fuck. I was beginning to fear you weren't ever going to come back," Tabatha says.

"What about Harry?" That's the thing that concerns me the most. More than ever, I don't want him to come with us. I don't think his company is doing Oliver any good. It's sad to think that way, but just because they're brothers doesn't meant they mesh well together.

"I don't know. I'll be too busy with work to entertain him. It'd probably be best if he comes later, after the inheritance bit is sorted."

The sense of relief that washes over me is almost over-whelming.

"How come I have the sense that Harry is kind of a poophead?"

"Tabby!" I say, trying my best to keep a serious face.

"What? He was acting like a little prick back at the bar. Did you see how he treated that poor waiter?"

Yes, there was that. Harry talked to the guy like he was a servant. Where the heck did he get that sense of entitlement? In a way, he reminded me of Charlotte's ex.

"I know he's your long-lost brother, Ollie, but he's kind of an ass," Tabatha continues.

"I was kind of an ass too," he replies, but there's no levity in his tone.

"Just when you went dark," I counter.

"When I went dark?" His lips break into a small smile. My comment wasn't meant to be perceived as a joke, but I'm glad it amused him.

"That's what Adeline said. In fact, she told me this wonderful story about when you broke your own pinkie on purpose so Harry wouldn't feel bad about his crooked finger."

Oliver frowns as if he's trying to remember, and then his eyes light up. "Oh bloody hell, I did do that. Man, I was such an idiot. It hurt like a mother, and in the end it was all for nothing."

"You know, of all the stories I've heard about you, boss, that's the stupidest thing you've ever done." Tabatha laughs.

Oliver joins her. "For the first time ever, I'll have to agree with you."

"Holy shit, is it raining elephants outside? Oliver and Tabatha agree on something? That's a first." I put my hand over my chest mockingly, but my smile vanishes when they keep staring at me like I've sprouted a second head.

"What?"

"How do you know we usually don't agree with each other?" Tabatha asks.

"Uh, I don't know."

Oliver smiles. "Sugar, I think you're remembering."

"But I didn't get any flash of memory this time."

"No, but you're remembering basic stuff and not even real-izing it. That's fucking brilliant."

He pulls me closer and kisses my cheek. Tabatha rolls her eyes and makes a gagging sound. As for me, I turn my thoughts inward, trying to find other memories I've recovered without knowing. Before long, we arrive at the new club and I've gained nothing besides a raging headache.

Anthony Bowman is everything Oliver described him to be. Quiet and polite, but with a dry sense of humor only a few people can handle. Harry not being one of them. He took offense to something Anthony said within ten minutes of meeting Oliver's former bandmate and stormed off to explore the club on his own. Good riddance. I hope he gets lost.

Not surprisingly, Anthony and Tabatha hit it off extremely well, and they soon disappeared together to God knows where. In fact, we've lost everyone.

Oliver wraps his arms around my waist and pulls me closer. "Alone at last."

My arms fold around his neck as I rise on my tiptoes to kiss him softly. His tongue breaks the seam of my lips, teasing a little before pulling back. Oliver is a master of sweet tortures.

"Dance with me," he says against my lips.

The club is crowded, and the techno music is loud, but somehow those three little words make this one of the most magical and romantic moments I've ever experienced. Not as romantic as his proposal, but...

Wait.

I freeze in his arms as my eyes fill with tears. They're rolling down my cheeks before I can stop it. I remember that day crystal clear. The clues Oliver left for me, the unexpected visit from my half-sister, the proposal—everything.

"Sugar, why are you crying?"

"I remember our wedding day, Ollie. I remember everything about it."

Oliver stands frozen for a couple of seconds before his lips unfurl in one of the biggest smiles as the news finally sinks in. He picks me up to swirl me around, disregarding all the people around us. When he finally puts me down, his cheeks are as wet as mine.

"Let's get out of here," he says.

"What about everyone else? And Harry. Wasn't he supposed to stay with us?"

"I'll text Allan and ask him to get Harry a room at their hotel. We're getting out of here now."

Who am I to argue when I'm one hundred percent on board with this plan? Oliver takes my hand and together we zigzag our way toward the club's exit. When we're two steps from the door, Allan appears out of nowhere, so angry that he doesn't even see us at first.

"Allan? Where are you going?" I ask.

"Have you seen Sticks?" he asks instead.

"No. What happened?"

Allan only glances at me briefly before he turns his ire in Oliver's direction. "I don't care that he's your brother or that you own the company. I don't want Harry anywhere near the girls."

"What did he do?" Oliver says through clenched teeth.

"I don't know exactly, but he said something to Sticks that really upset her. She took off before I could ask her about it."

I figure Oliver will come up with an excuse for Harry, but he shocks me when he says, "I'll get to the bottom of this."

I've never seen Allan so rattled before. He's like a different person, almost feral. I grab my cell phone and text Sticks, asking where she is. No answer. I text Remi and Tabby next.

Tabatha replies that Sticks went back to the hotel with Remi.

A sense of relief washes over me, but when I glance at Oliver's face, the relief vanishes.

"Sticks went back to the hotel with Remi."

"Okay." Allan turns to Oliver. "I mean what I said about Harry. If he comes to California, I don't want him anywhere near the studio."

Oliver doesn't reply, just watches Allan walk out the door. Whatever Oliver had planned for us, it's the last thing on his mind now.

Fucking Harry ruined everything again.

# CHAPTER 38
## SAYLOR

I don't know what Oliver told Harry after the club fiasco, but he didn't stay with us that night. Instead, Oliver dropped him off at a hotel—different than the one the girls were staying at. Harry went back to Hertfordshire the next day. No one was sad to see him gone. Well, no one besides Oliver. Even if he didn't say anything, I read the sadness in his eyes. Or better yet, the disappointment. He just found his brother, and it turns out the guy's an asshole.

It can't be easy for him to watch Harry act like an idiot and to have his partner tell him he doesn't want Harry around. In the few short months I've interacted with Allan, I've never seen him lose his temper. He's one of the most easygoing people I know. But it seems that Oliver is no longer seeing Harry through rose-tinted glasses. I'm glad he's not letting guilt blind him to the guy's faults.

Work keeps him distracted, at least. Between the interviews Allan managed to schedule and the studio time in London, there was no time to dwell on his family issues. By the end of the week, the ever-present shadow in Oliver's gaze was almost gone.

The band and Allan are staying a few extra days in London to go sightseeing. We're spending one last weekend with Adeline and then it's California, baby. Finally.

"I hope Felix is all right," I say on the drive back to his family's estate.

"Sugar, you checked the online feed several times in the last few days. He's fine."

We couldn't bring Felix with us to London, so we found a dog hotel. Three days without that furball is too much.

The song on the radio cuts off when it switches to Oliver's incoming ringtone. The little display on the car's dashboard say it's Charlotte. With a flick of a button, Oliver takes the call. "Hello, sis."

"Oliver, how far are you?"

"Twenty minutes or so. What's the matter, Char? Missing your big bro already?"

There's a poignant pause before Charlotte's voice comes through again. "Ollie, it's Grandma. Sh-she's gone"

It takes me a while to fully process Charlotte's words, and then utter sadness hits me. With already blurry eyes, I turn to Oliver. His face is ashen, frozen in an expression of completely misery. Out of the blue, he swerves the car to the left, scaring the shit out of me. I let out a yelp when we almost hit the stone fence lining the road.

Once the car stops, he asks, "How?"

"In her sleep. Gilbert found her this morning."

Before I can say anything, Oliver's gone, out in the poor weather. He walks to the front of the car, hands laced behind his head. Then he looks up to the gray sky and lets out the most gut-wrenching, anguished scream I've ever heard in my entire life. I'm out of the car just in time to prevent him from falling to his knees. He collapses against me instead, his entire frame shaking as he wraps his arms around my body.

There are no words I can say that feel right, so I just cry with him, feeling the loss of that lovely lady deep in my bones. I wish I'd had more time with her. If I'm feeling her death so profoundly and I've only known her for a couple of months, I can't imagine Oliver's raw pain.

Only when his body stops shaking do I find my voice. "Come on. I'll drive."

He takes a step back and watches me for a moment before kissing me so roughly it hurts. I don't mind, letting him take whatever he wants from me. His hands are on my face, trapping me while he punishes my mouth with his savage tongue. I can taste the desolation in that kiss.

My lips are tingling once Oliver has his fill. His gaze drops to them right before he runs his thumb over the now-sensitive skin. "I'm so sorry, sugar. I don't know what came over me. Did I hurt you?"

"No," I lie as I touch his cheek. "Let's get out of here."

"Okay."

I veer toward the driver side of the vehicle but stop when Oliver touches my arm. "Are you sure you can drive?"

Glancing down at my left hand, I open and shut it. "The car is automatic. I can handle it."

"Thank you."

He walks to the passenger side with shoulders hunched forward and a dead look in his eyes. My heart breaks even more at the sight. Sudden nausea hits me so hard, I can't push it down. I lean forward just in time to vomit everything I had for breakfast that morning, narrowly missing soiling my clothes. My forehead is clammy by the time I'm done, and I know it's not from the light rain. The whole episode doesn't last a minute, and I'm not surprised that Oliver doesn't come out to see what I'm up to. My stomach is still upset, but I think I got everything out.

Once I finally slide in behind the steering wheel, I find him staring out the window with a fisted hand covering his mouth. His cheeks are wet again. He's crying, but doing so in silence this time.

My vision become blurry once more, but I clench my jaw hard and fight the sadness threatening to take control. It's my turn to be strong.

# CHAPTER 39
## SAYLOR

Adeline's heart stopped beating sometime during the night, though the doctors won't know why until after the autopsy. The preliminary results will take four weeks. To me, it seems like an awful long time to wait.

Oliver seems indifferent to that. Actually, everyone's pretty much accepted that she died of old age. Charles, the lawyer, was the one who insisted upon the exam.

Right now, I'm feeling useless. Oliver took it upon himself to organize the funeral, just like he did with his father's, and dove headfirst into the task. I offered to help only to be asked to spend time with his sister, to distract her. I don't mind being given the role of babysitter, but from the get-go, it was clear that Charlotte didn't want my company. She spent most of the day yesterday locked in her room, so I was left alone with my grief. It didn't compare to Oliver's or Charlotte's, of course, but it was enough to make me hollow.

Oliver is out of bed this morning before dawn.

"Where are you going?" I whisper.

"Go back to sleep, sugar. I'm taking Felix for a walk in the woods. I'll be back soon."

He walks out the door, clicking it shut behind him. On the

other side, there's a quiet bark followed by Oliver's hushed voice.

I can't go back to sleep. The pressure caving my chest won't let me. I sit up in bed, bringing my knees up to hug them. Suddenly I'm hit with another overwhelming nausea spell. Jumping out of bed, I make a beeline for the bathroom, barely making it in time. I've never felt such sickness before, not even when suffering from a massive hangover or when I had the blood clot.

The sound of me hurling echoes around me. My throat burns, my skin clammy. Once I start, there's no stopping until there's nothing left. Uncurling from my crouched position, I stand on shaking legs as I wash my mouth and face. My reflection shows a ghost instead of a person, my skin ashen.

A nagging suspicion makes my breath hitch. *Shit, it can't be.* I grab my phone and pull up the calendar, counting the days since my last period. *Fuck.* I'm two weeks late. How did I not realize that sooner?

I sit on the edge of the bed, numb. Morning sickness plus missed period after weeks of sex nonstop can only lead to one conclusion. That's what I get for trusting the pill. What am I going to do? What am I going to tell Oliver? Now seems like the worst time for me to be pregnant. Does he even want kids? I'm sure we talked about it before, but I haven't recovered that particular memory yet.

There's no point in dwelling on endless questions. I need to know if I'm pregnant or not. All these symptoms could also be related to stress. The problem will be hiding my suspicions from Oliver until I'm certain.

♡ ♡ ♡

only manage to sneak into town to buy a pregnancy test in the afternoon. Hiding my worry from Oliver was easy enough; wrapped up in his misery, he didn't think anything was amiss when I gave him one-worded answers to his few questions.

I asked Linus, the family's driver, to take me to a big supermarket chain, not wanting my intentions to be obvious. He parks in front of a superstore, the kind that sells everything. Perfect.

As soon as I walk in, I see the sign pointing to the pharmacy. I grab a shopping basket and throw random shit in it as I make my way to where the pregnancy tests should be. My hair is hidden under a woolen hat, and I hope the thick scarf wrapped around my neck and covering my chin grants me some anonymity. I've only been recognized once, but considering Murphy's Law, the day that I'm on a furtive mission will be the day a fan will spot me.

I stop in front of the shelf containing all kinds of pregnancy tests, and I'm at loss. There are so many of them. Which one should I get? Since I don't want to make the trip back here, I grab several. It won't hurt to take multiple tests to be sure; I won't see a doctor until I return to Cali, after all.

At checkout, the cashier looks at the pile of tests, then at me. "You really want to know, huh?"

I ignore him. It's none of his damn business. I shove them all in my oversized bag, afraid someone else will notice how desperate I am. I pay in cash, not waiting for the change. I need to get out of here.

Linus is waiting for me just outside the store. Once I slide back into the car, he asks if I got everything I needed. *Yes, and then some*, I think sarcastically.

When we're about two minutes from the house, I text Oliver, asking him what he's up to. He says he's meeting with the funeral director and won't be done for another hour. Feeling guilty for not helping him at all—even if that was his choice—I offer to come by. He says his mother is there and he wants to spare me the displeasure of her company. Bless his heart. Even when deep in his grief, he still has time to worry about my well-being.

Instead of being relieved, all I get is more anxious. I'm terrified to take the test. If it wasn't so early in California, I'd call Liv.

*Stop being so cowardly, Saylor.*

Felix is sleeping in front of the TV when I walk in. He raises his muzzle when he hears me, then promptly shuts his eyes again. Good. In my jittery state, I don't have the mind to play with him.

My body is shaking as I lock myself in the bathroom. God, I never thought I'd be doing this. Thanks to the story of my conception, I've always been so careful when it came to sex. Granted, my situation is completely different than my mom's, but still, I'm unprepared to deal with a pregnancy.

Twenty minutes later, I'm sitting on the toilet seat, staring at all the white sticks that show the same result.

Positive.

I'm pregnant.

*Well, prepared or not, here it is. Now I can start to really freak out.*

A knock at the front door has me jumping. My heart gets lodged in my throat as I hastily shove all the test results in the cupboard under the sink.

Schooling my expression, I open the door to find Gilbert there. To say this is a surprise visit is an understatement. I even forget all the positive pregnancy test results in the bathroom for a second.

"Did something happen?" I ask.

"May I have a word with you?" The usual condescending tone he uses with me is gone. His eyes glimmer with a sadness I didn't know he was capable of feeling. Adeline clearly touched everyone's heart.

I move out of the way, letting him in. My eyes immediately

drop to the small wooden box Gilbert carries in his hand. Without turning to me, he says, "I can't believe she's gone."

"Me neither."

His eyes fix on nothing, as if he's stuck in his head or perhaps a memory. "I had just spoken to her the evening before."

"Were you the last person to see her alive?"

Gilbert turns to me, frowning. "No. Harry came by the house. He was the last person she spoke to."

I don't know why but a terrible feeling sneaks up my spine, making me shudder. *Where is this sense of doom coming from?*

Swallowing the sudden lump in my throat, I say, "You said you needed to speak to me."

"Yes. Before Harry came by, Adeline called me into her room. She gave me this box and told me to hand it over to you in case something happened to her. It was almost like she knew her time was near."

"Do you know what's inside?"

Gilbert's expression twists into a frown. "Of course not. I'm not a prying man. Whatever is inside this box is meant for your eyes only."

He sets the small container on the coffee table before veering toward the door.

Before Gilbert leaves, I blurt out, "What do you think about Harry?"

My out-of-the-blue question makes him freeze mid-step. If possible, it seems his somber expression turns even darker.

"I know my opinion doesn't matter. I'm only the *help*, after all."

There's no mistaking the bitterness in his tone.

Now that the question is out, I press on. "If I asked it's because I want to know."

He watches me for a couple of seconds, his beady eyes unreadable, before he finally continues. "There's something strange about him."

"What do you mean?"

"I'm very good at reading people. I can tell he's hiding something. She never said it aloud, but the way Adeline talked about Harry was enough to tell me she also had reservations in regard to him."

A terrible suspicion takes hold of my heart, squeezing it so tightly I have trouble breathing.

"Gilbert, you don't think Harry had anything to do with her death, do you?"

His eyes widen for a second right before he flattens his lips into a thin white slash. "I don't know."

Not the answer I wanted to hear. If he doesn't know, it means he has doubts, that he's considered the possibility. Gilbert walks out and I'm left battling my dark thoughts. I turn to the box, sitting there on the table so innocent and cute, but I'm terrified of opening it now.

I grab it with a jerky movement. No sense in postponing this, and I might as well do it while Oliver is away. Inside I find a vintage gold watch and a letter. Setting the box aside, I tear the sealed envelope as my heart begins to gallop at full speed.

"**D**ear Saylor,

I hope you never get to read this letter. If you do, it means I never got to talk to you in person. It's my own fault. It took me too long to accept what my heart had been trying to tell me from the start.

I'm afraid we've welcomed a wolf in sheep's clothing into our midst. The signs have been there all along, but it wasn't until very recently that I got the proof I needed.

The man posing as my grandson is most definitely not Harry. I know this now without a shadow of doubt, but I'm weak and old. No one will believe me. I'm leaving that task to you. You must protect the family from this usurper, and most importantly you must protect Oliver.

I don't want you to doubt my words, so I'm giving you a way

to know the truth for yourself. The watch inside this box belonged to my late husband, Oliver's grandfather. It was the possession the real Harry coveted the most when he was little. I promised him he would inherit it when he was older. Wear the watch and make sure the usurper sees it. When he doesn't recognize the heirloom, you'll know the truth.

It saddens me that we didn't have much time and that my final gift to you is this burden. For that, I'm truly sorry. I couldn't have wished for a better partner for my grandson. You are his lighthouse guiding him home in stormy weather. You are his entire universe. Take care of him for me.

Love,

Adeline"

read the letter again through blurry eyes. And again, and again, hoping I've understood her wrong. It's futile. Her words won't change; her accusations won't change.

I fold the letter and put it back in the envelope, knowing I can never let Oliver read it. I fold the envelope into a tiny square and shove it into my jeans pocket, then glance at the watch.

*Oh, Adeline. What did you ask me to do?*

# CHAPTER 40
## SAYLOR

don't get to wear the watch in front of Harry to see his reaction. I fall ill instead.

After I read Adeline's letter, I'm taken over by extreme exhaustion and go back to bed. I wake hours later with Oliver shaking me slightly. My entire body aches, my skin clammy and hot to the touch.

"Sugar, talk to me."

"Ollie, what time is it?"

"It's almost six." He puts a hand against my forehead. "Shit, you're burning up."

"I feel like I've been run over by an eighteen-wheeler." My voice is hoarse, my throat burning. It almost seems like Adeline's letter was cursed with the worst jinx imaginable.

"Let me see if I can find a thermometer and get you some painkillers."

Oliver disappears, returning a moment later not with what he went in search for but one of my pregnancy tests.

"Saylor, what's this?" The glow from the lamp casts strange shadows on his face, making the V between his eyebrows more prominent.

I open my mouth but no sound comes forth. I could be

delirious from the fever, but it doesn't sound like Oliver is overly enthusiastic about what that stick means. Closing my eyes, I roll onto my side, giving him my back. I can't deal with his rejection right now. The mattress dips behind me as he sits on the bed. Touching my shoulder, he rolls me over again and searches my face.

"You're pregnant?"

I nod as hot tears roll down my face. I don't know why I'm crying.

He touches my wet cheek with the tips of his fingers, frowning even more. "You don't want to be pregnant?" His question comes on a choke, as if it pains him to ask.

"It's not that."

"Then why are you crying?"

"Because I didn't mean to get knocked up. It's the worst possible timing in the world, and I'm sorry for no—"

"Shut up." He takes my face between his hands. "I don't care about the timing. This is good news, sugar. Don't ever apologize to me about it. You didn't make this baby alone."

*This baby.* Oh my God. He just made it so much more real. There's a tiny human growing inside of me. I'm going to be a mom. Oliver is going to be a dad.

In that moment, everything that Adeline revealed comes crashing down on me.

I cry harder, terrified of what the future holds. What if I can't find prove that Harry isn't Harry? What if I discover he's somehow responsible for Adeline's death?

"Please don't cry, sugar. We've got this. It'll be okay." He kisses my forehead before placing a soft peck on my lips. "I love you so much."

"I love you too." The lamplight shines on his wet cheeks. "You're crying."

He lets out a shaky laugh before wiping his face with the sleeve of his shirt. "I'm so fucking emotional these days."

"You have reason to be. So many things have happened in such a short period of time."

He shakes his head, then glances at my flat stomach. "This is surreal. I can't believe we're going to be parents."

"If it's okay with you, I want to keep the news between us. At least until we confirm it officially."

"Okay." He places a warm hand over my lower belly. "Do you feel anything yet?"

"Right now, all I feel is ache."

"Oh shit, sugar. I forgot all about it. I found the pregnancy test and got derailed."

He jumps off the bed, running to the bathroom once again and returning with painkillers. "I couldn't find a thermometer, but I got pills for the fever. You definitely have one." His eyes turn as round as saucers before he continues. "Oh fuck. Can you take painkillers? Do you think they'll be bad for the baby?"

I would laugh if I didn't hurt so much. "Relax. I'm sure you can find that information online."

"Good call." He grabs his cell from the side table and begins to type away, his face scrunched in concentration.

Warmth spreads across my chest despite the heavy weight there. Oliver is so stinking cute worried about simple things like that.

I wish doubts about my pregnancy were the only things we had to stress about, not whether his fake brother killed his grandma or not.

# CHAPTER 41
## OLIVER

Saylor was down for the count during the entire week. I was too worried when her high fever wouldn't relent, so I caved and called the family doctor, despite her protests. A cold caused by a virus was his diagnosis. I told him about the pregnancy, so he took some blood samples as well. The result came in on Thursday—one hundred percent pregnant.

I never thought I would become a dad at only twenty-four. In fact, if it would've happened a couple of years ago, I would've run for the hills. I'm terrified, I won't deny that, but I'm also fucking happy. My only regret is that Nana won't be here to meet her great-grandbaby.

I come home from the last errand before Nana's funeral to find Saylor moving around in the kitchen, wearing nothing but a tank top and shorts.

"What in the bloody hell are you doing up?" I set the groceries on the kitchen counter, removing my jacket to cover her shoulders.

"Will you quit worrying? I'm better."

"You were still coughing last night."

"Well, that was last night." She shrugs off my jacket and keeps opening random cabinets.

"What are you looking for?"

"Coffee, what else?"

"Sugar, you know you can't have coffee."

"Fuck that. I need coffee unless you want me to commit murder this afternoon."

"You don't need to come."

She glares at me. "I'm saying goodbye to Adeline."

I raise my hands to say I'm backing down. "Okay, but you're not having coffee. It's not good for the baby."

"Ugh! I can see the writing on the wall already. I'll cease to be a person and become only an incubator."

I stop what she's doing to hug her tight. "You'll never cease to be Saylor to me, sugar. In fact, I'm glad you're not an incubator, because I have plans for you."

"Are you putting the moves on me?" She narrows her eyes at me.

I let myself enjoy the easy banter with my wife. The day will be hard enough, and I need this moment of levity to keep me going. My lips curl into the grin I know drives her insane. "Say, are you already getting crazy horny?"

She smacks my arm, feigning being appalled. "I've been bedridden for five days, I look like a freaking zombie, and you're asking if I'm already a nymphomaniac?"

"Ah, sugar, you know you make a sexy zombie."

"Get me coffee and maybe you'll get lucky later."

I step back because my cock is already on board with the idea. "Why do you torture me so?"

She crosses her arms in front of her chest. "I could ask you the same thing. The doctor said I could have one cup of coffee a day."

"Fine, you win. I'll procure coffee while you get ready. People will be arriving by the droves soon. Nana was a popular woman."

"Yes!" Saylor throws her arms around my neck and kisses me with a resounding smack. "You're a good husband."

I forget what I just said a second ago, wanting to claim my prize for the coffee before the day is over. But Saylor's already sauntered away and out of my reach. I debate going after her, but it's best if I control my urges. She's still not fully recovered from her cold. I've gone without sex for a few days; I can wait a little longer.

I return twenty minutes later with steaming coffee in my hands. Saylor's still in our room, but the moment I say I'm home, she comes running. She's ready for the funeral, wearing a dress Nana would've loved. It's simple and black with a full skirt, but when Saylor moves, it reveals tulle in bright turquoise and purple. Mermaid colors.

She catches me staring at it and glances down. "Do you think it's inappropriate?"

"No, sugar. It's bloody perfect."

"I got it a while back with Liv. I told her that if I died on the operating table, she would have to wear it for my funeral."

A sharp pain flares in my chest thinking how close that came to pass. But I also realize something else. "Did you just remember that?"

Saylor frowns at me, confused. "What?"

"Your conversation with Liv. That must've happened a few days before the surgery."

Saylor's beautiful aquamarine eyes glint with understanding. "I didn't even realize I was remembering. It just came to me."

I breach the distance between us, grabbing both her hands. "One day very soon you'll remember everything."

She smiles at me and we stay that way, staring into each other's eyes. By all means, today should be one of the saddest days of my life, but I can't help the happiness that fills my heart while I stare at my beautiful wife. *How did I get so fucking lucky?*

Making lazy circles with my thumbs around her wrists, her

pulse accelerating beneath my touch, I feel a metallic band around one. *That's new.* I bring her hand up, finding a man's watch around her delicate wrist.

I know that watch.

"Where did you get this?"

She jerks her hand away, covering the accessory with her hand. "Adeline gave it to me."

"Why?"

"I don't know. Why are you looking at me like that? Do you think I'm lying?"

I don't get why she's so defensive. "Of course not, sugar. It just that...." I pause, running my hand through my hair. "That watch used to belong to my grandfather, and Nana had promised it to Harry."

I expect Saylor to remove the watch and hand it over—not that I told her the story to persuade her to do so—but she doesn't, which is bloody strange. It's unlike her to want material things. Plus, she's made it no secret that she doesn't like Harry that much. Why would she want to keep an heirloom promised to him? That's not like her at all.

"Well, she never told me that. She left the box with the watch under Gilbert's care. He only gave it to me after her passing. There was a note with the watch. She wanted me to wear it at her funeral."

I don't think Saylor's lying, but she must see something in my expression that leads her to believe I'm doubting her.

"I believe you, sugar. But don't be surprised if Harry makes a comment about the watch. He was kind of obsessed with it."

I see a strange glint in her eye as she says, "Oh, if he remembers the watch, I'll gladly let him have it."

# CHAPTER 42
## SAYLOR

The turnout for Adeline's funeral is far greater than for Dr. Best. I'm not surprised. Considering how the man treated Oliver, I highly doubt he was any better with strangers.

While the guests are being entertained, Oliver and I pay our final respects to her alone. I asked him if we could, mainly because I didn't want to lose my shit in front of a bunch of strangers. Oliver stands by me as we both stare in silence at his grandma. I thought it would be hard, but it doesn't seem like she's truly gone, only asleep.

"She looks so peaceful," I whisper.

"Yes. They did a good job."

He pulls me closer and kisses the side of my head. I know he's offering comfort as much as he's taking. I don't want to cry, but it's getting harder with each passing second.

"A few weeks back, Adeline asked me when we would give her a great-grandchild. I was mortified."

Oliver chuckles. "Why?"

"Well, because the topic started when she guessed what we had been up to earlier."

"Did you talk about sex with Nana?" There's humor in Oliver's voice.

"Don't laugh."

"I'm not laughing. I'm just wishing I was there."

I place a hand over my flat stomach. "Your wish came true, Adeline."

Oliver covers my hand with his. I stare at our hands together for a couple of beats before looking up. His eyes are brimming with unshed tears, just like mine are. My mood is all over the place. I don't know if I want to cry or laugh. Probably both.

Of course Harry is the one who interrupts our moment.

"There you are."

I step back and Oliver's hand drops from my stomach. *Shit.* Harry is the last person I want to know about my pregnancy. Did he see where Oliver's hand was before? It wouldn't take a genius to guess the meaning of that gesture. He strides toward us, wearing an impeccable dark suit and an unreadable expression. My skin crawls at his proximity, and when he leans over to kiss me on the cheek, bile rises in my throat.

"How are you feeling, sis?"

I'm fucking speechless. Even if I haven't read Adeline's letter, I wouldn't want him calling me that.

"I'm much better, thank you."

I turn to Oliver, raising my left hand to fix his tie. An excuse really—I want the watch to be in Harry's line of sight. Taking my time, I turn to him to gauge his reaction. "When did you arrive?"

"Ten minutes ago. I spent time making my rounds, introducing myself to Grandma's old friends." His gaze zeroes in on the watch and stays there for a couple of seconds before he continues. "They were surprised to learn I was alive."

No reaction whatsoever to the watch, but it's impossible not to notice his accusatory tone.

"Did you want me to issue a press release?" Oliver asks, clearly irritated.

"No, of course not. But I don't know. Perhaps a dinner party wouldn't be a bad idea."

"Are you seriously talking about a coming-out party for yourself while we're at your Grandma's funeral?" I level him with a glare.

In hindsight, his attitude shouldn't surprise me since I just got the proof I needed that this man isn't Harry.

He tries to save face by schooling his expression into one of regret. "Of course not. I'm sorry. That came out wrong."

"I'm going to check on Charlotte," I say to Oliver, completely dismissing the fake Harry.

"Okay, sugar. I'll catch up with you later."

I stride out of the room as my heart beats inside my chest at warp speed. I'm furious and scared at the same time. If that man isn't Harry, who is he? And how much danger are we in?

It occurs to me that today is the best day to pay the Jenkinses' property a visit. Despite Harry's claim that he's about to lose the house, he's still living there. But going there while Harry's here means I have to miss the ceremony. I hate to leave Oliver to face the ordeal by himself, but I just can't sit next to that conman and do nothing.

Instead of finding Charlotte, I stride out of the house, avoiding eye contact with any guest. The courtyard is filled with cars and more are coming. I veer toward the garage, hoping to find Linus there, but he isn't and the Land Rover is gone. *Fuck. What now?* I know the Jenkinses' property isn't too far from here, but walking would probably take too long. It doesn't seem I have a choice though.

I stop by the guesthouse first, changing from my fancy shoes into sensible boots. Felix greets me, as happy as he can be, and I decide it wouldn't be a bad idea if I brought him along.

Using the GPS on my phone, I discover I can reach the Jenkinses' within a ten-minute walk if I take a shortcut through the woods. I'm glad the weather isn't terrible; it's still cold, but at least it's dry.

My mind is reeling as I walk through the silent forest, the only sounds echoing around me of my boots and Felix's paws on the dried leaves.

The narrow path leads to a creek, and on the other side, a break through the vegetation reveals a manor. There isn't a way around it, so cross the creek I must. Luckily, there are a few mossy rocks protruding from the water, so I'm able to get to the other side of the bank without getting my feet soaked.

Felix cuts through the icy water as if this is a great adventure for him. I wish I shared his sentiment. The Jenkinses' house is smaller than Longview Manor, but I can tell it used to belong to people who had money in the past. It's lost its former glory though. Clingy vines have taken over the brick walls, and what used to be a garden now resembles a wild jungle. The paint on the windows and doors is peeling off, and I bet some of the wood is rotten.

I open the wrought iron gate, wincing as it creaks loudly. A gust of cold wind comes out of nowhere, making me shiver on the spot. This place is creepy to say the least. I don't know why anyone would want to buy this property. It's definitely not worth the amount Oliver had been willing to pay for it.

Felix takes off on his own exploration mission, stopping to sniff here and there. I veer to the front door, hoping to find it unlocked. I turn the knob, but the door won't budge. Of course not; I wouldn't leave my door unlocked either if I was hiding shit.

I circle the house, searching for another way in. Trying every single window, I find them all closed shut. I'm beginning to lose hope. I don't want to have to break a window to have access in. A drop of cold water hits my head, and I glance at the sky. *Just fucking great. It's going to start raining now.*

I spot a lonely balcony that doesn't protrude out of the building, but it's part of the upper floor with a balustrade only at the front. A high window rests behind the metal barrier, and it's open. Clingy vines stretch all over the wall surrounding the opening, but I don't think I can climb them. I search the back-yard for anything I can use to gain some height. I think I can pull myself up if I can reach the railing.

I almost can't believe my luck when the metal gleam of an old construction ladder catches my eye, almost entirely hidden under a bunch of junk that I can't even begin to identify. Care-fully picking my way through pieces of broken wood and discarded boxes, I have to climb over sacks of dirt to reach the top part of the ladder. It takes me a while to finally yank the rusty ladder from under everything in the way and I end up losing my balance, almost falling completely with the ladder on top of me. I'm able to remain standing by a miracle, but the sound of fabric tearing makes me curse. Sure enough, the tulle underskirt caught on a rusty metal rod and tore.

I make a grab for the piece of colorful fabric, dangling cheery and bright in this junkyard of solitude, when a breeze catches it, sending it flying away. I shouldn't leave any evidence of my clandestine visit behind, but I've wasted too much time already. Plus, the wind will most likely blow that little scrap of fabric very far away.

The ladder is high enough that it puts my waist on the same level with the balcony floor. Curling my fingers around the metal rods, I stick my foot between the bars and pull myself over. Felix barks from below. I shush him, not that he understands what I mean by it.

Heart stuck in my throat, I stick my head inside the room and am immediately assaulted by the smell of ammonia and urine. I have to cover my nose to keep from gagging. A hospital bed sits between two small tables with medicine bottles on them. I guess this part of the story wasn't a lie. He was taking care of the Mr. Jenkins.

Asides from the bed, the room is bare. I move on, walking out of the room to peruse the rest of the house. I have no idea what I'm looking for. The few doors I try are locked, so I keep moving down the corridor until one opens. Inside, I find an office. A great dark wood desk is covered with paper and books galore, with more tomes piled on the floor. A film of dust covers most of the surface, and the smell of mold is strong.

Shit, does the usurper know anything about cleaning? I'm surprised Oliver never mentioned anything about the condition of this place.

A grandfather clock chimes the hour somewhere in the house, scaring the shit out of me. A sense of urgency takes over and I begin to search with vigor, opening drawers and checking all the documents on the desk. I don't think anything of importance is on display, so I move on to the bookshelf behind it. The more time I spend here finding nothing, the more discouraged I become. I'm checking the last bookshelf to my right when I spot the corner of a yellow folder sticking out.

Pulling the folder out, I discover they're medical records for Simon Jenkins. A shot of adrenaline runs up my spine when I see the date on the label—these records are from last year. With eager fingers, I pull all the papers out, scanning through the documents as fast as I can.

I feel like I'm going to be sick when I realize they're medical records for a facial plastic surgery procedure. My arms begin to shake when I see the pictures attached to one of the files: before and after photos, plus the reference.

"Oh my God." I cover my mouth with my hand. I'm staring at the real Harry. He did survive the accident after all, but is he still alive?

I set the yellow folder down and start to look for more proof, anything that will give me clues about who the poser is. On the floor, there are a few pictures, frames facedown. One is a family picture, the Jenkinses and two boys who seem to be around the same age.

*Shit. Shit. Shit.* Is it possible that the guy posing as Harry is actually the real Simon Jenkins? My mind is reeling. I need to get out of here and bring all this evidence to Oliver.

Felix begins to bark like mad outside just before he lets a

whine and then falls quiet. My heart ceases to beat for a second.

I'm no longer alone.

# CHAPTER 43
## OLIVER

"'m really sorry for your loss, young man. Adeline was such an extraordinary woman. To lose her soon after your father passed, what a tragedy," says an elderly man whose name I can't bloody remember.

I only nod and make noncommittal sounds, looking at my phone from time to time. *Where the hell is Saylor?* She left to find Charlotte, but I haven't seen her in the last hour. My sister, on the other hand, is across the room chatting with some of Nana's friends.

I texted Saylor twenty minutes ago and I still haven't received a reply. *That's it, I'm going after her.* I give some excuse to the man in front of me and make a beeline for the front door, but I don't make very far. My mother gets in the way, launching herself at me for an awkward hug. She can barely stay upright and I know why. She reeks of alcohol.

"Oh there you are, my darling son."

"Mother, pull your shit together."

"Why bother? No one here cares about me anyway. All they can bloody talk about is your grandmother. Never mind that I just lost my husband not too long ago."

"Are you kidding me right now?"

"It's the truth."

I search for someone to help me with Mum. I don't care if people know that she's a crazy drunk, but I don't want her to ruin Nana's funeral with her antics.

"What's wrong with Mum?" Harry asks, coming to stand next to me.

"Drunk. I need to check on Saylor. I haven't seen her in a while, and she's not answering my texts."

I would ask Harry to take care of our mother, but I honestly don't think he can handle her right now.

"Do you mind getting Charlotte to check if Saylor is in the guesthouse?"

"I'll go check," Harry offers.

My gut reaction is to refuse his help, but I have no good reason to do so. Not wanting to come out as an arse and alienate him, I let him go look for Saylor.

What's the worst that could happen?

## SAYLOR

Hugging the proof I need tight to my chest, I run back to the hallway, but I don't go back the way I came in. I don't know who's outside, and going down an unstable ladder isn't the smartest escape route. I rush down the stairs, all too aware that I have no idea if there's someone waiting for me in the level below. Panic is making me careless.

I look out the front window, trying to see if there's anyone outside. The front yard is deserted and eerily quiet. *Shit. What happened to Felix?* My heart is beating so fast I'm afraid it's going to jump out of my chest.

Man, I'm so not cut out to be a spy.

The longer I stay here, the higher the chances that I'll get caught. I might as well run out the front door. I turn the knob, and barrel down the front steps, searching frantically for Felix. I don't call his name out loud, because that would be the dumbest move possible. I do, however, do something almost as dumb and circle the house again, going toward the back. I just can't take off and leave Felix behind. What if he's hurt?

*What if he's dead, Saylor? You could be next.*

I stomp on that negative voice until it dies. There's no sign of Felix anywhere. *Fuck. What now?* Okay, maybe I'm freaking out over nothing. Maybe he just got spooked by something and ran away. It's high time I do the same.

A tingling sensation on the back of my neck has my skin breaking into goose bumps. I begin to turn when I'm grabbed from behind and some sort of cloth is placed over my nose and mouth. I struggle against the hold, but whoever my attacker is, he's much stronger than me. My vision blurs, darkening around the edges until I can't see anything but an endless void.

# CHAPTER 44
## SAYLOR

Blinking my eyes open, it takes me a while to focus. Somewhere nearby, water keeps dropping, echoing around me as if I'm in a cave of sorts. The air is cold and moist again my skin. I try to move, only to discover that my wrists and ankles are tied. The floor is damp against my cheek, and also filthy if the smell is any indication.

Panic starts to set in, making it impossible to breathe. Memories from a past I want to forget come rushing back, rendering me utterly and completely useless. *No! I won't be dragged back to that hell.* I bite the inside of my cheek, hoping the sharp pain will save me from going down that rabbit hole. I cannot let my emotions control my fate; I need to remain sharp if I'm to get out of here.

Easier said than done. My body is shaking as I push myself to a sitting position. The world is pitch black around me, so I focus on my other senses. I count the beating of my heart—one, two, three. My pulse is the loudest noise reverberating in my ears, until the sound of fabric scraping against the dirty floor makes my panic rise to the highest level possible. I curl into a ball and whimper softly.

"You're finally awake," a voice in the darkness says.

"Who's there?"

"Harry."

I begin to shuffle as far away as possible from the disembodied voice, knowing how futile it is to try to escape. I'm at his mercy.

"I know what you've done. You're an impostor. Adeline knew it too."

"Nana? Is she still alive?"

"Don't fucking play games with me."

Suddenly the room is no longer dark. A soft glow emanates from a corner not too far away. Sitting on the floor next to the small lamp, a young man with longish dark hair stares at me.

"I'm not playing games."

Despite the light, his face is still partially hidden in shadows, the gauntness of his cheeks even more pronounced. He looks familiar. I squint as my brain processes what I'm seeing. When the truth finally hits me, I'm shocked that it took me so fucking long to recognize him.

"You're the real Harry." The truth comes out of my lips in a hushed whisper.

"Yes, and you must be Ollie's wife."

"H-how do you know about me?"

"Oh, Simon likes to torture me with tidbits of information about my family."

"I don't understand. Why is he doing this? Because of money?"

"That too. But also because Simon is a psychopath. He didn't need me alive after he took my samples for the DNA test, and yet he lets me live here in these inhumane conditions so he can torture me."

"Where are we?"

"The crazy runs in the family. Mr. Jenkins had a bunker built deep in the woods behind his property."

"How long have you been here?"

"I don't know. I've lost count of the days. Simon snapped

when his father died. He drugged me, and when I regained consciousness, I was already here."

Absolute fear threatens to take control of my sanity again. To think that deranged man is now with Ollie and Charlotte. *Oh my God. Why didn't Adeline tell me about her suspicions sooner? She could still be alive.*

"What is he going to do to me?" My voice is shaky, mirroring what my body's doing right now.

"I don't know. Simon brought you in and left without saying a word to me. He seemed to be in a hurry."

I struggle against my binds again, wincing as the hard plastic digs into my skin.

"I don't see any binds on you. You've never tried to escape?"

Harry laughs without humor. "Simon doesn't need to keep me chained to anything. I can't walk."

"What do you mean?"

"When Mr. Jenkins hit me with his car, he paralyzed me from the waist down."

*Oh my fucking God. The story keeps getting worse and worse. Who were those people? When Oliver finds out the truth—because I will get out of this hell hole to tell him—it'll devastate him.*

I try again to break free. I cannot let that sucker win.

"We need to find a way out of here. Do you think you can help me out of my bindings?"

"He used plastic zip ties to bind your wrists and ankles. I would need something sharp to cut through them."

"How about your teeth?"

I don't wait for his answer as I begin to crawl toward him. I'm getting out of here and I'm taking Harry with me, even if I have to carry him over my shoulder all the way back to Oliver.

That fucker Simon messed with the wrong woman.

# CHAPTER 45
## OLIVER

stare at the empty closet in disbelief. Gone are all of Saylor's clothes and her suitcase. Felix is missing. An hour after Harry went looking for Saylor, he still hadn't returned, so I locked my drunk mother in my father's study and set out on my own search. I found the guesthouse empty.

That was twenty minutes ago. I've called Saylor a dozen times and left endless messages. Now all the calls are going straight to voice mail. I've gone through the list of her friends and no one knows anything. This seems like déjà vu; she pulled the same stunt back in Hawaii, leaving me alone in that hotel room without a goodbye note.

No. She didn't fucking run away this time. I knew something was off back in Hawaii. I don't know what to think now. Saylor wouldn't take off like that, not in the middle of Nana's funeral, not in her condition. She was happy despite everything.

I hear the front door open and run out of the bedroom to see Harry coming in, not Saylor. My heart sinks like a boulder in the ocean.

"Where the fuck have you been? I called you several times."

"I'm sorry. I forgot my phone in my car. I came here to look for Saylor like you asked, and when I saw all her things were gone, I went to find information."

"And?" I can't believe it hadn't occurred to me to question Linus or Gilbert.

"Nothing. No one's seen her. She must've taken a cab and slipped away while everyone was busy with the funeral."

"That's bullshit. She wouldn't do that. She had no reason to."

"Are you sure, Ollie? It was clear to me that she wasn't happy here."

My hands curls into fists as I stalk toward my brother. "She wouldn't run away," I say through clenched teeth.

Maybe if this had happened a couple of weeks ago, I could've believed it. I stop in my tracks, veering toward the second bedroom where we've kept some of our stuff. Inside the closet, Rita's case is still there. I open it for good measure, finding Saylor's beloved guitar inside. Instead of feeling a wash of relief, my stomach churns.

I run back to the living room to grab my phone. "I'm calling the police."

"Why?"

"Because she didn't run away."

I don't look at him as head out the front door. There are still guests at the main house, but I don't care. The operator's voice comes through, but before I can speak, sharp pain explodes behind my head and I'm propelled forward. I turn in time to see Harry come at me again with a shovel, hitting the side of my face this time. The blow knocks me down, and I'm too stunned to do anything to protect my body from the impact with the ground. The acrid taste of blood fills my mouth as my world turns off-kilter.

"What the fuck are you doing?" I ask, still not catching on that my fucking brother just attacked me.

"Why couldn't you just accept that your wife left you, brother? Why did you have to be so stubborn?

He hits my jaw with his fist this time and it's the last thing I see.

♡ ♡ ♡

## SAYLOR

"Come on, Harry. We don't know when he'll be back."

"Do you think it's easy cutting through these bloody things with my teeth?"

He resumes gnawing the plastic restrains around my wrists while I look around the bare room, trying to find anything I can use as a weapon. The only object I can think of is the little lamp in the corner. Even so, I don't think it's big enough to inflict any damage.

I feel a slack on the plastic tie and help Harry by putting pressure against the restraint. The skin around my wrist is probably raw at this point, but desperation trumps pain. The plastic zip tie finally snaps. Two red bands mark my wrists now. They are also covered in blood, but I don't think it's mine.

I turn, noting that Harry's lower lip is split, blood pouring from the gash. "You hurt yourself."

He wipes his bloody lip with the back of his hand. "Yes. Those zip ties are sharp."

"I'm sorry."

"I don't think I can chew the ones around your ankles."

I look down at them. Even if my fingers weren't numb from the lack of circulation, there's no way I could break those ties with my bare hands. However, I notice there's some slack on them. It's not enough to pull free, but maybe I can unzip my boots and take them off. After a lot of struggling, I manage to move my left foot in front of the right. It's an odd and uncomfortable angle, but I can reach the zipper now.

"What are you doing?" Harry asks.

"Trying to get my damn shoe off." I focus on the task, but the damn thing won't budge. "Ugh, come on!"

"Maybe I can help?"

I switch my position on the floor, placing my bound legs over Harry's lap. He holds my boot with both hands and tells me to try to pull my foot out.

"What do think I've been doing for the past minute?" I didn't mean to snap at him, but I'm too nervous to care about anyone's feelings.

"Getting sassy won't help one bit."

He wiggles my boot left and right, and with me pulling in the opposite direction, my foot finally begins to slide out. With a final pull on Harry's end, my foot comes out, the jerky movement making me fall backward on my elbows.

"Victory!" Harry brandishes my freed boot like a trophy.

No time for celebration, though; we still need to find a way out. I grab the accessory from Harry's hand, putting the boot back with haste. I'm wobbly on my feet as I stand up, the vertigo taking a moment to pass.

"Where's the way out?" I ask.

"I believe we're underground, so look for some kind of stairs."

The farther away I move from Harry and his lamp, the darker the room becomes. I can't imagine that a bunker buried deep in the ground wouldn't have some type of illumination, so I find the nearest wall and search frantically for a light switch. In my scrambling, I bump against something metallic.

"I think I've found the stairs."

Getting familiar with the way out by touch, I quickly realize the stairwell is a spiral type, narrow and steep.

*Fuck. How am I going to carry Harry out of here?*

*One problem at time, Saylor.*

I venture up the stairs blindly since I couldn't locate a light switch. The staircase shakes as I go up, proving it's not very stable. Fucking fantastic. After a slow ascension, I finally come to the door. Holding my breath, I turn the knob and push the heavy metal door forward. It moves slowly with a loud creak, but it opens. Late afternoon light comes pouring in, and I want to weep.

I debate going on my own to get help, but I forget the idea the moment it enters my mind. I can't leave Harry behind. Pushing the door open all the way, I find a rock big enough to hold the door open, but I have to bend and stretch my body to its limit to reach it without letting the door shut. What if I can't open it from the outside without a key?

Once the rock is in place and I'm sure it'll hold, I go back inside to get Harry. Going down the stairs with the path illuminated is much easier.

"Come on, Harry. It's time to go."

"You should run for help. I'll slow you down."

"Not a chance, buddy." Crouching next to him, I throw his arm over my shoulder. "Ready?"

"Are you sure you're strong enough to carry me?"

"There's only one way to find out."

I unfurl from my crouched position, lifting Harry with me. I soon realize it's hard to keep my balance when I'm holding him upright like that, his entire body weight on me.

He sighs. "This is not going to work."

"Jesus, will you quit with the negativity already?"

"I dare you to spend months locked in a bunker and maintain a sunshine attitude."

"Touché. Okay, let's see if all those months in physical therapy will pay off."

I lift Harry into my arms like he's a child. The only problem is that, despite his obvious emaciated condition, he's a tall guy, and bones are fucking heavy. My arms are already shaking and I haven't even started up the stairs yet.

*Come on, Saylor. You can do it.*

Gritting my teeth, I concentrate on taking one step at a time. The ascension is too fucking slow for my liking, but we eventually make it out of that hole. I can't hold Harry any longer though, so I drop him onto the leafy ground not too far from the entrance of his hellish prison.

Bracing my hands on my knees, I try to catch my breath.

"You should go now, get Ollie. I can crawl my way into a hiding spot."

"Not happening. I'm not leaving you behind."

"You're such a stubborn woman. No wonder Simon didn't like you. He knew you wouldn't be easily manipulated."

I open my mouth to reply when a distant call for help freezes on the spot. I almost didn't hear it, but I recognize the owner of that voice.

*Oliver.*

Forgetting my earlier promise, I leave Harry behind, sprinting toward the direction I think the call came from. Branches get in my way, scratching my face and snagging my clothes, but I don't stop, even if I'm not sure I'm going in the right direction. Then I hear the sound of a shovel hitting ground, louder than the call for help had been.

I don't even try to be stealthy as I run toward the new noise. Breathing hard, I come upon Simon, who is presently covering a hole in the ground with dirt. There's no sign of Oliver, but I have a terrible suspicion as to where he is.

*No. I can't be too late.*

I let out a guttural scream as I jump on Simon, knocking him down. My sudden attack stuns him a little, granting me the opportunity to punch him in the nose, but he recovers fast and quickly overpowers me. He pushes me off him to strike me next, his rough hands wrapping around my neck in an iron grip.

"Stupid bitch! Why did you have to get in the way?"

I try to pry his fingers off to no avail, then buckle and thrash on the ground, which only makes him squeeze my neck tighter. I'm winded and tired from carrying Harry up the stairs and from the run here. The little bit of strength left is quickly waning.

"I knew the old hag had something up her sleeve. I could see the defiance in her gaze before I smothered her with her own pillow."

Dark spots begin to take over my vision from lack of air. I don't think I have much time left before I pass out. The last thing I hear is a growl before a blur collides with Simon, knocking him off me. Air rushes through my lungs now that the passageway is finally unobstructed. With shaking arms, I push my upper body up to see that Felix is the one who saved me.

I turn to the hole in the ground, heart stuck in my throat. As I feared, I find Oliver there, unconscious. A whimper escapes my lips as I take note of the patch of bruises and dried blood on his face.

"Ollie, my love. Open your eyes."

I brush the dirt off him, fearing the worst. *He can't be dead. He can't be dead.* Looping my arms under his, I pull him out of the hole, my muscles protesting with the effort. Oliver stirs, twisting his face as he does so.

*He's alive! Thank God.*

Felix lets out a whine, making me turn to the scene behind me. A bloody Simon is standing over Felix's limp body, shovel in hand. He raises his arm, ready to deliver a killing blow.

"No!" I yell.

He looks over his shoulder, the devil's face staring back at me. I've never seen so much evil in anyone, not even in my former attacker.

Simon smiles at me, a cruel and twisted upturn of his lips, right before he brings the shovel down. I close my eyes, refusing to bear witness to such an act of violence.

*I'm so sorry, Felix.*

A gunshot echoes in the forest. My eyes fly open just in time to see Simon collapse to the ground. On the other side of the clearing, Gilbert is there with a rifle in his hand. He brings the barrel down and steps closer to Simon's unmoving form.

"Is he dead?" I ask.

"Yes. I never miss a shot."

"Saylor?" Oliver says.

"Yes, Ollie. I'm here."

"Are you okay, sugar?"

"You're the one covered in bruises and you ask if I'm okay?"

"Did he do anything to you? I'll kill him if he did."

"Don't worry, your butler's already done that for you. That's what I call top-notch service."

# CHAPTER 46
## SAYLOR



There's an entire committee waiting for us when we walk into our home in Hermosa Beach. After the horrible ordeal at the hands of Simon Jenkins, it feels like it's been an eternity since we left California.

We finally learned the truth of what happened to Harry. Mr. Jenkins did hit him with his car, then decided to take care of Harry himself to avoid going to jail. That part of the story was true. Bound to a wheelchair and confused, Harry began to believe the lies the Jenkinses told him. He learned the truth much later when he first saw Oliver on TV performing with Boys Future. Then he began to plan his escape, but Simon suspected what Harry was up to and took away his wheelchair.

I still don't know how that monster figured out I was on to him. I guess it's a truth we'll never know thanks to Gilbert and his sharpshooting skills. Who would've guessed the stuffy butler was an Olympic gold medalist for rifle shooting? Thank God he was around when Felix returned to Longview Manor covered in blood. Knowing something was amiss, Gilbert armed himself before following our dog into the woods.

I push those memories aside and focus on the situation at hand. My bandmates are here, plus Liv, Bas, and even someone I haven't seen in years, Sebastian's cousin Shane.

Mom flew to the UK as soon as she heard what happened to us, so she's with me, Ollie, Harry, and Felix. Charlotte decided to stay a little longer in the UK with her mother.

Remi and her little sister Cassie are holding handmade 'Welcome' signs. The house is decorated with colorful balloons, and I spy a delicious food spread outside on a long table. Bright sunshine gleams on the pool. Even the weather decided to welcome us.

Felix spots Liv's dog, Fritz, outside and runs out to greet his friend. I lock gazes with Liv before we both break into a run and hug each other in the middle of the living room.

"I'm so glad you're back," she gushes.

"Me too."

"I'm sorry I couldn't take time off to see you." She pulls back, wiping the tears from her cheeks.

"Don't apologize, chica. Mom was there."

I turn to Oliver, as he hugs everyone in his path, introducing his real brother in the same breath. The bruises on his face are finally beginning to fade, but the sight of them still makes my blood churn. I almost lost him that day. I'm still plagued by nightmares of him in that shallow grave.

Harry has recovered by leaps and bounds. The gauntness is gone from his face. Clean-shaven and with a proper haircut, I can see some resemblance between him and Oliver. Something Simon and all his plastic surgery procedures couldn't replicate.

Despite the ordeal he's been through, not only at the hands of that psychopath but also the Jenkinses, his spirit isn't broken. He speaks fluent sarcasm like a master, always ready to crack a joke here and there. It's his coping mechanism, no doubt, but it's helping Oliver deal with his own guilt. They still have a long way to go, but the road no longer seems bleak.

Harry seems a bit shy with all the attention he's receiving.

Remi stops in front of him, watching him intently. "Boy, you're ten thousand times better than the other Harry."

"I sure hope so. How dreadful would it be to lose a popularity contest to a psychopath," he's quick to reply.

And just like that, Remi declares Harry will be her date for the day.

I'm hit with a bit of nausea, which reminds me that I have to tell Liv the news before Oliver breaks it to everyone else. We'd agreed earlier to let our friends know I'm pregnant, but Liv, being my best friend, deserves to know first.

I pull her into the privacy of my room and close the door. "I have to tell you something."

"Me too." A spark of mischief glints in her eyes.

I squint at her, thinking there's no way her news is the same as mine.

"You're pregnant," I say.

She nods, fighting to keep from smiling from ear to ear. "You too?"

"Yes."

A moment of silence follows as we both digest the news. Then we scream like two crazy teen girls meeting their idols for the first time. The ruckus is so loud that a few seconds later, Oliver and Bas burst into the room, ready to fight an invisible threat.

They both relax when they realize what's going on. "You told her?" they say at the same time, then glance at each other.

"What the fuck?" Oliver speaks first. "Liv's knocked up?"

"Is Saylor pregnant?" Bas asks right after.

I trade a glance with Liv, who rolls her eyes. Glaring, I return my attention to the duo. "Hello? We're right here."

Oliver grins sheepishly. "Sorry, sugar. I'm just speechless. Life just isn't this picture perfect."

"Considering the shitty hand destiny dealt us, I'd say we more than deserve a happily ever after ending."

"Well, it's definitely an ending all right. We're all gonna be parents. Life as we know it is over." Bas hugs Liv sideways, kissing her cheek.

"Nah, it's not the ending. This is just the beginning." Oliver smiles at me, melting my heart.

My memories are still trickling in slowly, but I'm no longer obsessing about them. I also quit stressing about the future. Oliver and I faced our greatest fears and survived; we can tackle any curve ball life throws at us.

I place my hand over my stomach, letting joy and the greatest love I've ever known wash over me. Oliver's hand covers mine and I bring my face to his, staring into his tear-filled eyes.

"I love you," I say.

"I know." He smiles.

"How long have you been waiting to use that line on me?"

His answer is to kiss me.

No. I won't worry about the past or the future. The only moment that matters is now.

**** The End ****

**Continue reading for a preview of *Love Me Like You Do*, the conclusion to Bas and Liv's love story.**

# LOVE ME LIKE YOU DO SAMPLE

## LIV

My eyes are bleary as I read the contract with the catering company for the thousandth time. I knew taking the week off to attend the funeral for Oliver's father would cost me big-time. I tried to do as much as I could before the trip since I cannot trust my coworker Celine to even do the bare minimum. It's not hard to see how she landed the job in the first place—she's a natural bullshitter. What is hard for me to grasp is the reason she's still around. She totally fucked the contract I'm trying desperately to fix. I miss Mellie and Lloyd so much right now.

My phone beeps, and with a quick glance, I see my sister's name pop up. It's the tenth message in less than an hour. It's a mistake to ignore Kimmy, but I know once I acknowledge her, it won't be a quick call.

With a sigh, I write a quick e-mail to the catering company, attaching the revised contract. Hopefully that's the last one of Celine's screw-ups that I have to fix. Glancing at the desk she usually occupies, I find it empty. No surprise there, since she always leaves work at five on the dot. I'm the only idiot in the department who works past eight most days. It's six now, and it's just me besides my boss, who is locked in his office on a conference call.

I take the opportunity to read all the messages Kimmy sent me. Gah, she has so many questions. She's helping me organize our parents' surprise anniversary party, something we decided to do months ago, but thanks to my high-demand job and also my unexpected trip to England, she ended up handling most of the preparations. Some event coordinator I am.

I answer her first question about the flowers and her response tells me she's pissed. She already made all the decisions without my help. Crap. She's mad at me. I'll be in the doghouse for a long time. Kimmy holds a grudge like no other.

I call her. It rings and rings. I'm afraid she's going to let the call go to voice mail when she finally answers. "I don't need your help anymore."

"I'm sorry. I had a ton of things to do by the end of the day."

"Yes, you're always so busy. I don't know why you sign up to do anything outside your day job if you're going to bail in the end."

"I didn't bail. I'll be there on Saturday to help with the final preparations."

"You'd better be. This was your idea, after all. I'm not an event planner."

"I know." I rest my head in my hand, feeling the first signs of a headache approaching.

Bill, my boss, steps out of his office and makes a beeline to my desk. He doesn't look pleased.

"Kimmy, I have to call you later."

I end the call before she can get a reply in.

"Is there something wrong?" I ask him.

"Yes. I need you to attend the conference this Saturday."

My heart sinks. He can't possibly be serious. "Bill, it's my parents' thirtieth anniversary this Saturday. I'm helping organize the party. I mentioned this to you months ago."

"I'm sorry, Liv. It's out of my hands. This is one of the biggest events Reinhardt Corp takes part in, and it needs to go smoothly. Our CEO is one of the keynote speakers."

"Yes, I'm aware of that. I thought you were going to be there with Celine." Not that she counts for much.

"Change of plans. I have to attend the roadshow in Europe, and Celine is coming with me."

I open and close my mouth. There's nothing I can say, really.

"Listen, you don't have to stay until the end. As long as everything is under control, you can leave early."

"Sure, Bill. You don't have to worry. I'll make it work."

He knocks on my desk twice, something he always does that annoys the heck out of me. "I know I can count on you, Liv. You're my best employee."

He walks away, exuding his usual confidence while I glare at his back. The ladies in the office think he's attractive. I don't see it. Maybe because I work with him on a daily basis and have to put up with his narcissistic personality. Patty Sanders, my former boss, was a tough cookie, but at least she was a hard worker too. I honestly don't know what Bill does.

Instead of going home, I open the folder containing all the documents pertaining to Saturday's tradeshow. Celine had some tasks assigned to her, and knowing how incompetent she is, I'll have to double-check everything she did.

It takes me two hours to make a list of the items I need to fix besides taking care of my own list of to-dos. When I get home, I find cold dinner waiting for me on the stove. Shit. I had promised Sebastian I would come home earlier today. I didn't even text him.

"Bas?"

No answer. I put my keys and purse on the kitchen counter and lift the pan's lid. Pasta carbonara, one of my favorite dishes, but only good if eaten as soon as it's prepared.

I forget eating for now and head to our bedroom. Sebastian steps out of the bathroom with a towel wrapped around his waist at the same time I enter the room. He pauses when he sees me, but instead of saying hello, he continues to the walk-in closet.

"I'm sorry I didn't call," I say.

"Don't stress. I'm used to it by now."

His clipped answer twists my heart.

"Celine left me a mess to fix."

Sebastian returns to the room wearing loose PJ pants and nothing else. I know he's not showing his sculpted abs to seduce me, but my eyes linger on all that exposed skin just the same. He doesn't acknowledge my reply, choosing to jump on the bed and turn on the TV instead.

Since he's pissed at me already, I might as well tell him all the bad news.

"Bill asked me to cover for him this Saturday at a conference."

Sebastian finally looks at me, frowning. "It's your parents' anniversary. Or have you forgotten already?"

"I haven't forgotten. I'm not staying at the event until the end."

"Right."

His sarcastic tone makes my blood boil. He knows I hate it. "What do you want me to do, Bas? This is one of the biggest events for Reinhardt Corp. I can't say no to my boss."

"That's the problem, Liv. You *can* say no. You don't need the measly salary they pay you."

I cross my arms in front of my chest and give him the death glare. "I *do* need it. I don't want to depend on you financially. Why is that so hard to understand?"

He turns to me, his eyes dark with contained anger. "I'm not asking you to quit your career. I'm asking you to quit this job and look for something better. Preferably a place where you're not overworked, underpaid, and under-appreciated."

I scoff. "What do you know about working in the real world? You went from party boy to instant celebrity."

I realize I said the wrong thing the moment the words leave my lips and Sebastian's glare turns glacial.

"You're right. I know nothing about how things work in the real world." He throws his legs to the side of the bed and stands up.

"Where are you going?"

"I think it's best if I sleep on the couch tonight."

Oh shit. I think I pushed things too far this time. "Bas, I'm sorry."

He stops in front of the door and looks over his shoulder. "You know, Liv, I'm really tired of hearing you say that."

He walks out, closing the door behind him with a soft click. I remain frozen, staring at the closed door. Part of me wants to go after Sebastian and talk things through, but I'm afraid I'll only make things worse. I sit on the edge of the bed, feeling at a loss. Sebastian has never looked at me like that—*ever*.

A sob escapes my lips as a shudder runs through my body. Newly married and already failing at it. I don't know what can I do to fix this mess.

***** End of Sample *****

♡ ♡ ♡

**Download *LOVE ME LIKE YOU DO* now.**

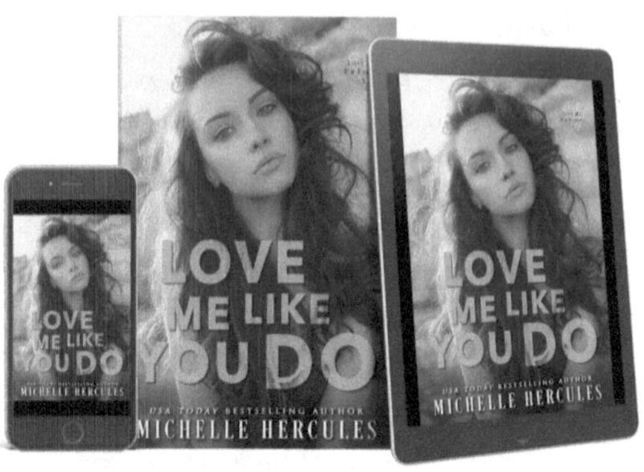

Liv and Sebastian's love has been put through the test time and time again. Terrible circumstances kept the young couple apart for five years. Now finally married, it should be smooth sailing. But that's the funny thing about real life, there is no magical happily ever after once vows are exchanged.

Liv and Sebastian will soon discover marriage is hard work. When life throws another curveball their way, they'll have to face their biggest challenge yet. Will this new storm bring them together or break them apart for good?

**ONE-CLICK NOW!**

# FREE NOVEL

## CATCH YOU

Want to read another deliciously fun contemporary romance by Michelle Hercules? Then **CLICK HERE** to get your FREE copy of *Catch You*.

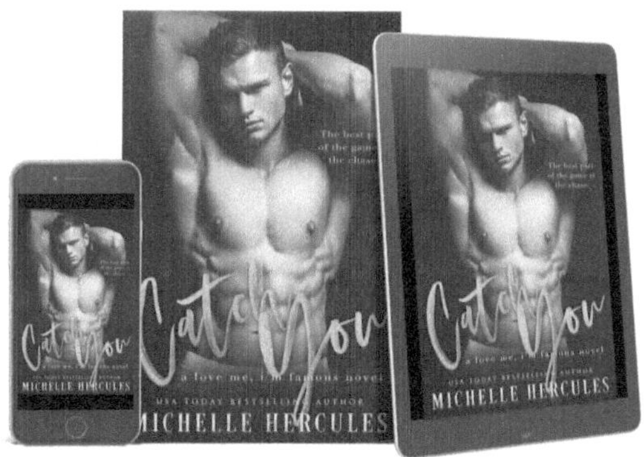

**Pride and Prejudice meets Veronica Mars in this enemy-to-lovers romance.**

KimberlyI had always thought Owen Whitfield fit the mold of

the brainless jock perfectly. Group of idiot friends? Check. Vapid girlfriend? Check. Ego bigger than the moon? Check. As long as he stayed out of my way, coexisting with his kind was doable. Until one day our worlds collided, changing everything. He pissed me off so badly that I had no choice but to give him a taste of his own medicine. Little did I know that my act of revenge would come back to bite me in the ass. How was I supposed to know Owen would turn out to be the best partner in crime I could hope for?

Owen never paid much attention to Kimberly Dawson, but I knew who she was. Ice Queen was what we called her. She was gorgeous, no one could deny that. But she was also a condescending bitch, which was enough reason for me to stay the hell away from her. She thought I was a dumb jock, and that was okay until she came crashing into my life. Against my better judgment, I let her embroil me in her shenanigans, forcing us to spend too much time together. It was my doom. She got under my skin. She was all I could think about. I never thought I would be the knight in shining armor to anyone, not until she came along.

**CLICK HERE to get your free copy!**

**OR**

**Scan the code!**

# ABOUT THE AUTHOR

*USA Today* Bestselling Author Michelle Hercules always knew creative arts were her calling but not in a million years did she think she would become an author. With a background in fashion design she thought she would follow that path. But one day, out of the blue, she had an idea for a book. One page turned into ten pages, ten pages turned into a hundred, and before she knew it, her first novel, The Prophecy of Arcadia, was born.

Michelle Hercules resides in Florida with her husband and daughter. She is currently working on the *Blueblood Vampires* series and the *Rebels of Rushmore* series.

**Join Michelle Hercules' Reader Group:**
https://www.facebook.com/groups/mhsoars

**Sign up for Michelle Hercules' Newsletter:**
https://mhsoars.activehosted.com/f/11

facebook.com/michelleherculesauthor
instagram.com/michelleherculesauthor
tiktok.com/@michelleherculesauthor
bookbub.com/authors/michelle-hercules
patreon.com/michellehercules